YESTERDAY'S TOMORROW

DORIAN KEYS

A Cozy Reads Publication
Release – November 2022

Copyright © 2022 Dorian Keys

All rights reserved.

YESTERDAY'S TOMORROW
By Dorian Keys

ISBN: 978-1-7777646-9-2

TABLE OF CONTENTS

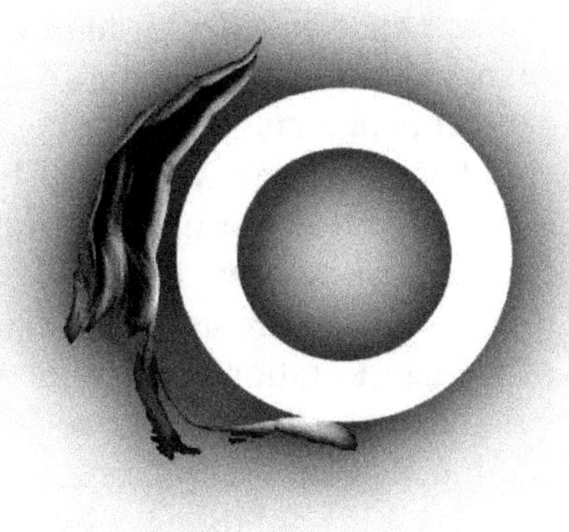

I

CHAPTER 1

You could say I come from a broken home. A broken planet. Physically and figuratively. A leftover of an era when we still talked. Fellow citizens weren't afraid to look one another in the eye, and friendships were still a thing.

At the edge of the Earthly town where I lived as a child, nestled near a series of fields and hills, was Section Eight — the westernmost neighborhood of the city where I was born. It was filled with three-story red brick buildings. The one we lived in had four entrances, and there were three families per floor, which meant that there were plenty of children roughly my age to play with.

Because we had no real toys, all of us kids would run laps around the pothole-ridden, run-down side streets, which seldom experienced any traffic. That made Section Eight anything but quiet. Noise exponentially increased when one of my neighborhood friends had something to celebrate.

To be a little more detailed, I fondly remember Lira, our next-door neighbor, mainly for the cakes she baked. Our families were close before I was born, so she was in our apartment at all hours of the day. Lira usually came in to chat, gossip with my parents, or hang out with my grandmother while she babysat me. Other times she would ask for eggs or sugar or whatever other scarce commodities she needed, and we did the same. Anyway, one specific night Lira was baking a cake for her daughter's birthday, her third. Of course, my parents would help in any way they could. Even if it meant we had to ration some milk and sugar for a few days until they were available in the market. The celebration that followed had all our friends, including my best, Tony, Lori, and Suela, crammed in the short and narrow hallway of the building we lived in. We partied until the first-floor neighbors chased us out of the building, waving their flip-flops in their hands.

An uncomfortable chuckle followed by a long sigh always escaped whenever one of these memories overtook me. Everything was so intense back then, happiness, excitement – sadness.

I remember my past. Dirty clothes full of patches, empty stomach … but surrounded by friends, and happy. At least I was. Though I might be reserved as to who I share these memories with, I'm not ashamed or embarrassed by them.

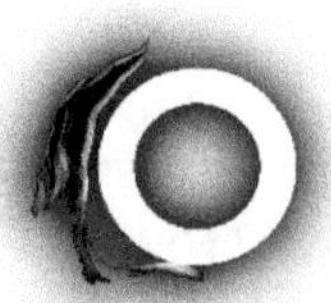

Sighing, I placed the back of my hand near the lit white circle on the right side of the doorframe. Above it, a series of numbers accompanied by a large square quick response code was enclosed by a thin rectangular frame with rounded corners. The most visible digits were '38-42.' I understood the number 38 indicated the floor level, and the rest of the characters and the quick response code were used by the EvoGens and maintenance personnel when repairs were needed. These blocky white numbers label all residences, which here and there would be out of place. In fact, just last week, the System cranes inundated the area, replacing a row of units around mine. I did see some new faces for a few days. Then, as usual, nothing. These changes happened so often, I stopped checking who lived next to me. The door in front of me rapidly dematerialized, revealing the inside of my personal living quarters.

I didn't know where the System found the inspiration to design these accommodations, but I could feel the psychological soothing they projected. The bottom of the interior wall was painted in a milky white color, which, going up to the top, gradually faded to blue. About half an inch in diameter, several small LED lights were sparsely laid out on the ceiling and evenly illuminated the area.

Dropping my bag on the top of my bed, to my left, I walked inside the room. Materializing behind me, the front door silenced the persistent electric hum filling the dome. I walked into the bathroom, which was in the farthest left corner of the room, turned on the faucet, and splashed some water on my face. Raising my head with my hands still on my cheeks, I felt water drip from my chin.

Rectangular in shape, the mirror, about six feet above ground, was at the perfect height to see my reflection. My dark hair, pressed against my forehead by my hat, was slightly leaning to my left side. Because of the lack of sunlight, my skin, pale as it usually was, had become even paler. Dark circles under my eyes showed my lack of sleep. I rubbed the water out of my eyebrows and looked at them through the mirror. As I stared at my reflection for a few seconds, I slowly focused on the TV wall unit behind me.

"Open the window and show me the commercial district," I commanded it, grabbing a towel from the shelf on my left.

The TV wall had a panel along its edges as a form of an analog regulator. That wasn't the only way to control it, however. It also came with a little booklet detailing every possible voice command it accepted. One could, of course, control it by voice, which was the most convenient way of doing anything in Ceres2. The ever-listening microphones picked up any perceived voice instructions from our communicators and, based on context, would perform the actions needed to complete such commands. I could remove my communicator to avoid the System listening. However, everything in Ceres2 required human residents to have one. I didn't remember all of the directives the TV wall accepted, but most were based on the System, intuitive. This one wasn't, though I could clearly see why it existed. These units were designed to be survival pods. Apart from the air circulation holes, which led to a filtration system, they were hermetically sealed. I couldn't just open the window to get some fresh air. In fact, the air inside the residential units often felt fresher than the air in the dome.

Multicolored pixels rapidly flashed as the large monitor flickered and displayed a slow rotation of live video feeds taken from different cameras near the commercial district.

"Stop here," I commanded the screen again as my favorite feed displayed. Likely from a camera mounted on top of a streetlight pole, it showed the tall neon-lined commercial buildings, all of which projected advertisements on their sides. In the middle of the screen were the traffic lanes, all three layers. As transports and the occasional train moved on the ground floor, other vehicles floated on the second and third levels.

After drying my face, I threw the towel back on the shelf and crossed the room to the small kitchen area.

"Play some ambient music," I commanded the TV wall once more as I walked to the fridge. There were three tubes labeled with tiny LED lights in the shape of a water drop by the handle. The one with a blue dot dispensed drinking water. Half an inch to its right, another tube labeled by a white dot dispensed milk, or "milk-like product," rather. The one next to it had a different color depending on what drink was available that month.

Inside the refrigerator were several compartments: bread, fruit, vegetables, and so on. The System would replenish whatever I consumed. My account would be billed based on what I expended for the month— no need to shop or borrow from friends or family…no need for a neighborly chat.

A box labeled "fruit" caught my eye. Peeking, I saw the usual dried fruit, grapes, apricots, and such. Not feeling like consuming any of that, I closed the door. A month in this place, and I was already tired of its food. But it kept me alive, so I tried to make the best of it. Then I remembered that special drink I'd bought a few days ago, in the sealed metallic bottle.

As slow but steady ambient sounds played from speakers nested in the ceiling, I sat on my bed, pushed my pillow out of my way, and opened my backpack. Tucked in a special pocket in the main compartment was the tablet I used to read books and articles during my commute. All the way at the bottom was my water bottle. Next to it, the sealed metallic jug.

My mouth salivated before I even reached for it. What a strange feeling to have. I knew that what was inside wasn't tasty. The smell of fermented liquor immediately emanated as I twisted the cap open. It reminded me of homemade grappa. It reminded me of Earth, of home. Something my grandmother would serve to my uncles when they would come to visit us.

The lady who sold it assured me this drink wasn't what I thought it was. Taking a sip out of it, I immediately felt the alcohol burn its way down my esophagus, finally stopping in my stomach. As a familiar buzz clouded my head, I kicked my bag on the floor, adjusted my pillows against the wall, and sat on my bed. The initial fruity flavor was quickly replaced by the unforgiving liquor aftertaste, which persisted.

Soaking in the sounds and sights from the wall-sized flatscreen TV, I took another sip of the liquor. Though the wall in front of me displayed images of the futuristic city I was in at the moment, my mind drifted toward home. I took another sip.

Leading with C-3 Live Feed, C-3 meaning Colony Three, of course, the obligatory chyron scrolled on the bottom of the screen displaying stock market stats across the colonies and news of the day. As my eyelids got heavier and heavier, I took another sip from the metallic bottle. Placing it on the ground, I finally closed my eyes and fell asleep.

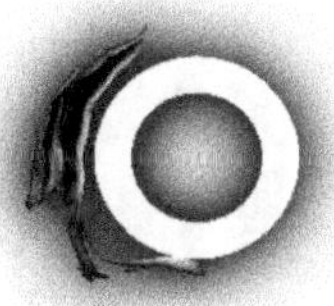

A cold feeling on my cheek made me raise my hand and wipe at it. In a moment of laziness, without looking, I simply rubbed my fingers across it to get a feel. It seemed like water.

I finally opened my eyes after a few more drops hit my face. Above me, Weeping Willow branches blocked out the sun as the sound of a gentle breeze hushed through its thin leaves. Supporting myself with my hands, I sat on the green grass. It also felt wet. Dew was dripping from the tips of the thin tree leaves onto the ground where I was sitting. Smiling, I looked at my hand, then observed what was in front of me and saw what I expected: the Blue Eye Lagoon. Emerging from the ground, its water formed a short, silent stream before disappearing inside a small, two-foot-tall cave.

Hearing my childhood friends' playful screams behind me, I got up and looked in their direction. Waving his water bottle above his head, Tony was chasing Lori, spraying water in her direction. Suela was a little further in the distance, admiring one of the crying trees.

The warm sensation of home enveloped me. The sun was beaming, the birds chirped, and the bees flew from flower to flower. I walked to the stream and bent over to splash some of the cold liquid on my face. *Strange, I can't see my reflection.* My warm feeling disappeared. Swallowing, I dipped my hands in the deep blue pond, looking for my reflection somewhere within. Nothing. As the sun hid behind a dark cloud, everything around me changed its color to a subdued grey. The wind picked up.

In a fit of panic, I sat back down on the grass and closed my eyes. Together with my friend's cheerful voices, the whooshing sound of wind blowing through the leaves was replaced by a muffled version of it. I took a deep breath and opened my eyes again. The blue ceiling lined with small LED lights greeted me. Grunting, I rubbed my eyes with the meaty parts of my thumbs and sat up on my bed.

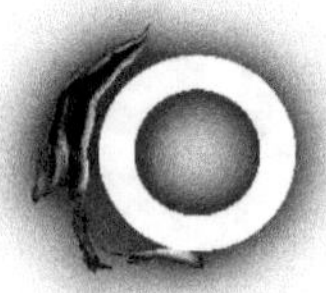

The soft birdsong-chirp message notification brought me further back to reality. I raised the device to my view.

"Mister Nett, please report to the registrar's office. We need to update your credentials." The same message echoed through the ceiling speakers.

Yawning, I laid my head back on my pillow and continued rubbing my right eye with my index finger. After that initial wake-up tingling worked its way out of my body, I curled my toes. That's when I realized that in my sleep, I had kicked my shoes off my feet. On Earth, and subsequently, Mars, my parents always made a point to ask me to remove my shoes once home. Though Ceres2, which the System at times referred to as the Third Colony, seemed to be warm and welcoming, thus far, it didn't feel like home.

My communicator vibrated as it followed the notification, prompting me to acknowledge it. I sat on the bed and placed my hand over the screen. That usually did the trick of letting it know that I had received the message and would stop vibrating. The white ring on the side of my front door lit up in anticipation of my approach, but I ignored it. My head spun as soon as I stood up. The alcohol was still in my system. After taking a shower and changing my clothes, I grabbed my backpack and headed out.

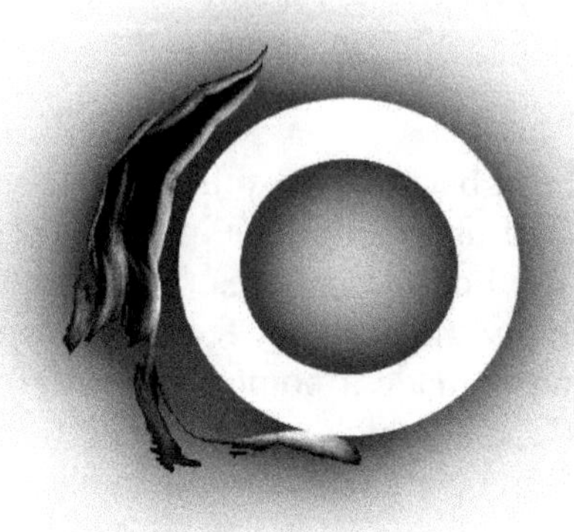

CHAPTER 2

Contrary to what I expected to see when I arrived, mostly because of the advertisement posters on Mars, these new megastructures the System decided to build in Ceres2 weren't that tall. The tallest was seventy stories high, and that was only the town hall. The rest of the structures were forty.

But they ran wide.

Hundreds, no, thousands of city blocks were paved with concrete. Magnetic-strip streets were placed on top. The buildings themselves were modular. They consisted of either living quarters, like the one I lived in, or utility blocks. They were attached to each other with rails which allowed construction robots and maintenance crews to lift sections to work on plumbing, electrical lines or completely replace them.

Large transportation, the maglev trains, ran on the ground. On the twentieth floor were the magnetic lane streets, where electric cars served as a more private mode of transportation. On the fortieth floor was another transportation level. Elevators from the personal living quarters led directly to the nearest stations.

Ceres2 had a combination of all the vehicles I'd ever seen. Because of their weight, magnetically levitating trains generally traveled only on the ground level. They ran on electrified tracks in the middle of the traffic travel lanes and ranged from five cars to about fifteen. Aerodynamically shaped, they reached speeds averaging several hundred miles per hour and were mainly used to move humans, androids, and other resources between domes.

Most small vehicles varied in shape, some relied entirely on the electrified magnetic lanes. The absence of engines made them lighter; instead, they had generators that produced a countercharge to the roadbed. Electromagnets in place of tires created the necessary force to keep the vehicle above ground.

The cabins where we would sit, reflected the form of the vehicle they surrounded. Some looked like cars I used to see on Earth. Others resembled jets and airplanes; the one I'd just gotten in had an aerodynamic shape. I pressed the button on the side, and the door, much like the living unit door technology, retreated slightly and faded. It re-materialized behind me as soon as I stepped in. In front of the left front seat, a U-shaped steering wheel signaled that this vehicle was capable of outside movement between domes. On the dashboard, the familiar white circle pulsated once again. I took my seat and waved my communicator in front of it. The electromagnets whirred. Feeling that the vehicle was now floating, I strapped on the seatbelt harness.

"Destination accepted," the vehicle confirmed. "Please make sure all loose objects are fastened, then press 'begin journey.'"

Tucking my backpack under my feet, I pressed the digital button. The magnets under the vehicle's undercarriage pushed the car upwards through a hazy white cloud emanating from a nearby exhaust vent. Because of these vapor puffs, the numerous red laser directional pointers which helped the car stay on track were visible the higher I got. I felt the vehicle move forward, merging with the traffic lane above me. Though traffic vigorously floated in different directions, being alone gave me a sense of peace and quiet. The noisy rush of the surrounding machines seemed so distant.

Unbeknownst to me, transformation had already begun before I even left Earth. Nostalgically, I still retain a mental image of the life I was separated from. Childless, still filled with potholes, Section Eighth streets fell silent. My grandmother's death hushed our apartment as well. And that's when we immigrated to the Mars colony. Conversion, though only visible through retrospect, gripped me once we settled there. Unable to find a job in her field, my mother helped around the house as much as she could. Eventually finding employment in the local kindergarten, she was home less and less. My father, whose formal education and trade were in automated engineering, was only able to work in construction. All along, wanting to pass his craft and knowledge, he taught me about robotics: how the components came together, how the code worked, and finally, how to integrate them with the System.

Time progressed, and all I have left are bits and pieces of memories of those last days I spent with my parents.

"You know how you know that as a leader, you have failed?" His complaint, while we watched an increasingly longer TV show called 'Another Murder on the Red Planet,' still rings in my ears. "It's when you find yourself forcing others to do your bidding. Do what you want them to do, no questions asked. And whoever doesn't agree, they're your enemy. Nature has placed a failsafe in humans for that specific reason. It's called conscience. These canners," he pointed at an android on the screen. "They don't know what that is. They are made of electrical impulses. Then again, I can name quite a few humans that are like that."

I was aware that during those times, protestors were destroying and defacing everything they could get their angry hands on. But in general, being outside during the day was safe.

"Someone is always using someone, someway…somehow," He told me the very next day before leaving home to join a protest against the System. "We're all zombies and robots to those in power. A number on paper, or worse, a statistic to the System. Whatever we do, we can't let them use us as they see fit. We are humans, damn it! We are better than this!"

That was the last conversation I had with my father. He didn't come home that night. The morning after, my mother called the factory where he worked. She was told it had no record of him ever registering to work on the Mars colony. Thinking that the System was glitching, as it constantly did during the turbulent protests, I went to school. The principal pulled me out of class, telling me that my mother had been hospitalized.

I took a taxi-transport to the facility, where the nurse told me my mother had had a nervous breakdown. They brought me to the room she was admitted, heavily medicated. She woke up five hours later and explained that everywhere she went to look for my father, they told her that no one had a record of him ever registering.

The hospital released my mother later that night, and we walked home. Holding my hand tight, her head at times seemed as if it was on a swivel. Her eyes darted everywhere as though she were hoping that somehow my father would walk out of a random corner. He didn't.

It wasn't until a few days later that we discovered that the bank account that we used to save money to pay bills, which was under my father's name, didn't exist anymore. Neither did his System Registration number. Having only recently moved to the Mars colony, we had very few friends; most of our neighbors had already moved out because of the constant riots in the surrounding residential areas. The rest of them didn't even acknowledge my mother's pleas for help.

A week later, a solar flare ravaged Earth. Wiping petabytes of data, the power grid was down for months, years in some Sections. Moments after the flare impacted Earth, we in the Mars colony experienced power loss. Shutting down parts of the cluster, the System inadvertently revealed the fundamental technical flaw of a totally computerized governing structure.

Maglev trains and travel lanes collapsing preceded food and energy shortages. The System, however, had ways to prioritize tasks efficiently. On Earth, politicians blamed each other for their shortcomings instead of tackling the real issue, and, as usual, riots and a few wars followed.

Nonetheless, hysteria induced by the flare marked the beginning of civil disobedience on Mars, and anger became prevalent. Most of it was directed toward the System. Strangely enough, some of the anger was directed toward fellow human citizens. Initially, it was considered a political divide, but fear and confusion dominated once people from the same backgrounds and political views began to attack each other, seemingly at random.

System's response was swift. It segregated anyone and everyone who dared to speak, write, or attend a rally against it regardless of political stances or citizen background, but the violence did not stop. Unlike Earth, which at the time was just adopting the second generation of robots and androids, Mars security forces were comprised of only EvoGens. There were no middlemen, human lawmen, for the public to complain about. A complaint against the security EvoGens was, in fact, a complaint against the System itself. Human to-human aggression was ignored. Bloodshed increased.

People just stopped talking to each other out of fear of who was tied to who. Message boards raged with hatred. Though void of potholes, the Mars neighborhood streets emptied. Most announcements on social message boards, requests for help and such were artificially boosted, hence largely void of concrete actions.

Shaking, the vehicle began its descent, and before I knew it, it parked itself. I exited the craft and walked along the sidewalk to the entrance of City Hall, where the Registrar's office was located.

A thick mist enveloped the inside of the dome today. It was usually created when the chemicals released by the atmospheric processors the System had installed on Ceres2 would precipitate on the ground, surrounding the domes. They would start their reactions there. That subsequent temperature variation resulted in precipitation, or rain, as we sometimes called it.

"Looks like we are going to have some weather today, huh?" the EvoGen standing by the front desk said when I approached, blinking its digital eyes.

"Thanks a lot, canner." Wanting to yank its battery latch and shut it down, I bit my inner lip. I stopped myself. On Earth and lately on Mars, most dissenting humans referred to any System android, no matter what generation or iteration it was, as a canner. *It's not human. It will **never** understand human emotions,* most agreed. Couple those statements with the fact that to most, androids were seen as the defacto executive branch of the System, and one would begin to see the clear and increasing divide. Though on both planets, things were a bit more complicated. While Earth still claimed to be governed by humans, the system was the one with the power to change anything. Mars was technically still governed by people, but we all knew they were System puppets. Their mere presence angered a good portion of the population. Ceres2, on the other hand, was completely governed and managed by it. The EvoGen androids the System had implemented here were advanced. They looked somewhat different from the previous generations. Though, mechanically some things were the same. On Mars, my father taught me that the augmented Metal-hydrogen battery on all the android units was located in the torso area. A latch, holding it in place, was marked by a red vertical lever. It ended in the middle of a circle with the same color.

While the second-generation androids had two visible cameras and speakers - no facial expressions, EvoGens had oval-shaped heads with a screen for a face. They displayed a digital rendition of eyes when they indicated that they looked at a particular object. They sometimes showed colors, such as red for danger, yellow for hazard, etc. Generally, when found in office settings with human resources around to communicate with, they would display a digital face.

"It would seem so," I modified my initial response, placing my wrist next to the pulsating white circle on a pole about three feet off the ground.

"Ah." EvoGen's robotic voice echoed through the hall. "Mister Nett, we require your updated immunization and genetic profile."

"I was told the records would arrive today," I replied, "with the transport shipment."

"Transport?" The android slightly tilted its head.

"Yeah, they're Earth records. Manual." I huffed.

"Please let me get a human for you." The EvoGen turned around and disappeared past a door behind it. A few seconds later, a woman, probably in her late twenties, with black hair and deep blue eyes, emerged from it. Walking toward me, she wore a white mask covering her mouth and nose. She looked at the screen the humanoid robot had prepared.

"Mister Nett," she said, looking at me before shifting her gaze to the screen in front of her, "I see your file needs updating, and the transports have been delayed a few hours. Weather issues." She adjusted her mask.

"We will track your file manually. Meanwhile, I would ask you to wear a mask when using public transport and while in communal spaces."

"A mask," I cleared my throat. "Of course."

"The EvoGen will provide you with one," she continued.

I squinted; while this wasn't the first time I'd seen a person wearing a mask, I'd always gathered what was being said better by looking at the other person's face, lips, and eyebrows. Covers made it much harder for me to conclude that information.

The young woman walked back to the entrance she'd emerged from. System's ring next to its frame pulsated white and green as soon as she hovered her communicator above it. A few moments later, the same EvoGen reentered through it. In its hands was a mask.

"Thank you for your cooperation, Mr. Nett." It handed me the face cover.

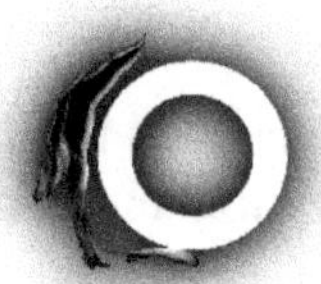

Ceres2, or its concept at the very least, was everything I ever wanted. Nay, everything I ever dreamed of, since my pre-teenage years when I used to walk to the Blue Eye Lagoon on that narrow dirt road surrounded by corn plants. So much so that ever since I arrived in Ceres2, I would ask the TV wall to show me the commercial area of the colony. The buildings, the sidewalks, and the transports, which floated midair, gave the settlement the futuristic feel I'd craved all my life. The saturated-color neon lights lined up on the buildings, not only illuminating the immediate area but also signaling that the establishments were open for business.

Nevertheless, as they say, be careful what you wish for; it might come true. The factual cost of having my dream of living in a futuristic city was enormous. So far in my life, I had left the planet where I was born and my extended family with it. I soon found myself adrift. My father disappeared on Mars. My mother – institutionalized. In the beginning, I had no idea what was happening to me. I was too young. I dealt with my father's disappearance the only way a teenager would. I rationalized the

System messed up its code and that he was fine. When the System decided that it was going to distance my mother from me, my complacency and rationalization turned to contempt. Contempt towards the System. Alas, it had its 'innovative' ways of handling these emotions. Like a dark cloud, the omnipresent information collection hung above everyone's heads. Especially those who grew restless of its unremitting shift of nebulous rules.

Communicators, cameras and sensors served as an all-seeing eye for it. The rumored human spies, on the other hand, were the ones to deal the largely 'invisible' damage. I had never met one of them, but I had heard stories of how people, like my father, had disappeared because of their actions. That was the straw that broke the camel's back. Those last days on Mars, I only spoke to Erica. Similarly, one of the very few people I had even exchanged words with, on Ceres2, was Randy. An optimistic, high-energy, manager. But that's where the parallels ended. He greeted me as soon as I exited the inter-colony transport, helped me with the application to join Ceres2, and, since I didn't have a job designation, also assisted me with obtaining some money in the form of digital currency from the System.

That struck me a bit peculiar. The System essentially paid for me to stay in my living quarters. Mostly doing nothing. Randy, a chubby man with conspicuous feminine features and a large beard, however, checked on me almost daily. I must admit, his energy was substantially annoying. Don't get me wrong, I have always considered myself to be a man with patience and drive, but hearing the phrases *this is a great program,* and *the System is the best thing to happen to humanity* every day for three weeks was where I drew my line. Not to mention his favorite phrase, *Utopia requires compliance.* I still remember what he told me as we crossed the interplanetary transport pathway to the processing area. "The System is creating a utopia in Ceres2. It only exists when everyone understands that what is being done, whatever it is, it's for our collective good." He said, slowly rubbing his hands.

"The System is ensuring that all our needs are met, while we help it better itself. Therefore," I specifically remember this moment because he stopped. I had to stop as well. "In Ceres2, Utopia equals compliance. It's important that you learn this one principle, Mr.Nett." Those phrases, his unusual praise for the System, immediately reminded me of the rumored human spies on Earth and Mars. I looked at him again. Randy was wearing a trench coat covering all of his body. Most of his face was enclosed by one of those facemasks with small filters on both sides. I could only see his grey eyes, the overflowing beard sticking under his mask, but nothing else. Exhausted from the trip, I nodded 'yes,' so I could get him to stop talking.

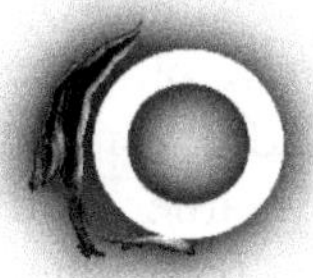

Town Hall's main entrance was on the ground level in the colony's center. However, one could access it by elevator from the higher floors of that same building. Across from it was one of the pathways that led to the commercial district. I strolled by that area every chance I got. Seeing the neon lights from afar through a TV screen was nice, but walking on the ground floor, especially by where the shops were, was an experience. One, I needed to drown my sorrows.

A large projection on the wall next to me depicted accessories sold to augment our personal communicators. Though the minimalistic utilitarian devices simply combined a flexy screen, held in place by bands, with two flat microphones and speakers on both ends. Numerous colorful elastic straps and screen extensions were available for purchase in the market. Once the word UTOPIA faded in and overtook the entire windowless structure, I leveled my eyes, gazing at my surroundings.

People and androids getting in and out of one of the levitating trains, which just arrived at the station, filled the area. Above me, floating cars accompanied by the red laser stabilizers piercing the puff of vapor from one of the nearby heating vents whooshed about. Once the bustling crowd somewhat dissipated, I walked closer to one of the glass-covered parks, which the System would sometimes use as an entertainment center.

"Glass House." A placard posted to its side read. "Each panel constituting the Glass House is made from the same technology as your TV walls: tiny LED lights embedded in small glass squares. When not on, the glass appears transparent. When the dots are switched on, they act as pixels creating a colossal screen."

I peeked inside. EvoGens and human construction workers were milling about. Some carrying steel beams, others adjusting machinery. They were installing some side panels, which seemed to be supported by scaffolding. The EvoGens were laying small rails on the floor. Off to the corner, some seats, usually installed during movie nights, were laid loose on the floor. The dome itself was off. Outside light shone through.

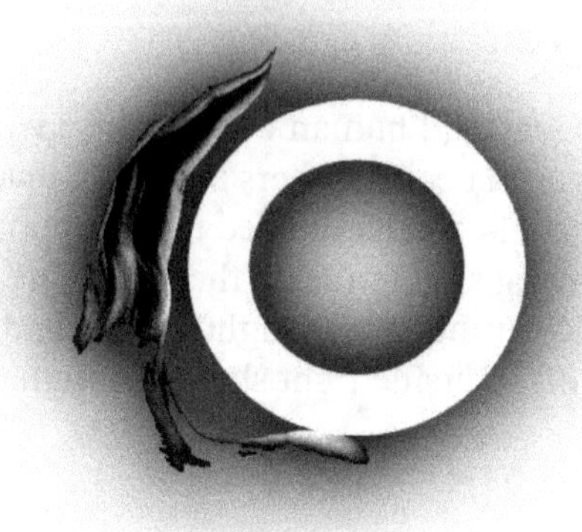

CHAPTER 3

O nce the rush cleared, the pedestrian zone, which spanned the surroundings of the Glass House, remained primarily populated with commercial androids. In contrast to the highly specialized and refined EvoGens who worked in the sensitive parts of Ceres2, power plants, rescue operations, and so on, these ambled predetermined paths as they held various pieces of merchandise with their hands.

A noisy group of people walked in front of the Glass House as another man, wearing a black suit and a subtly lit facemask, got out of a car that stopped a few feet from me. He joined them. As they walked away, I stood in front of the car, contemplating whether to go inside and check out what was on display or return to my living quarters. Contemplation was the contradicting result of my desire to sit and stay there for as long as I wanted versus wanting to be alone and away from people. Another few vehicles descended and parked in front of me. The subsequent flow of people yanked me out of my thoughts. They all seemed to be going somewhere. Laughing. Chatting. I had no friends or acquaintances I'd hang out with to have a good time, so my residence sounded pretty good. I got in the car and ordered it to bring me back to my place.

Transport ascending, I pulled my tablet from my backpack, dropping the latter on the floor next to my seat. It greeted me with the wallpaper of my father and me working on an android together. My mother had taken that picture on Mars. The application icons, unchanged for years, always elicited a feeling of home, back when I had both my parents with me.

Tablets like the one I had, weren't sold on Ceres2. This one was a gift from my father, and I made sure I treated it carefully. The device itself had come with an outdated wireless charging system, a method in which the device still had to contact a surface with energy flowing through it. Still, I'd bought the attachment, which allowed it to be charged dynamically as I passed flow charge ports. They were everywhere in maglev trains, transports, and our living quarters. By doing this, the device was always powered even though its internal battery might have outlasted its time.

I had intentionally disabled the code which enabled interlinking. This way, the information I had on the tablet would stay frozen in time. I had several books I'd enjoyed reading on the device since I was young. Still, the interlinked applications rotated titles based on the trending books the System chose at any given season. I didn't like that. I didn't like the System dictating what I should read and its overreach of removing files from my devices whenever it felt like it.

The reading application, which I periodically checked to ensure my books were still intact, was on the top left. Tapping on it opened a page, which showed my books and audiobooks in list form. *It's all there.*

An unusual link without an icon, which generally meant it was an article I had saved in a hurry, caught my eye. "Rise of the Code" by Darimund Penman, an old college friend of mine who became a journalist. Consequently, declared to be an undesirable by the System, he disappeared on Mars. And with him, all the articles he had ever written or contributed vanished. We all knew he loathed the System, and I downloaded whatever I could find in a hurry as soon as I heard about his troubles.

I looked around one last time. It wasn't illegal to read articles of this kind. In fact, no one really knew what was legal or illegal in Ceres2 since the sale of all kinds of drugs, alcohol and anything that could pretty much kill someone, if abused, was unregulated. But the possession of dissenting articles, coupled with whatever events one would get caught and tangled with the System, could… had, resulted in ejection from the colony.

Throwing my communicator on the seat behind me, I took one last look around. I knew that as long as I kept the screen tilted against the camera, which I knew was on top of the driving seat, the System wouldn't be able to see what I was reading. Moreover, as long as I remained quiet, the System wouldn't have a clue what I was doing. I tapped on the article, opening it. I began interpreting it with Darimund's typical manner of speaking. Unusually exaggerated theatrical highs, lows, and his general contemptuous scratchy voice.

"THE SYSTEM, THE SYSTEM! ALL HAIL THE SYSTEM!" The opening sentence read in big, bold lettering. "But what is this System you speak of, dear writer? – You might ask. And furthermore, where did it come from? Take a seat and allow me to convey the most accurate chain of events a human can put together.

Our story begins with a man, Frederick Einst. Born on Sector Eighty-Nine to a wealthy family, Frederick pursued an early career in politics. But soon, he found out that there was no money or power in it. So, he changed his career to financing and banking. Using his numerous family contacts, because, of course, Frederick was BORN in Sector Eighty-Nine, he was able to create a small piece of software called TLC (The Logical Conclusion.)

After almost crashing several companies, Frederick finally got his break. TLC successfully predicted a company's demise. Knowing this, our 'friend' Freddy offered them a way out. It was publicly ridiculed. However, a few months later, Frederick was avenged, and the company, I believe it was a toy store chain, he previously predicted it would falter, failed. TLC was validated in front of the financial world. And though most of us never heard about it, I bet *you* didn't know. That very event propelled TLC to astronomical heights. Everyone wanted The Logical Conclusion.

With his newfound fame, Frederick sold and offered financial asset management to all Earth's banks. And before anyone knew it, The Logical Conclusion was being used, one way or another, by everyone. Let me repeat it, EVERYONE! Payment information collected from every venue, from arts to … zorb football. Your local grocery shop, news corporations, utility companies, and… let us not forget… governments. Money and information go hand in hand.

Because Earth was, and still very much is, fractured in all word senses, different nations found different ways of abusing… I mean, implementing it.

This brings me to Section Nineteen, my place of birth and the last free election humans on Earth experienced. To say that the appointment of our nation's prime minister, Cintra, was different than the other elections would be an understatement. Do you, precious reader, remember that? Yeah, that was a … an… I can't find a single positive adjective to describe it.

Even so, strange events surrounded it since the campaign was announced. People who opposed the results were deliberately called out on the internet and on TV. Entire articles were published, much like this one, analyzing every word of what was said and their perceived meanings. They were initially dismissed by the regular person. "Who the hell cares about the internet and TV anyway," most uttered. Prolifically.

Sadly, all our cries were drowned. Waters calmed down in the following months. Business carried as usual. Then, the first bells of doom rang. TLC had arrived. I remember my father coming home with a newspaper. "Creating a perfect utopia by automating our services," the front-page article read. Two paragraphs, embedded with a slew of political slogans, explained how the law, yeah, you read that correctly, the law, could be impartially applied despite the ever-changing political atmosphere. (A little disclaimer here, I know the writer of that awful article personally, and he is a real piece of… work.)

The Logical Conclusion's algorithm was cheered and applauded when it was implemented. Initially, it begged us to use the myriad of interlinked devices it was peddling. Soon enough though, and this seems to be the case with all small companies which gain any iota of power, it stopped begging and began demanding. But all along, The Logical Conclusion always relied on the digital information siphoned from the slew of devices we used, mostly involuntarily. This was mainly accomplished by their insidious method of promotion. Remember the old carrot on a stick called 'free upgrade?' Yeah, it was over once most of humanity got hooked on those small 'cool-looking' devices. The final iteration of such devices is what you are most likely wearing right now. The almighty personal communicator. Those pieces of junk provided The Logical Conclusion with all the information it needed. They likely still do.

This was the first time that an algorithm was publicly implemented by a government, and man it showed. They twisted the original code to automate payroll, other administrative jobs, and more sensitive issues. Its first and significant addition was incorporating Traffic and Parking Laws. Red light, speed, and other cameras popped up all over the Sections in a record amount of time, almost overnight.

A little personal story here, I got three speeding tickets before I even got notified that I had gotten the first one. I got a stack of them in the mail, you know. And do you, dear reader, know what *they* told me? I should've gotten a … you guessed it right, personal communicator. Yeah, that would've solved the problem with surveillance. Alright, personal rant over.

In just under four years, Cintra together with Mr. Einst, hired a literal army of computer coders to add more functionality to The Logical Conclusion.

They rebranded it before Cintra's term was over, calling it **the System**…"

The vehicle slowed down and began its descent. I closed the application, put the tablet back in my backpack, then reached on the back seat and retrieved my communicator. The transport dropped me off on the ground floor. So I headed for the elevator. Its doors opened shortly after I approached them, revealing two men and one woman. The one on my left had dark hair and was wearing a white suit with no tie. Chest hair protruded from the top of his unbuttoned shirt. The other - blue jeans, a polo shirt, and white sneakers. They continued their conversation with each other as I entered the elevator car. The woman had short black hair and brown eyes. She was wearing a yellow shirt, black business pants, and black shoes. A white cloth mask covered most of her face.

Ah, yes. I pulled my mask and hooked it on my right ear, slid my finger underneath, and hung up the rest, covering my mouth and nose.

I'd had a complicated relationship with masks ever since they were introduced to the mass population. On the one hand, I liked hiding my emotions. The System cameras, which were everywhere, analyzed people for any signs of System Hysteria, a condition declared dangerous on Mars. On the other hand, I couldn't read or convey my emotions to another human like this. I really wanted to say "hi," but the mere presence of the mask on my face did what it always would: completely sever the human in me. After pressing the thirty-eighth-floor button, I just looked down and walked to the left far end of the large cabin. The doors closed, and I felt the upward pull. Like everything else in Ceres2, these lifts weren't moved by wires; they were magnetically pulled and pushed. It would take the cabin maybe ten seconds to cover ten floors.

The elevator stopped, and the two men stepped out. The woman took a few steps and stopped at the end of the cabin, next to the control panel on the corner opposite me. As she turned to face the doors, we briefly made eye contact.

"Just arrived?" I asked as soon as I saw her looking my way.

"No." She looked down. "I transferred from the east wing. The hospital. I have been serving there for the past six months."

"You're a doctor?"

"And a biochemist." She chuckled. "A steady schedule is one of the perks of being specialized in Ceres2."

"Eh." I pointedly adjusted the mask on my nose. "I'm the relatively new arrival."

"Relatively?" I saw her eyebrows go up.

"I got here about three weeks ago," I explained, "from Mars."

"You were born on Mars?"

"No. No." I paused, "I was… I was born on Earth."

"So was I." Her eyes smiled. "I wondered if I was right about your accent."

"I have an accent?" I chuckled, instinctively looking down. I think I blushed. *Thank god for masks.*

"I think that those who weren't born in the old world can't tell. I can." She tilted her head. "But what does your mask have anything to do with your birthplace?"

"Yeah, about that. It's the paper records." I explained. "How long have you been here?"

"I left Earth when I was little. The System provided most of my education on Mars and then here."

"My name is Elton." I extended my hand almost by instinct.

"Arlinda." She didn't reciprocate. "Let's not shake hands yet."

"Oh, yes, masks, viruses and all." I sighed as the elevator car shook and stopped.

"This is my floor." Arlinda looked out as the doors slid open. "I hope we'll meet again, Elton."

"Likewise, Arlinda." I smiled behind my mask.

It was always refreshing to talk to another human being. Especially a friendly, pretty girl. I didn't get a good look at her face, but I thought she was pretty. Magnets whirring, the elevator cabin lifted one more time. Once the doors opened on the thirty-eighth floor, I exited and turned left at the elevator bank.

I walked along the extended metal platform supporting the road heading toward my living quarters. On my left was a lifted mesh barrier, which extended about four feet above the floor. It prevented accidental falls, which would be fatal for any human from this height. Beyond them, the city center glowed in the distance. Its light illuminated the rooftops of the living quarters and maintenance modules leading there. On my right, the magnetic roadbed was guarded by raised plastic and metal barriers. Rectangular signs hanging every ten feet or so warned of electrocution and magnetic wave hazards.

She sounded pretty anyway. I paused and leaned on the rails, still thinking about Arlinda. *Eh, she's already forgotten about me.* I continued walking along the sidewalk. Bright neon lights illuminated my left; at times, they slowly pulsated.

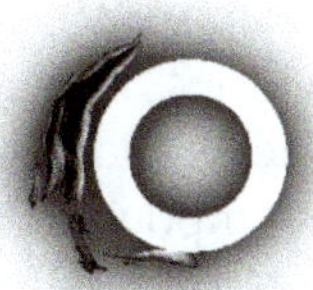

The last woman I had thought this hard about was Erica. I'd met her while I was in high school on Mars. My little desk was in the third row, by the wall. Hers was on the same row but all the way on the other side, by the window. I loved how the light shone through her natural red hair when she turned her head to look my way. That first time we made eye contact, I got utterly lost in her deep green eyes.

I remember it like it was yesterday. When the teacher caught me staring at her during class, she asked me to tell her what the topic of the day was. Obviously, I had no idea. My attention was elsewhere. And she proceeded to embarrass me in front of the entire class.

Later that same day, however, Erica said hi as she left the classroom. Unable to process what I was going through, all I could muster in reply was, "you are beautiful." What I did know was that I really, *really* liked her.

I became good friends with Erica, and we confided in each other for the remainder of our time on Mars. She confessed to me that her family was well-known among their circle of friends—I believe her father had been a high-ranking official somewhere on Earth. They, as a family, remained secluded from the rest of the human population. Erica told me that her parents didn't like participating in any social events the System created. And with the rising tension between citizens and government, he'd given everything up when he moved to Mars to protect her, his daughter.

I was absolutely absorbed in my relationship with Erica and vaguely remember the subtle but numerous changes in the world around me. Happiness in my life abruptly ended with my father's disappearance. As a result, my mother and I lost everything. That shattered the rose-tinted glass I had been looking at Mars through. Paranoia and stress dramatically increased. My only saving grace was Erica.

Life was no longer easy and happy. It seemed as if people no longer talked. They just insulted each other. Though I'd been living on Mars for most of my adult life, daily protests and general disorder made it feel less and less like home. That was compounded by the televised instances of such events. At times, the streets were filled with more System androids than people. And, together with the newcomers, diseases began to spread. That was about the time when my mother had her final mental breakdown. The System wasted no time in diagnosing and institutionalizing her with the newest syndrome, System Hysteria: a condition where a human blamed all their ills on the System whether it was in fact to blame or not.

Initially, I was allowed to visit her but soon enough, citing a new viral flareup, the System barred me from seeing her. And with my family practically nonexistent, Erica was the only person that was there for me.

Soon after, the System announced that in-person college classes were canceled due to the latest pandemic quickly spreading on Mars. Though deep inside, we knew that the System was actually limiting who could go outside and protest its progressively anti-human policies, no one dared to voice that opinion. An increasing number of people who did so got seriously hurt by savage mobs of people who indiscriminately attacked anyone disagreeing with what the System dictated. Or worse, they disappeared.

It got harder and harder to live in a place where all I witnessed were protests, angry people in the maglev trains, and the general feeling of dread. Every day I woke up and walked onto the street, I noticed changes. There was a new graffiti on a building wall just outside my house—the usual, "DOWN WITH THE ROBOTS," the same stuff I had seen on Earth before we left. A garbage can that had been tipped onto the street three nights ago, during a protest, was still there, rolling in the Martian wind. The store next to it was looted, and all its windows were broken. All the commercial entrances on that street had boarded doors and windows. I would look down to try and shield my mind from what was happening around me, but the sight of the garbage spread on the street wouldn't let me shake it from my head.

A month after the in-person classes and other events were canceled, the System displaced humans based on their age and immunization statuses.

Without even notifying me, my mother was relocated to an ambient-controlled dome on the other side of the planet. I tried protesting and received a notice from the System that I was showing signs of System Hysteria.

Cameras and sensors were everywhere, and the notification meant they were observing me. Simultaneously, the System flooded the entire planet with advertisements about this new colony, "Ceres2: Utopia awaits!" They proclaimed, "Apply today!"

Because my parents, the people who supported me, were forcefully taken away, I barely had money to buy food, let alone pay rent. I mainly slept in the alleyway behind the restaurant where I occasionally worked. Though I would do my best to stay clean every time I meet with Erica.

I still remember that cold morning when she skipped class to see me. We sat on the park bench in front of the college I used to attend.

"I don't think the System will reverse these isolation rules anytime soon." I looked at Erica as she shifted her gaze to the floor.

"I don't know what to say, Elton," she replied after a brief and awkward silence. "It seems the System no longer cares about us." She swallowed.

"I haven't been able to pay my rent in months." I confessed, rubbing my neck, "the landlady locked me out of my apartment yesterday." I was too embarrassed to tell her the truth that I had been living in the back alley for weeks.

"What are you going to do now?" Erica stared at me with disbelief.

"Up there is my only chance." I pointed to the big poster above us, flashing the words Ceres2 and UTOPIA. "If I stay here, I'll end up…" I tightened my lips and looked down.

"This is not right. It's not!" She exclaimed, shaking her head in disapproval. "If you go, then I want to come with you."

I had no more words left in me. The System was effectively draining all my energy, one crisis at a time. Swallowing, I looked at the sign again.

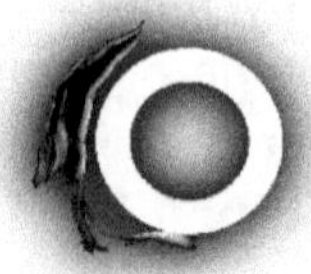

The loud whirring of the elevator's magnets brought me back to Ceres2. Somewhat startled, I followed it with my eyes as it passed my level, descending to the lower floors. A few cars sped in the traffic lane to my right, rattling the plastic mesh barrier in some places. Sections along the dome roof diameter, which stood several hundred feet above me at this height, made their usual clanging sound. I continued walking along the extended metal platform as the distant voice from an advertisement projected in the commercial spaces across me echoed. *What's the point of having advertising with audio in these things when one can't tell what they're selling?* Another car whirred on the street on my right. *Well, it's probably meant for those who are nearby.*

A bitter smile quickly faded as I caught myself mumbling. I used to do that on my way to and from school, back on Earth. I would look at an advertisement or a license plate or listen to the strange and jarring sound the large trucks made as it echoed through the buildings, and I'd just daydream while walking to school.

What do I know: here is number 38-42.

CHAPTER 4

My wrist communicator vibrated as soon as my front door closed behind me. "A kind reminder," it read, "that the residency application associated with Elton Nett is still under review. We will notify you when there are further developments. Or if there are any changes to your status. Your current status is: PENDING." Sitting on my bed, I groaned.

The application I'd had to fill in to enter the Third Colony amounted to about five hundred gigabytes. It contained all the data gathered from my birth until my family moved to Mars. Education, grades, behavior analysis; the Mars System compiled it all. It had video clips, work ethics narratives, and interviews from my coworkers and friends. The System didn't hide it; in fact, we were responsible for ensuring the information was as complete as possible based on the checklist provided.

Before I handed the big manilla envelope and other documents to the System android, who processed me at the port of entry on Ceres2, I read the worksheet stapled on the outside. It had a catalog of the items included. The only document marked in red lettering was my actual genetic profile and the first list of my vaccination rounds, the ones I got up to the age of ten, which were missing. Yet the Third Colony System required original copies. *All specimens must be healthy*, the fine print read under the red markup.

My generation, especially those who were born within my decade, were the ones to be cursed to have multiple forms of information, digital, and paper. The System identified and developed successful vaccines for a sizeable number of highly infectious and deadly diseases during my childhood. But many new ones were spreading to pandemic levels as soon as another one was brought under control.

Three years after the first pandemic, the System permanently locked Earth-Nation borders. Anyone who crossed, and it wasn't hard back then, had to provide their universal genetic and vaccination evidence. Obviously, that information was private, but the System decided to include that with the digital passport pedigree data.

I didn't have a digital passport on Earth. Hell, no one did. After my grandparents died and my family moved to Mars, we were digitalized. That happened during the one-month mandatory quarantine my parents and I were subjected to when we landed. As soon as we exited the transport ship, all of us were rounded up and sent to a building that reminded me of my old elementary school. The only difference was that this building smelled like bleach.

I celebrated my tenth birthday with a small cake and five other kids from the same corridor.

After everyone sang happy birthday inside a room lined with tiles, floor to ceiling. My parents brought a small white cake with a candle in the shape of the number 10. Because we weren't allowed to shake hands, let alone kiss and hug, everyone unceremoniously left after I blew it. I saw people with yellow hazmat suits spray the room with a white liquid as soon as we exited.

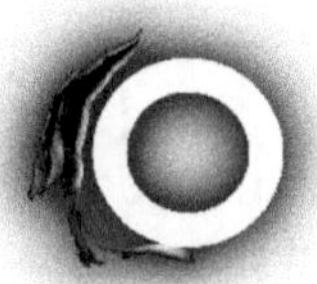

After setting the TV wall screen to my favorite feed, I opened my refrigerator door and asked the System to play ambient music. A bowl of soup and a few breadsticks caught my attention on the upper tray. Behind them were some of what I called "hockey pucks," little green saucers of compressed seaweed, and some soy-based sauce next to them. Below them were several bread products, cookies, and such. On the bottom were vegetables and fruits, which didn't attract my attention at this point.

So far, my diet had consisted mostly of dried fruit, vegetables, and the rare worm and bug-meatball mixture. Of course, as on Mars, I would go out to the colony center, where humans would sell cooked recipes of their own. Very few tasted like what I used to eat on Mars, even less like my grandmother's cooking.

Since I hadn't yet tried eating meat in Ceres2, I pulled out a small bag with pre-cooked meatballs and placed them on the counter next to me. I rummaged through the lower tray and found some cooked potatoes and broccoli.

Sprinkling on some salt, I ate the contents as soon as I pulled them out of the microwave. I remembered how my mother would tell me what her father had told her about how he used to live by himself on Earth. He would wash, cut, and fry potatoes in a frying pan and eat them directly from it. As a result, the dinner table he had usually stayed untouched. I went to bed and stared at the screen. I dozed off as my stomach digested the food I'd just eaten.

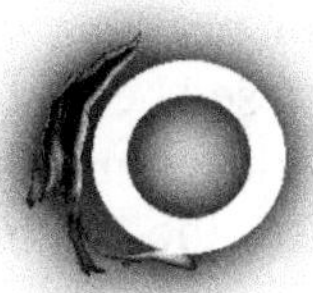

A loud church bell ringing attracted my attention. Faintly trailing it, I could hear Tony's laughter, followed by Lori's giggling. Looking in the direction the sound was coming from, I got up. The floor was cold and wet, and the room was dark. I looked down, but I couldn't see neither the bottom nor my feet. Extending my hand, I helped myself up by holding onto the wall, which felt as if it was wet as well.

A white light blinked into existence. My friends' echoing laughter intensified as the church bell bangs faded. Initially, it seemed as if the light emanated from a small nearby source. But I soon realized it was a large light, far in the distance. As I paused and observed it for a moment, I coughed. The area around me had filled with a dense layer of what appeared to be smoke. Waving my hands so I could move some of it out of my face, I slowly walked toward the light, using the wall to my left as a guide.

As if someone flipped a switch, the area around me lit up. I still couldn't see the floor, and the white wall to my left was covered with a red substance. It resembled blood. My heartbeat rising, I looked around, trying to see if the other walls were also covered in blood. But I couldn't see through the thick white mist around me. Above, though, I saw a dark, starry sky. And the wall I was touching continued up as far as I could see.

Leveling my head to see what was ahead of me, I followed the wall in the direction I remembered seeing the faint light. The bright light surrounding me made it hard to discern it in the distance.

I walked for a few seconds next to the white wall, now covered with red bands. Unlike the surrounding area, an opening in the smooth surface, free of blood streaks, looked like a door. I could see light penetrating through the cracks on its side and bottom. Its hinges squeaked as it opened. The light from the other side created a band on the mist brighter than my surroundings. Shielding my eyes with my hands, I looked around and went through the door. It closed behind me with a loud boom, and the area darkened. Instinctively I closed my eyes and rubbed them. Once I could see again, I noticed that the white door, which had the word BLOOD, quickly faded away.

Breathing hard, I frantically looked around. I recognized this place. This was the backyard of the building I'd lived on Earth. Instead of the rest of the buildings, though, the natural spring and Weeping Willows surrounded me. Tony was still chasing Lori with his water bottle. Next to me stood Arlinda, pointing at the sky.

I lifted my head to see what she was pointing at. Above us, a round craft shone down a floodlight. Its light surrounded me as a loud generator hum filled the area. I swallowed. Arlinda stared at me and, at the same time, took a few steps back. I wanted to walk to her, but I couldn't. Looking down to see what was preventing me, I felt as if an invisible hand had grabbed me from under my armpits, swiftly pulling me up.

Before I knew it, I found myself high enough to see the windows on the third level of the building. I looked down. The light emanating from under the natural spring made it seem like the blue eye was staring at me.

My teeth grinding, I opened my eyes. The lights, which worked based on motion sensors, turned on, and the room took on a blue hue. I was clinging to my bedsheets. Exhaling through my nose, I let go and relaxed my jaws as much as I could. Feeling my heart wanting to burst out of my chest, I sat on my bed. Elbows on my knees, I rested my head in between my hands and stared at the floor.

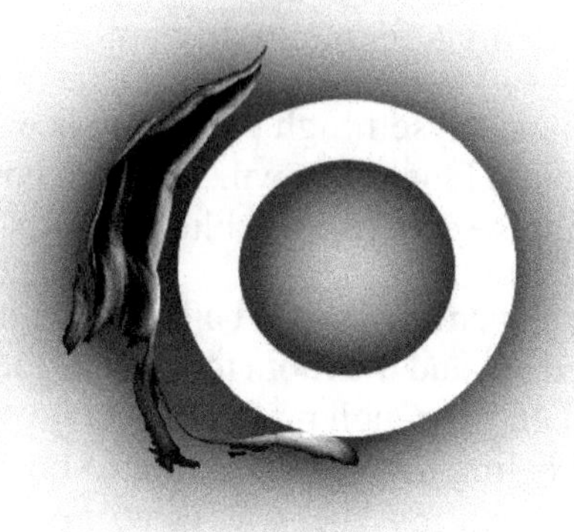

CHAPTER 5

These once pleasant recurring dreams, now twisting my soul through nightmares, constantly reminded me of the very first time I journeyed without my parents. Disregarding their 'monster' warnings, Tony, Lori, Suela and myself, ventured into the 'forbidden zone' – hills and fields surrounding Section Eight.

The trip, stemming from one of Tony's many adventures when with his parents, proved to be quite unnerving for me. Partly because up to that point of my life, I was used to being with one of my parents when this far from Section Eight. But mostly because of… monsters. Though I never got a visual of what they looked like, I always imagined teeth, red eyes… and black fur. However, the intrigue of the Blue Eye Lagoon, of how water just came out of the ground for no apparent reason was compelling enough for me to accept.

For hours we hiked on the dirt road leading to the ever-distant hills. Stopping every once in a while to inspect the larvae inhabiting the many potholes filled with leftover irrigation water and to remove little pebbles sticking in between our feet and sandals. I had never been so close to corn plants, certainly not ones that towered me by over two feet. But I was thankful they did, the sun was unforgiving, and they provided the only shelter from its rays.

A small wooden house surrounded by a low dirty picket fence greeted us shortly after we reached the top of the nearest hill. Trees behind the cot cast a shadow on its top while flowers peppered the front yard. A dog barking within summoned an old lady wearing a white scarf over her head. Dragging her long grey dress, she stopped on the other side of the fence and calmed down the canine. She asked us if we were lost, and I instinctively looked back the way we came. I could see Section Eight, but not where home was from there.

We told her we were going to look at the natural spring, and she said that we were too little to go up there by ourselves. Of course, we disregarded her. She insisted that we take a bottle of water with us, at the very least. We accepted it. After drinking some, and oh boy, I had been thirsty, and I hadn't even realized it, we resumed our hike.

By then, we had passed the first hill, and I could no longer even orient myself to look at the corn fields, which should have been somewhere below us. In front of us, another mound, and I could see a taller one behind it. Surrounded by trees and bushes, I could only hear the bees and other insects buzzing by. In the sky, a large bird flew in circles. The path we walked on was no longer a straight line; instead, it twisted and turned around multiple of what appeared to be banks of dirt.

After what felt like another hour of hiking, we finally reached the top of the tallest hill we had been seemingly hiking toward all along. There were no houses there. No streets. No power lines. Nothing, just us, the trees, birds, and insects that accompanied us all the way. Below us was a valley. In its middle were patches of trees and a sizable green pasture. That was unusual because, on our way, we only saw dirty grass and shrubs.

The closer we got, the more significant that area appeared. Once nearby, I could see a clear difference between the dry, sun-beaten grass behind and the field with knee-high grass in front of us. There were white flowers, the small ones that looked like tiny crystals, and yellow ones I'd only ever seen in pictures. About twenty or thirty feet away from us were a lot of Weeping Willows. We called them *crying trees*. Their branches, too long and thin to stay upright, bent and pointed to the grass. I could hear water rushing but couldn't see where it came from.

We continued walking past the crying trees, and there it was: a tall rock and the spring next to it. The water emerged from a wide opening in the ground, maybe ten feet in diameter, and was deep blue. I had never seen water that color. I knew that the ocean and sea were blue because I had seen them on TV, but I'd never witnessed them myself before.

Tony walked over to it and dunked the now-empty water bottle the old lady gave us. "Ah!" He chugged the contents. "Here, drink some." He handed the bottle to me. "It's water!"

We explored the surroundings for about half an hour, and once the sun passed the middle of the sky, we decided to head back. Curiously enough, the hike back home felt a lot shorter. Maybe because at this point, we anticipated the hike down would feel as stretched as the trip up felt.

That was my first experience going out to the "forbidden zone."

After that day, we would head out there periodically. The following year, though, Tony's family moved to Mars. A few months after, Lori's family relocated to Section 15, and Suela ended up at a different school. Sadly, I was the only one from our close circle of friends left in Section Eight.

I walked to the spring a couple of times myself. One day, I noticed that the house where the old lady had given us the water was no longer standing. Instead, the area was littered with what the house once was: wooden beams and dirt. The brick chimney laid broken on the top of a damaged flowerbed where flowers were no longer growing.

Even twenty years later, I still remember that natural spring. I dreamt about it on Mars, but lately, they had become more frequent.

CHAPTER 6

Since I arrived on Ceres2, every time I enjoyed something, the guilt of my loved ones not being near me—or alive, for that matter—to enjoy it as well, ate at my core. At first, when I disembarked three weeks ago, I would break down and cry while looking at the TV screen. Once that deep depression subsided, I found myself spending a lot of time in my unit. Some days I would just catatonically stare at the TV wall. Then apathy settled in. I wondered if that was the way life was, not only for me but everyone else. After all, the transport I took from Mars was filled with grown adults who, at times, broke down and cried. Everyone tightly held their big manilla envelopes. I knew what that meant—we all went through a lot of trouble to get all those documents together. We all intentionally left everything behind. Yet, the heartache was evident.

As if I was on autopilot, I got up, made a coffee, and turned on the TV wall. My living quarters took on the typical blue hue while the screen showed the usual feed I requested: the commercial district. I knew the time on my communicator said it was around noon, but the dome looked no different than any other time of the day.

"Mister Nett, your volunteering services are required. Please report to Bay Three for further instructions," my communicator announced.

Though Randy explained to me in length how it worked, volunteering, or rather paid volunteering, as they called it, confused me initially. The System's concept adapted in Ceres2 was pragmatic; anyone could be called to do any job at any time. It was a departure from how things ran on Earth and Mars, where jobs were assigned and fixed. And because of the nature of the assignments, scheduling wasn't really a thing. Mainly because when a job was to be done, and a human factor was needed, the System would select the next person available from a rotating roster. Randy explained that the selection process prioritized those with a formal education in the specific job the services requested. Still, the System would embed an android with the human team without a human expert. It usually had detailed instructions regarding the given assignment.

Conversely, the only humans who knew their schedules ahead of time were doctors, System's engineers, and managers. While generally, the System would fix most mechanical and complicated issues that would occur to androids, they also needed human robotics experts. Because of my general experience in robotics, I thought the System would dispatch me more frequently in assignments of that nature. So far, that didn't seem to be the case.

I headed for the shower. But before I could even turn it on, the communicator vibrated again. Someone was at the front door. I grunted. I knew it was Randy, the only person who would visit me at random times.

"Mister Nett!" Randy exclaimed, entering my unit, "what a great day in utopia!" he did the usual hand rubbing as he looked around. "Wouldn't you say?"

"Hi Randy," I rolled my eyes as I turned my back to him and walked to the coffee machine. "Yes, it's awesome being here."

"That's what I'm talking about!" he said and paused for a moment. "Making some coffee, I see." He followed up.

These types of awkward moments accented all our meetings. I knew Randy was forcing a friendship between us, most likely because he knew I was so isolated.

"Yeah," I took a sip from the mug I prepared. "The System notified me of a job today."

"A job!" I felt his hand touch my shoulder, "look at you!" Randy exclaimed once again, "finally joining the utopia efforts!"

"Utopia," I cleared my voice and swept his hand away from me. "Yep. That's what I'm here to do."

"Look." Randy continued, "it's not that much different than what you experienced on Mars. Both Mars and Ceres2 were built similarly, see?" He took a deep sigh. "The buildings and structures are enclosed by retractable mega domes..."

"I know, Randy," annoyed, I interrupted him, hoping he would take the hint, shut up, and hopefully leave. "I have seen the holographic exhibition of the entire Mars colony in the Museum of Human History."

But, of course, Randy lacked any form of social cue understanding. "I love how they showed how the System created the domes by using the existing materials on Mars. It's like it was recycling Mars. You know."

"Yes, Randy." I pulled some clothes from my drawer. As he continued to talk about how the System had built the domes. "It built them," he said, referring to the domes, "so elegantly, yet in such a practical way. Am I right?"

"We are living in cages, Randy," I huffed, placing my coffee cup on the counter, "what's so elegant about it?"

"Boy, they told me you would be a little difficult on the uptake." Randy followed. "But I think you will be one of our star members. I can feel it!" Swept under his own enthusiasm, he clapped his hands twice. "Anyway." He smirked, "what kind of assignment are you going to?"

"I don't know," I replied. "Something to do with Bay Three."

"Ah, the fire." Randy looked at me. His smile faded. "Well, someone has to clean that up."

"There was a fire?" I picked up my coffee cup and took another sip.

"Yeah, last night." He rubbed his nose and cleared his throat. I didn't say anything on purpose, waiting for him to get his usual verbal diarrhea and tell me what happened. But he didn't.

"Well, I'll leave you to it." Randy finally blurted after the brief awkward pause. "Carry on." He smiled, "for utopia!" He ended his sentence and headed for the door.

Groaning, I looked at the front door reappear. I turned around to head for the shower and noticed that the TV wall had switched feeds. The System had picked up our conversation. The screen was now displaying some form of documentary about Ceres2. It showed the different domes sparsely laid on the surface as it compared both colonized planets, Mars and Ceres2. And because they were presented as holographic images, I couldn't tell how far apart they actually were from each other. Maglev trains and other vehicles traveled in tubes that connected the domes. As that imagery rotated, I could see that on the opposite side of each planet were the power generators, nuclear fusion reactors, and sewage treatment plants. The hydroponic plants were placed opposite them so they could be protected from any possible radiation if the nuclear reactors malfunctioned. Mega tunnels and trenches were used to lay the cables and canals to connect these structures to the domes which hosted humans and other facilities. I leaned on the bathroom door frame, took another sip from my mug and continued watching.

The atmosphere processors came to view with a transport used next to them for comparison. They were huge plants that released controlled amounts of chemicals on the planet to create an atmosphere on its own. Placed along the planet's midline, they were equally distant from all the other domes. "The processors are gradually shut down once they accomplish their mission. The metal domes would then initially retract halfway to allow air inside. Slowly but surely, they weren't needed anymore." The ever-present bottom scroller on the screen read. "In fact, they are still used on Mars, but not to hold the atmosphere in. They are usually deployed as protection against dust storms. As you have already noticed, on Ceres2, the domes are still used constantly. The air is not entirely safe to breathe for extended periods due to CO_2 overabundance."

"Cycle to my favorite feed," I commanded the TV wall. As the imagery reset to what I instructed, I took one last sip from the coffee mug and went to take a shower.

II

CHAPTER 7

Located in the easternmost part of the dome complex, Bay Three faced outward. High above the residential units lined against the supporting walls, a magnetic travel lane lead to outer space. Surrounding the residences, mega hatches marked the tunnels and piping housing Third Colony's electrical, water, and sewage ducts.

Wearing my facemask, I approached an area brighter than the surroundings, where the meeting point on my communicator led me to.

"Ah, here is the last member," a man, probably in his mid-thirties, wearing khakis, a polo shirt, and a yellow construction helmet, said as soon as I approached a group. "Get a little closer!" He motioned with his hands.

Group gathering, the man spoke to us through one of the emergency vehicles loudspeaker system. "My name is Samuel!" His voice filled the vicinity. "I am managing this emergency repair job!" He looked around. "There are twenty-six of us here, and I think it won't take us more than two hours to do this. Here's the situation."

Behind him, there was a typical forty-story residential block. Each residence, like mine, was about fifty feet wide and ten high. The System had redirected street light lamps to illuminate the building.

"There has been a fire in Unit Eight," Samuel continued. "We suspect the fire began with an electrical short caused by water buildup in a routing box. As a precaution, we've cut power from the entire block."

Two maintenance trucks got on the magnetic lane as soon as the maglev train which had dropped me off departed. Two more vehicles, resembling large forklifts, joined them.

"We will completely replace these damaged residences." Samuel pointed at the charred building behind him. "And swap them with new units."

Several oversized transports carrying the new parts filled all magnetic travel lanes. EvoGens rappelled down from the highest one. They immediately walked to the machinery and began activating them.

"Our job is to make sure all the units are installed properly. Everyone should have a message detailing which EvoGens you are supervising." Samuel finally stepped down from the vehicle.

My wrist communicator vibrated as the machines began their coordinated movements. A series of random characters scrolled across the screen. Settling, it showed a GPS location for me to follow. I looked up to see that only about three other humans remained in my vicinity. Checking their wrist communicators, everyone fanned out.

That must be it.

I followed the path the System usually laid for me when I would go to places I'd never been before. It didn't last long. Three blocks later, my communicator's screen flickered so severely, I couldn't see where it led. *It's never done that before.* As soon as I turned the corner, the surrounding lights went out. "What now," I muttered, looking behind me. As far as I could see, the block I was on was the only one without power. I could see lights in front and behind me. "Well, they did say they had electrical issues," I rationalized, resuming my walk.

A faint flicker inside the nearest housing unit grabbed my attention, mainly because the doors would always be closed. Also, none of our living quarters had doors facing the street; they would generally face the hall on the other side of the housing complex.

"Hello?" My curiosity piqued as I walked to what appeared to be a doorway.

No one answered, but the ceiling lights wavered, revealing graffiti on the inside wall. I couldn't read it because the flickering light only briefly illuminated the abandoned unit.

Wait a moment. I stopped and squinted in disbelief. *Abandoned? That's odd.*

Uninhabited residences were generally securely locked up, unpowered and all. *Perhaps there was another fire here? Something Samuel and the rescuing crews missed? And where the hell are the EvoGens?*

"Hello!" Taking a step inside the unit, I raised my voice.

Crunch. The dry sound of a branch breaking or possibly a glass panel giving in under my weight faded. I looked down but couldn't see much through the darkness.

Smelling burned flesh, a horrifying stench I experienced on the filthy streets of Mars after the System 'quelled' riots, I stopped moving. Panicking, the hair on the back of my neck stood up. A strange feeling to have in the self-described Third Colony utopia. This unit didn't belong here.

Before I could turn around and head out, the lights, still flickering, lit up the surrounding laser-burned bullet-hole ridden walls. Under my shoes, a black, crunchy substance, almost as if I was standing on charred tree branches. I read the word "Robots!" on the wall to my right before the lights flickered yet again.

I immediately recognized that type of graffiti. I remembered seeing the phrase "Down With The Robots!" on storefronts when my mom walked me to school on Earth. Here though, its placement was very peculiar. *Inside living quarters? Where nobody could see it?*

Apart from the strangely placed front door, the inside was very similar to my living unit. On top of the dirty sheet-less bed mattress was a black case. Approaching, I placed my hand over where the identifiers would usually be, on the bottom left of each face. Wiping that section clean to reveal the silver metal casing. The letters O.W.C-C1, which stood for Off-World Colonies, Colony One, appeared. Their blue color was severely scratched.

Gasping, I immediately coughed out the stale, burnt-flesh-smelling air I'd taken in. Transport containers like these were only used to carry official documents, and only the System and its devote followers referred to Earth as a colony. Lights flickering once more, I felt for the locking mechanism, which moved freely. *This container is unlocked.*

Nestled in black cushioning foam, two metallic cylinders, about two inches in diameter and eight in length, lay within. *I have seen cylinders like these before.* Shaking me out of my thoughts, the monotone sound of metallic footsteps echoed. Recognizing that androids were approaching, the first thing I thought was, *I don't think I'm supposed to be here.*

Panicking anew, I placed both containers inside my jacket and zipped it up, then replaced the lid on the container and hurried out. As if someone was controlling them, the flickering lights turned off as soon as I stepped out.

"Mister Nett, you are in the wrong section." Two Second-Gens, System rings pulsating red, were waiting for me outside. One of them extended its hand and guided me further away from the damaged unit. Both walked behind me, physically pushing me to the end of the block.

"That room had fire damage as well," I said once the androids weren't pushing me anymore. Hearing their mechanical sounds getting more distant, I turned around only to see the two robots extend their arms toward me.

"You cannot walk there, sir," they said in unison, "the area is dangerous."

The Second-Gens who'd escorted me out of the zone evoked feelings of Mars, but, given my predicament, I didn't feel inclined to have a conversation with them.

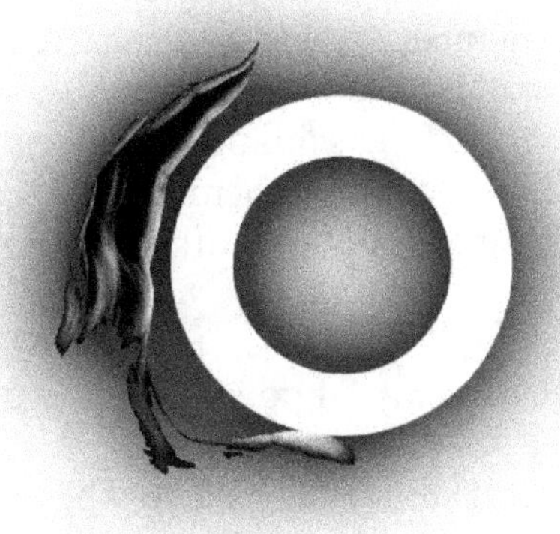

CHAPTER 8

Leaving the robots behind, I briskly continued walking toward the construction zone.

"Mister Nett." Samuel approached as I got closer to the construction site. "Can you please take control of these droids and place them on the outer perimeter?" He pointed to the magnetic lane leading into Bay Three. "A few vehicles slipped past it, and nearly hit the new apartments we are installing."

"I'm having difficulties with my communicator," Lifting my left arm, I showed him the device. "It sent me somewhere that way." I turned around, pointing to the area I had just come from while ensuring he didn't see the containers inside my jacket. That's when I noticed that the Second Gens who escorted me out of the area were gone.

"Yeah, that's been happening lately, especially at the edge of the colony's core." He got a little closer, examining my wrist communicator. "It looks like it's working now," Samuel continued after he pressed a digital button on it. "You can go to the management office and get it checked when we're done here."

To my surprise, the device now showed my correct location and time. On it, a button with the number twelve flashed. Reaching over, Samuel pressed it. Slowly, twelve EvoGens surrounded us.

"Cover that spot over there," he said, pointing to the area where all the vehicles were parked. "Just place them evenly across the road and sidewalks. Let's keep everyone out till we completely replace the damaged units."

"There's more damage that way." I pointed back again.

"Yeah, we know." Samuel shifted his gaze to where I was pointing. "The System is slowly replacing the old residences."

We watched from the sidewalk as robotic cranes slowly slid out the units from the vertical frame beams, placing them on the flatbed self-driving vehicles on the magnetic roadbed.

"I'll get to my spot," I said, making sure my jacket was zipped up before facing him.

Curiosity got the better of me again, and once I got the EvoGens posted, I scooted inside one of the transporter cabins. Removing my wrist communicator, I took both tubes in my hands. **Earth original documents, authorized use only,** was written across their length. Twisting the top of one of them, I felt fabric-laced rolled papers akin to court documents within. Skipping past the opening paragraph, I stopped on a list of names. Before I could read further, the transport shook. I quickly hid the papers behind my back before an android opened the front door. "Mr. Nett," it popped its head inside, "our assignment is over. We are resuming
normal operations."

"Acknowledged," I replied as the android left the cabin.

Breathing shallowly, I hurriedly rolled the certificates back into the tube and placed both inside my jacket. My carotid and jugular arteries throbbed on both sides of my throat; I coughed, then took a deep breath. *Original documents in a place like this? How? Perhaps there was an accident?*

Zipping my jacket, I exited the cabin. Noticing that the rest of the helpers had already left, I walked to the bay so I could take the shuttle back. "This is an automated message from the System," my wrist communicator echoed. "Please report to management at your earliest convenience for an examination of your device. Thank you, and have a nice day."

"God damn canners!" I groaned.

I was worried that the video of me removing the documents might've been captured by the System's extensive camera network. I approached, entered a nearby parked transport, and gave it my address. As the vehicle moved, I sat on the chair and lightly touched the tubes. *Maybe I made a mistake.*

My calm facial expression did not reflect the turmoiled panic state I was in. I just stared at my surroundings. Transport slowing, it descended then stopped. Apprehensively, I walked to my residence. The front door, however, didn't open after I waved my wrist communicator. Instead, the ring rotated in yellow and orange. "Mr. Nett, please report to the management office," the same generic monotone female voice the System used to render text to speech reverberated.

Trying to maintain a calm demeanor, I huffed in annoyance. Now I had to go to the management offices. I couldn't shake the fear that they were calling me, personally. That somehow, a camera or a sensor picked up what I took inside that damaged unit. I had never experienced something like this on Ceres2, and knowing what just happened, my biggest fear was that the Second-Gens who escorted me out had the evidence.

Maybe they saw me removing the closed cylinders? I had no idea how the System would behave if I handed in two opened tubes that once were sealed. I had no choice but to head down to the transport station. As if it knew I would need it, the same vehicle I'd taken home was still waiting for me, doors open.

Heartbeat through the roof, I asked the vehicle to bring me to the management offices. As the electric transport moved, I wiped a drop of sweat from my forehead. I coughed. Breathing through my mask was getting harder and harder. I took it off and placed it in my pocket.

What if they just wanted to check the device? *The area didn't have power. There's no way they would know,* I reassured myself.

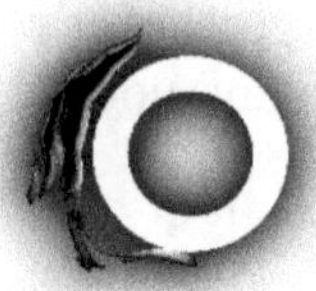

The transport shook before slowing down. I had arrived. Biting my inner lower lip, I adjusted the tubes into my belt and exited the vehicle. I walked through the open doors of the management office and approached the front counter.

"Ah, Mr. Nett," the android standing behind it greeted me, "the System inspectors are expecting you. May I have your communicator please?" It extended its hand.

"Of course," I replied. "I couldn't open the front door of my living quarters."

"We are aware. Please wait here for a moment." The android walked back through the door as another walked to the front desk, replacing it.

"Is this going to take long?" I asked, trying to make conversation with the machine as the front door opened and a young woman entered the large hall.

That's a familiar face. Is she…? She placed a mask across her face and adjusted it to cover her nose. *She's that doctor I met in the elevator!*

"Hi," she said after approaching the front desk, "my communicator said to…"

"Yes, Dr. Duro. We are aware. May I please have your communicator?" the android interrupted her. "It will only take a couple of minutes," it said in answer to my question.

She handed her communicator to the robot, who walked back to the same door. This time no one replaced it. The doctor turned her head and looked at me. I couldn't see the rest of her face, but her eyes drooped in indifference.

"We meet again," I blurted out.

"Again?" She raised her eyebrow.

"We met before, in the elevator." *Maybe it wasn't her?* I blushed and added, "I think?"

"Maybe, you had a mask on back then, right?"

"Yeah, I don't know where I put it." I looked at the floor. I didn't want to insert my hands into my pockets out of fear that the tubes might move.

"You got your paperwork sorted out?"

"No. The transport is delayed, apparently. I'm here because my communicator is acting up. You?"

"Same, and my residential unit lost power."

"You think it's just the two of us?"

Before I finished the question, the EvoGen walked back in. It approached the two of us and said, "Mr. Nett, Dr. Duro, please follow me this way."

"I'll go out on a limb here," Arlinda said with a sigh, "and say I think our questions are about to be answered." She followed the android, which headed for a door on the far-right end of the hall. Adjusting the cylinders I'd tucked in my belt, I followed.

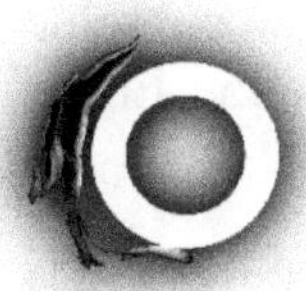

I'd been in and out of City Hall and official offices frequently over my life. In fact, no matter how different these buildings were, they projected the same sensation. Every time I would enter one of them, I would get the feeling of helplessness. As if I was asking a complete stranger to help me with a very personal issue. On Earth, my mother took me everywhere with her to get all the necessary paperwork for our eventual immigration to

Mars. And each and every time we had to queue for hours, I had to endure the strange smells of everyone around me. Cigarettes, alcohol mixed with body odor, and the occasional fried food someone in the hall would be eating. But at the end of each visit, we managed to receive the almighty manilla envelopes the records came in.

But back then, the highlight of the day was what happened *after* we got the papers. It was the ice cream my mother would get me.

They were sold at the ice cream shop in the center of the town. It was part of a variety store nested in a small brick building in front of a bus stop. One of those places that had some kind of pastry or ice cream for every season. They even had cream-filled cones—I called them warm ice cream.

Generally, we would make it there before it closed for the day, but I remember one night we were late. The shopkeeper was just about to shut the window as my mom knocked on it with her wedding ring.

"One more, please!" My mother waved as the shopkeeper pointed at the clock—it was seven in the evening. "It's for a child," my mother continued. "Please!"

I think that was the first time I'd experienced anger in my life, seeing my mother pleading for something. I tugged her hand. "Come on, Mom. I don't want ice cream," I lied to her. I really wanted it. But the ball of tears in my throat wiped that desire.

"I'll get you one tomorrow," she said reluctantly as we continued walking down the sidewalk toward Section Eight. "You were a really good boy today."

The very next day, riots against the newly implemented System ravaged the city center. They lasted for months. I never saw that shop open again.

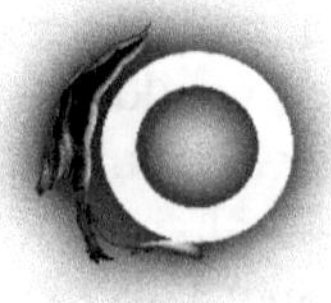

The android walked to the end of a very narrow hall where a door vanished, revealing a room filled with people. Some dressed in formal suits, others in construction clothes with yellow helmets.

"Please wait here," the EvoGen said after we both entered the area. "The System is analyzing the anomaly and will get to everyone in the order in which you arrived."

Before the android finished its sentence, Arlinda turned around and walked to the end of the room. Feeling left alone, I slowly strolled to an empty area and leaned against a panel. I was afraid the cylinders might fall if I sat down.

The wall on my left dematerialized and an EvoGen accompanying more people entered. The robot told them the same line the other had told us and walked away; the door closed behind it. A group of five or six construction workers and a man in a suit next to me were speaking in a language I didn't understand. Three young women stood in the middle of the room, one of them wearing a black sleeveless, seamless latex mini dress with a mock neck and cutout chest. Another was wearing something similar but red; she had long black boots on. The third was wearing a spaghetti-strapped mini dress with a flared skirt and knee-high platform boots. A white bow was affixed on her head, clearing her bangs from her face.

A man wearing teal shoes, deep-blue jeans, and a pink shirt approached them with a smile. "The System has determined that you ladies are too sexy," he said with a smirk as they giggled in return.

"I think I know why we're here. I think the System knows about the refugee shuttles," a whisper came from my left. Without turning, I looked in their direction over my shoulder. Two men and two women dressed in business attire talked to each other in a low tone.

"Shush!" one of them whispered a bit louder, "are you nuts?" He made eye contact with me, then quickly looked away.

"Relax," another man in their group, who didn't notice me, continued. "They took our communicators."

"You know the walls have ears here, right?" The man who made eye contact with me whispered. I lowered my eyes, turned around, and walked in the direction of the young ladies who were flirting as the man in blue jeans and teal shoes continued to crack jokes with them. I wasn't interested in the small spectacle they were making of that encounter. I just wanted to walk away from the group that seemed to have different, more concerning worries at the moment.

Shaking my head, I looked around the room for Arlinda but couldn't see her. Many people were strolling back and forth by themselves, while some groups seemed to be having a get-together. Just add glasses in these people's hands, and this would seem like a big party. I walked along the wall, trying to head in the direction I'd last seen Arlinda.

Suddenly the room went silent. Unaccompanied, an EvoGen had entered through one of the unmarked doors. It went directly to the group of people who had been talking about the refugees. "Please follow me," it summoned them with its monotone voice. "Your communicators are ready."

Several other security androids entered the room from other doors. They approached different groups and repeated the same phrase: "Please follow me. Your communicator is ready."

The pounding in my chest intensified. Partly because the EvoGens had approached the group talking about 'refugees,' or rather illegal stowaways, since refugees weren't allowed on Ceres2 but mostly because of the cylinders I had tucked away. Maybe they know about what I took from the cargo crate? As more and more people left the room, escorted by EvoGens, I could now see through to the other end. Arlinda wasn't there.

An android approached. "Please follow me. Your communicator is ready," It told me before it proceeded to walk to the nearest wall. A door, usually marked by a frame of some kind but not here, dematerialized, revealing a very narrow corridor, about three feet wide and six tall. It led me to another, smaller room where three EvoGens stood in front of a small table. A communicator was on it.

"Mister Nett, thank you for your patience. Before we hand you over the communicator, we have a few questions."

"Of course." I looked at the table.

"What do you know about the power loss that occurred today?"

"I was on a construction site. A cleanup operation, really. We were replacing some units which had caught fire. I did notice one section that had no power. Maybe a block."

"Anything else?" the EvoGen in the middle asked.

"As I said, the power loss seemed localized to that block that was damaged by the fire, and then, two androids did point me in the direction where we initially rallied."

"These androids were inside the blackout zone?"

"You're making it sound like there was a large blackout. I only saw one block, and yes, the androids were inside the zone. They showed me out." I squinted in confusion. "Was it a solar flare?"

The androids ignored my question. "Your record states that you are proficient with robotics. Is that correct?"

"Yes."

"Then we will need you to work with the System to identify some bugs we are encountering."

"Of course, but I'm—"

"That will be all," the System android interrupted me before I could add that most of my experience was with the mechanics of the androids. At this point, I just wanted to leave.

"One more thing," the android in the middle said. "We still need your genetic profile."

"I was told it would come today with the transport."

"That transport suffered an accident. The records couldn't be found. We will make a notation on your record. If the records cannot be recovered, we will schedule a testing session here." It grabbed the communicator and handed the device to me. "Meanwhile, here is the updated communicator. Please contact us if it misbehaves."

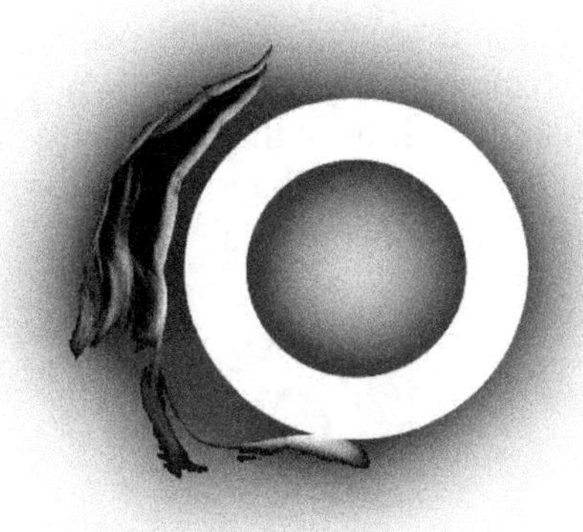

CHAPTER 9

Sighing with relief, I walked out of the building. Those narrow all-white corridors made me feel like I was navigating through one of my nightmares. I turned left, then right, and went through a dematerializing door. Finally, exiting out through the lobby, I walked over to the street as three individuals wearing construction uniforms got off their transport.

"All right, let's get our stories straight," one of them whispered after they passed me. They seemed a little concerned.

They're still interviewing people? What's happening?

"Please input your destination," the System requested as I approached the vehicle the group just walked out of.

"Home." I waved my communicator next to the white circling light.

"Destination accepted," the computer confirmed. "Please make sure all loose objects are secured, then press begin journey."

Pressing the digital button, I leaned back on the seat and buckled myself in. Do I check the cylinders now? My paranoia piqued. I can't risk it.

The sad truth was that even though Ceres2 was the beacon of the System, with all-new equipment and machinery, the people that managed it all came from Mars and Earth. Some were happy to have removed themselves from the harsh realities of the dysfunction the System brought to both planets. We all had old-world baggage, so to speak, no matter how far from it the System would transport us.

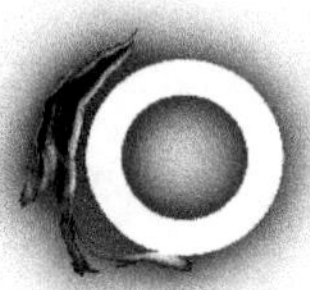

My front door dissolved as soon as I placed my wrist communicator near it. Everything inside was in order except for my TV wall. It was off. I stared at the black screen while I took off my communicator and dropped it on the top of my bed, then walked to the bathroom. I inspected the walls and the air vents. I don't think there are any cameras here.

I sat on the toilet and removed the cylinders from my waistband. Under proper lighting, the metallic tubes looked as if they had been used for a long time. There were scratches, little bumps, and evidence of several seals placed on top of each other. One of them had some adhesive exposed. It stuck to my hand.

The cylinders looked precisely like the ones the smugglers showed us on Mars. Just before Erica's departure. They said that they had intercepted System lists and databases which contained names of the next wave of accepted people in Ceres2. "as long as the System doesn't have its precious data," the man said, showing me the cylinder and its contents, "It doesn't know what to do. We send stealth shuttles and give people fake identities. Of course, we also help the resistance. He looked at Erica, then shifted his gaze to me. "Which makes this business extremely dangerous. Do you understand?"

"Yes." Erica swallowed. "I have to do this." She grabbed my hand.

"Are you sure about this, Erica?" I was beginning to get concerned.

"It's the only way, Elton. The System has denied both my parents and me any movement from Mars."

"Then stay." I grabbed her other hand and faced her. "I'll get my work in order, then come help my mother and get you."

"I'm afraid you'll never come back." Her lower lip trembled. "Elton, I want to come with you."

That was the last time I spoke with Erica. Three days later, I saw a special announcement from the System. It was warning human citizens against dealing with smugglers. The communicator showed several interplanetary transports which had crash-landed on Mars. One on Ceres2. I tried contacting Erica and her family several times, but no one answered. And, of course, the System, which likely was observing my every action, kept notifying me of early System Hysteria symptoms. My behavior was getting too erratic.

The very next day, two weeks before my official departure, the System released the names of the deceased humans found inside those transports. I broke down and cried as I read Erica's name among the dead.

Swallowing, I twisted one of the caps open and removed the rolled papers. I put the cylinder on the floor, then unrolled the documents by placing them against my thigh. The header showed a governmental logo with an eagle on the top middle of the page. There was only one sentence under it, written in blocky letters: Find the complete information in the micro-dot followed by a list of names. Some of the names had a red circle next to them.

I looked through all three rolled forms inside and found my name. It had a red dot next to it. That's what this was. The official transmission of our names?

I knew that by holding on to these lists, the System wouldn't be able to correctly count and verify the number of humans in Ceres2. And I would be happy if I could throw even a little wrench to interfere with its plans. I knew the System kept tabs on all of us. We'd all realized that on Mars. And if my parents had been with me, I believe they'd agree. One way or another, the human-governed System on Earth surveilled most of its citizens as well.

The second piece of paper had more names. The third piece had a large square with black borders on it and another smaller square with black edges in the middle of that. Likely the microdot with all this information. Shaking my head, I rolled up the papers and inserted them back into the cylinder. The small shipping container was clearly meant to deliver these cylinders to a smuggler.

Seeing only a list of names and having no means to even check what information would be in the microdot, I looked at the other cylinder on the floor. I coiled the documents, inserted them in, and picked it up. Twisting the cap, I instantly felt that this one was filled with heavier contents. They had a different feel than the papers in the other tube. These were covered in a thin layer of what felt like wax.

Taking them out of the cylinder, I unrolled the first one. Top to bottom, the entire page was filled with red squares and a small black square in the middle; more microdots. All of them looked the same. What am I looking at?

I rerolled all the pages and inserted them inside the cylinders. Placing both inside the cabinet under my faucet, I walked outside of the bathroom after quickly washing my hands. The TV wall was on now, showing the default slideshow of Ceres2 live video feeds. More places than I thought had lost power.

The city's center was as lit and beautiful as ever, but the stock market and news chyron were missing. The pit in the bottom of my stomach intensified. I can't speak for the motives other people had to move to Ceres2, but throughout my journey, I had moved from planet to planet in hopes of bettering my life and, in the process, escaping horrible realities. So far, the Third Colony seemed stable enough. But considering recent events, the shiny façade Ceres2 had, was beginning to show cracks.

The hologram displaying advertisements cycled through accessories, drinks, and other merchandise images. I lay on my bed, pushed the communicator off of it, and just stared at the TV wall. I was surrounded by stimuli that constantly reminded me about what I left behind, but holding the cylinders in my hands felt as if I touched a live wire. It brought back to those cold Mars days when I used to sleep in a box in the back alley and washed up only when I met Erica. They reminded me that most of my loved ones had, one way or another, perished by System's machinations. I got up and paced back and forth a few times. The thought that I had to do something with these cylinders clouded my head. I couldn't just go to the colony's center and wave them around. Groaning, I rubbed my nose. The only thing I could do for the moment was to keep them safe. Taking a deep breath to calm my nerves, I sat back on my bed. Grabbing my alcohol bottle, I chugged from it. Watching the occasional car floating between the neon-accented buildings on the TV wall, I calmed down enough, and at some point, I passed out.

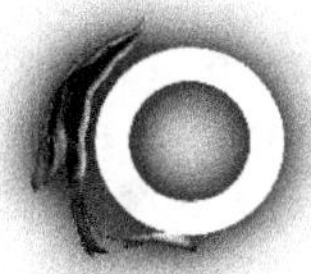

The interior lights in my living quarters lit up soon after I sat on my bed. They gradually illuminated the entire room as the TV wall slowly and simultaneously increased its brightness. I grabbed my communicator from the floor and wore it. Stretching, I got up.

For a few moments, I stood as still as I could. The ensuing dip in my blood pressure often obscured my vision so much, it was impossible to see where I was going. The cylinders. I thought after taking a deep sigh. My sight slowly restored. What am I going to do with these? I can't just destroy them. I could help someone escape Mars. But how would I do that? Cycling through the same thoughts I had before I went to sleep I sat on my bed, staring at the floor. I knew this was going to bug me immensely, but once my ears popped, I walked to the refrigerator. One of the drops had changed colors since I last checked it. It was now green.

What kind of drink is green? Bringing my wrist communicator closer to my face, I squinted and swiped the information boxes displayed. Cucumber-infused water? Out of curiosity, I placed a clear plastic cup under the tube, which automatically dispensed the drink. It wasn't green, though it looked cloudy. I brought the cup to my nose. The liquid smelled sweet. I took a small sip.

This is good! I immediately took another sip, then gulped down the rest of the contents. I always asked myself how did the System know how to come up with these combinations, every time that color changed. There had to be people who submitted these recipes, probably the same people who came up with the drinks I bought down by the colony center.

Placing the cup on the counter, I brought my communicator up. Swiping the digital display boxes on it, I revealed the time. It was 0300. It had been a while since I had seen a sunrise or a sunset; in fact, all days blended.

Ever since I'd arrived on Ceres2, I had been trying to establish an internal clock. But the random assignments, the light situation, and the fact that I had no one else to base it around, meant that I struggled to find a consistent regime. Though it was three o'clock in the morning, I didn't want to go back to sleep. Not everyone had my problem; there were established eight-hour shifts in which everyone rotated for work. But my assignments so far hadn't been consistent.

However, I was restless enough, and I knew I wasn't going to fall back asleep anytime soon, so I put on my shoes and walked out by the street. The sidewalk was empty except for a System droid standing about fifteen feet from me. Unlike me, the entire dome was quiet and had a sleepy feel. Leaning on the barrier, I stared at the glowing buildings. The elevator rose past my level and disappeared above as a few vehicles whirred on the roadbed. Initially, I didn't understand why I so much enjoyed being up in the middle of the night. Then it hit me; I hadn't had this feeling of safety in a long time. I certainly couldn't do this on Mars. Not without hearing the constant buzz of the System drones, heat-scanning the streets and the occasional gunshot. After staring at the distant lights for a few more minutes, I headed for my residence.

Getting closer to my unit door, I recognized the unmistakable teal trench coat. Randy was ringing the bell. He wasn't wearing a mask this time. Not him again, I turned around. What does this goblin want with me now! I huffed.

"Mister Nett!" I heard him exclaim. "Come-come! I want to hear everything about your first job in utopia!"

Goddamnit, he saw me! I grunted to myself before I turned around to face him. "Randy!" I faked a smile, "What brings you to the thirty-eighth floor at this hour of the night?"

"I knew the first job would make you restless." He laughed, taking a few steps toward me. "I know it happened to me. Come, tell me everything! I want to know everything!" he exclaimed, pointing his index finger up.

"What happened there, Randy?" I asked him as soon as we entered my unit. "That wasn't a fire. I saw bullet holes and laser burns. And I smelled burnt flesh."

"You strike me like a smart guy, Elton. Would you say you're smart?" Randy adjusted his coat whilst looking at me.

"Average." I rubbed my nose. "At best."

"Come on, Elton. Your file says that you learned robotics from your father. I'd say a little above average. Yeah?" Randy put his hand on my shoulder. Sighing, I removed it.

"Ahem." Randy turned around, facing the door. Clasping his hands behind his back, he looked up. "Achieving utopia isn't easy, Mr. Nett. Right now, we have to fight to preserve it. These illegals want to infiltrate us. Resisters. Wrongdoers. Wrongthinkers!" He did his usual finger-pointing to the ceiling motion. "These people are like a virus. And they will destroy what we have. Make no mistake about it." Randy turned around and faced me. His trench coat flapped. "But," he paused and smiled. "We have the System to help and guide us."

Randy was either having one of his utopia moments again, or he was intentionally avoiding answering my question. Maybe he didn't know what really happened there. But the fact that he mentioned illegals made me think that it might have been another refugee shuttle that had landed on Ceres2.

"Do you have a family?" I tried prying a little into his mind.

"They died on Earth." Randy curled his lips almost as if he was disgusted about what he was about to say. "Sector fifty-four. I told them to leave. But they said that's where they were born. They stayed. They should've left." He rubbed his nose, "Now they're dead! I was right!" The grimy way he spoke about his family's death disgusted me. I just stared.

"What you saw, was the aftermath of the System clearing an illegal refugee ring. Sent here by the resistance. That's what they're doing now. Smuggling civilians to do their dirty work. But the System showed them." His face lit like a candle. "Do you know what utopia means, Mr. Nett?" Condescendingly, Randy tilted his head, talking to me like I was a child.

"I don't know, Randy." I sighed, "A perfect place?"

"Utopia, first created in a dead language, long ago, means; a place that doesn't exist." He lifted his eyebrows, looking at me. "The ancients didn't believe that such a faultless place would even be possible. I mean, given what they had, it's not hard to imagine. Creative people some centuries later," he said, smirking in contempt, "gave it the meaning we know. Utopia, therefore, is the place we all strive to live in. A place where everything is equal. Everyone looks the same, is the same! Money has no meaning, and love is… pointless. Other than love for the System, that is. Imagine it," Randy pointed to the TV wall, which seemed to have already picked up on his speech. "Evergreen fields as far as you can see. Surrounded by those who only validate your feelings. No hostilities. And look," he grabbed my head and pointed it to the TV screen, "the System has already achieved that. Everything in Ceres2 is provided for. Food, shelter. And all the System asks in return is cooperation. I believe that's reasonable, right?"

"Randy. On Mars, the System couldn't care less for human welfare."

"That's not System's fault. Some humans are impossible to deal with."

"These are people, Randy. Like you and me."

"They're not people!" He furrowed his brows, "more like rats. Trying to destroy whatever maze they find themselves in."

"So, the System just kills everyone who tries to illegally come here?" I asked. My blood boiled at the thought that he probably cheered when Erica's transport was shut down.

"No, Elton. Come on. Only the ones who aren't included in the databases." He stared at me, then burst into a peal of maniacal laughter. "Cheer up!" he placed his hand on my shoulder again as my eyes widened in shock. "Anyway, I'm not privy to that information. I have no idea what the System does with the illegals. As far as Human Resources tells us, they are sent back to wherever they came from. At any rate," he smiled, "you were part of an important job on your very first assignment. That's awesome."

"You just told me that people died today, Randy. There's nothing awesome about it."

"System," Randy raised his communicator, "how many dead in today's incident?"

"No deaths incurred today in Ceres2," System's voice came through his device, "three humans were admitted to the hospital. Two with third-degree burns, and one with a miscarriage."

"See?" Randy raised his eyebrows and tapped me on my shoulder. "The System has this under control."

"It would appear so," I forced a smile. At this rate, I was afraid I was going to end up punching him if he continued talking.

"Well, then," Randy nodded. "I think it's time for me to get some sleep. What do you say, Elton?" Randy headed for the door.

"Swell idea," I groaned, following him.

"And get ready for another day in utopia, right?" Randy walked out.

"Yes, Randy." I rolled my eyes as the door rematerialized.

I sat on my bed, staring at the TV wall. Every time Randy would come visit me, the TV wall changed the feed automatically based on the conversations we had. The more Randy spoke, the more I learned who he was. A very disturbed person who seemed not to care that his parents died away from him. And as far as I'd caught, he had no other family to speak of. In a way, I wasn't that much different from him. I had no family. At least not with me. Saddened, I propped my pillow against the wall and leaned on it. "Reset to my favorite feed," I commanded the TV wall. Oversize screen showing the dome's center, I dozed off.

CHAPTER 10

The sound of the automated ambient music woke me up. Sitting up on my bed, I took a deep breath and stretched my arms upward. For a moment, life was as perfect as it could be; the room temperature was optimal, the dim lighting didn't assault my eyes as soon as I opened them, and I felt well-rested. I looked at my wrist communicator; it was noon, local time. "Perfect," I whispered as I took yet another deep breath. "Utopia." I instinctively blurted. That caught me off guard. Randy's nonsense was beginning to seep into my life.

Swallowing, I looked down as I put my feet on the floor. I was still wearing my shoes. The TV wall automatically turned on and showed me my favorite feed as I made myself a cup of coffee.

Because of planetary time differences, the stock markets on Earth and Mars were closed for the day. Their status was marked by blue numbers and letters while Ceres2's stock market was still trading. A System notification interrupted the stock scroller: "Virtual Earth and Mars walk: How it all began."

These events required the Glass House to be reconfigured to allow augmented reality sensors. So, they were pretty rare. The awful way Randy spoke about his parents made me miss mine. It also made me want to read Darimund's articles. So, I took my backpack and walked out of my living quarters. My next-door neighbor, apparently a young woman, was stumbling into her unit. She entered her room without even looking around.

Walking toward the maglev terminal, I passed a couple of EvoGens who were standing next to a charging point. I entered the station and walked past a few more people chatting as a train slowly came to a stop in front of me. Differing from long haul cabin setups, bigger, reclining seats and dedicated cars to effectively store androids. This one seemed like it belonged to a local route, given the narrow cabins and chairs along the sides. I sat down by the door as an android stepped inside.

Further down the cabin were more people wearing Augmented Reality glasses. None of them were talking to each other. They were in their own virtual worlds. I pulled out my tablet and opened the reading application. It displayed the last article I was reading. "Rise of the Code" by Darimund Penman "… rebranded it before his term was over, calling it the System." Ah, yes. The Cintra article about the creation of the System on Earth. I dimmed the screen and continued reading. "Once someone received a parking ticket from a human agent, that information would be entered into the System. It would then be cross-referenced based on maps available for time, exact place, weather information, etc. If such a ticket was disputed, a judge wouldn't be a human. The System decided if the summons was valid or not.

For a very long time, no one knew that this part of the System was fully automated. Eventually, someone from Section twenty-five dug in and realized that they weren't speaking with a human during any step of the dispute.

Civil rights advocate associations and numerous lawyers launched lawsuits, but they went nowhere. The human judges, little puppet bastards, reasoned that it was still fair even if the System was automated. Based on existing laws, if a violation was recorded, it was immediately cross-referenced with weather reports and triangulated to display its exact location. We have complete and total control over what laws dictate, the judgment stated, while the defense lawyers argued that some laws were antiquated and didn't fit this new application method. The cognitive dissonance of the outcome of the lawsuits versus the reality on the streets was evident to the human population. It inspired some localized but violent protests; the System's expansion continued. Several other branches of public services were quietly added to it: weather notifications, power outages, tide alerts, etc. They all fed the algorithm.

Eric Mundo, a welder from Sector nine, was arrested after entering City Hall. A government facility supposedly put there to help people. The System, however, had decided that the biometric data it collected matched to the man was accurate within a three percent error margin to a dangerous fugitive last recorded being in the same town. Mundo spent fifteen days in jail until the System was provided with paperwork from the man's lawyer clearly showing where the man was over the previous months up to three years via job logs. The following lawsuit revealed that the System had been expanded to encompass facial recognition.

During the trial, it was discovered that students and researchers had found out that in comparison to human authority, people were less inclined to dispute anything the System generated because the facts were laid so precisely. There were crystal-clear images, all with corresponding times, even if some points were guessed or "derived," as they called it.

Soon after Mr. Mundo's trial became a public spectacle, and inspired by the fury of controversies at the time, Jeremy Gauss, a System technician, duplicated his ID badge and leaked a trove of classified documents. That led to the first fully formed riots. His shocking article made the rounds across the planet for months. It precisely detailed how much information was collected by the governments, how much of it was erroneously used, and how much was sold to the corporations.

"We demand to be judged by our own peers!" the slogans out of the courtrooms read. "Down with the robots!" And justly so. Effectively, we are allowing a machine to decide what humans can or can't do.

However, the riots accomplished very little for all the destruction they caused. By that time, the System was fully integrated with the law enforcement emergency notification system. All calls were filtered through it, and human units were dispatched accordingly. That's why sometimes people expecting a police car would only receive an ambulance.

The scandals didn't end with Mr. Mundo, however. Shirley Jenga, a retiree, got pulled over by the police; his license plate had been revoked because of unpaid System tickets. He resisted the seizure of his property and was consequently arrested. Witnessing this event, other motorists joined his resistance, resulting in that highway being shut down. The services were restored the next day, but it was all over. For weeks after Mr. Jenga's arrest, motorists routinely stopped and blocked motorways, streets, and even facilities where humans would dispute tickets. Fueled by the opposing political party, the scandal got widespread exposure from the media and the internet.

At this point, the political and social brew was boiling over the pot. Citizens stopped paying for their tickets. Motorists disobeyed the System, and protests got even more violent. Arrest orders and vehicle seizures that ensued didn't sit well with people. And, of course, the opposing political party continued to manipulate the citizens for their purposes.

The System responded with the letter of the law: arrest and ticket the offenders. This feedback loop, created by the same scheme meant to protect and serve the citizens, revealed its major flaw.

Discretion.

Or the lack thereof, rather.

The force used by the System was overwhelming. We all knew it, but it became more and more evident that it monitored all internet, phone, and other forms of communications. It selected and filtered reports it deemed dangerous. Only sanctioned articles were allowed to be published. It then went on to deliberately and unilaterally delete internet business pages. Especially lawyers and other financial resources belonging to the "resisters" or "wrong thinkers." (Their words – not mine.) Anyone seen as a threat to the System would be publicly called out on national TV channels and the internet. That seemed inconsequential until people realized that their financial means were being disrupted.

The System, which had total control of the laws, emergency services, and even some military parts, created an atmosphere of entropy. While everything seemed fine on a surface level, fear of what would happen if anyone aired out their grievances reigned.

"Down with the robots!" persists.

The page ended with a string of unreadable characters. That usually happened when the article I had saved continued. I knew that the System would encrypt these dissenting human essays and censor them as much as it could. And if I had left the interlinking application as it was, the System would've removed this article along with the other books I owned long ago. I scrolled down the list of books passing a few favorites, and stopped by another unnamed piece. But before I could open it, my wrist communicator vibrated, notifying me that this was my stop. Adjusting my backpack, I exited the train, which stopped a block from the exhibition dome. The human crowd became thicker; many more people walked with me, likely to the same destination. Some were wearing masks, but I'd forgotten mine.

My communicator vibrated once again as I automatically paid my way in. As soon as I passed over the threshold, the dome illuminated. I was presented with broad daylight, blue skies with the bright sun hidden behind a seven-story yellow building on my left side. The sidewalks were bustling with people, some virtual, some real. I couldn't tell who was who, so I avoided crossing paths with anyone.

On my right side was a narrow one-way street where gasoline cars traveled. Further beyond that were another sidewalk and a river. This is Earth! I was home! A smile crept up on my face as I slowly strolled on the sidewalk.

A group of five or six people walking toward me attracted my attention as I inched toward the building, making way for them. Among them, I recognized Arlinda.

"Arlinda?" I raised my voice slightly as the group passed me.

"Elton!" she exclaimed as the people she was with looked my way but continued to walk. "I'm really not surprised to see you here. The nostalgia this place has!"

"I know." I sighed longingly. "I saw the notification, and I couldn't resist. Feels like home!"

"It so does!" She smiled and looked around. We stood there next to each other for a few seconds until the group that was with her stopped, letting the augmented reality ghosts go through them. "I gotta go," Arlinda said, turning to face me. "It was so nice meeting you here, of all places."

"Likewise, Ari." I shook the hand she extended.

She walked past me as I continued my trip farther inside the simulation. I did look back once, but her group had disappeared into a crowd of people.

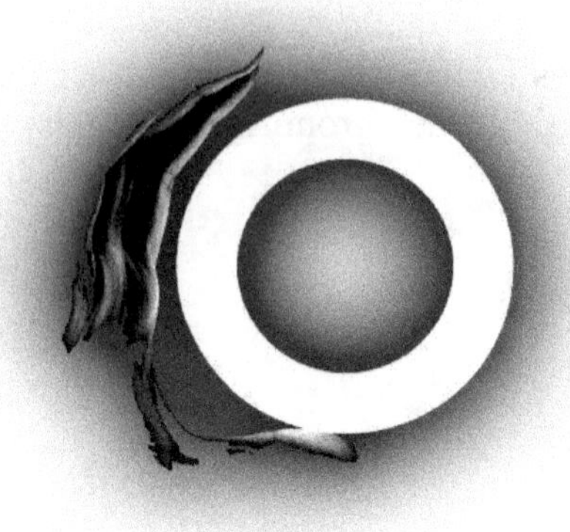

CHAPTER 11

The following day, the System summoned me to their technical building. They needed technicians to assist in retrieving and reintegrating some android units that were deactivated outside the colony walls. Yeah, I think this was all caused by another solar storm. The System thought it was immune to them. I guess they were wrong.

The notification specified a time and a particular uniform for the job it requested. I had to wear my maintenance ensemble, which fit under the Extra-Vehicular Activity Suits. After wearing the uniform, I put the equipment I'd need in my duffle bag and walked to the maglev train station just below my living quarters. Inside the train were a lot of human workers who were putting on their modified search and rescue suits, complete with compressed air tanks, rebreather masks, and open helmets. As the train left the station, I slipped into mine, sliding the visor up, adjusting the mask, and slipping it under my chin. I wore my boots but left my gloves on the side. No point in wearing everything on the train.

The maglev train stopped at the end of the tracks just outside the colony walls. Its doors opened, and the first thing I noticed was how dark it was outside. Adjusting my air mask, I turned around and saw a beam of light directly illuminating the dome. We were far enough from it that the five-hundred-foot walls that supported the dome seemed a mere few inches tall. In the distance were several similar beams illuminating the nearby domes.

We followed our communicator coordinates deeper into the darkness, away from the light stream as a group. It wasn't long until we found ourselves walking into an area made up of old, unpowered living quarters. I found that strange. Given the information I had, this colony on Ceres2 was brand new. We were the first to inhabit it. Were these the foundations for a new colony dome? Before I could look into them, one of the human workers raised his hand. "Let's turn here."

I looked back. "No androids?" We had no robots with us.

"They're too scared of some static." Another guy walking alongside me chuckled from behind his re-breather mask. "Screw them."

"Scared?" I squinted and slowed my pace as more people passed me.

"They said that the planet has gotten hit with a series of EMP waves, especially the area where we're going to. The System has classified this spot as dangerous to them," another person explained.

"Oh, hey, Leslie." He made an uncomfortable face from under his breather mask. "Didn't see you there."

"Yeah, I missed the train, apparently. The System sent another one to pick me up." Leslie adjusted his air tanks.

"Of course, the System will take care of your needs." The man laughed ironically as he shone his flashlight to illuminate the way. Because Ceres2 was so far from the Sun, only a faint light penetrated the dark and low cloud cover that persisted. Though the Sun was as high in the sky as it could be, it was dim outside.

These living quarters were single-stacked, only one floor high. But just as the colony grounds, they spread as far as I could see.

"Change of priorities," a robotic voice said from my communicator. The same message played on the communicator of the person standing next to me. "We need your crew to salvage one cryogenic pod. It is located several miles away from your position. Additionally, please keep your communicators on, and record radiation levels wherever you go. More resources and transports are on their way."

That message was followed by three beeps. Simultaneously, a path to a different destination was displayed on my communicator.

"Great." The guy standing next to me snorted.

"All right, people, you heard the message. Look lively! We have a new target!" Leslie raised his voice above the background noise of the atmospheric processors chugging in the distance.

After a thirty-minute hike in the cold outer Ceres2 atmosphere, we reached the top of a hill. At this point, I could see some two-story structures around us made of stacked-up residential living quarters. We walked along the middle of the road. The orbital mirrors lit up the valley below us.

"My communicator is working," someone commented, "so why can't the EvoGens do this?"

"I think they might be coming. What do you think, Leslie?" another added.

Leslie stopped and examined his communicator. "I think our destination is where the light beam is pointing. That's what I think." He adjusted his mask and continued the hike downhill. We all followed. Approaching the lit area, which had looked pretty small from the distance when we first noticed it, I realized it wasn't so small. The beam was illuminating a wreck.

"Is this the transport that was supposed to arrive a few days ago?" someone asked as he checked his communicator.

"Let's fan out!" Leslie called, raising his voice again. "Find this container and get it back! I don't want to be out here for longer than I have to!"

"Who is this guy?" I asked a person who walked next to me as Leslie headed toward the still-smoldering wreckage.

"He's a System administrator," he informed me. "He's booted more people than anyone else." He adjusted his gloves.

"Booted," I said softly in my helmet before raising my voice so he could hear me. "What do you mean booted, man?"

"Booted, as in, kicked the hell out of the colony." The man whispered with an angered voice as he took a step closer to me. "If you're asking, that means you don't really know how things work around here. Watch what you say around him, all right?" He pulled a flashlight from his side pocket, turned it on, and followed Leslie.

I adjusted my air tanks and followed the group, shining my flashlight at the large pieces of fuselage debris littering the ground. The light from the mirror was enough for me to see where I was going and what was in front. Strangely enough, It also provided some warmth.

"Hey, get over here!" Someone's scream attracted my attention. As people gathered in the area where the voice was coming from, I headed that way too.

Thinking that it would be faster to cut through the debris, I walked inside what appeared to be a storage compartment for the wrecked transport. Its roof was missing, likely destroyed when the craft crashed. It was filled with smashed Second-Gen androids.

Oh. This reminded me of the two Second-Gens that had led me out of the room where I found the cylinders. I stopped and looked around. They didn't look like they were damaged because of the crash. They seemed to have been intentionally destroyed. Some of them had bullet holes and laser burns. I kneeled so I could examine the remnants better.

Another member of the team walking nearby noticed me. "Is this where he is?" he asked, referring to whoever called out.

"No, I think everyone is that way." I pointed toward a ripped area of the compartment. He briskly walked to where I pointed. Getting up, I followed. As I passed the rip, I slipped and fell.

What is this stuff? Shell casings? I pushed myself up to my knees. Why are shell casings here? Before I even had time to finish that thought, loud gunfire came from the direction where all the team members had headed.

We didn't have any guns. Who is shooting?

Someone wearing a yellow hazmat suit with lights on its helmet came running in my direction. This person was clearly not one of our team. Evidently, he didn't see me because he tripped over my knee and fell. A handgun slid through the shell casings a few inches from me.

Grumbling, he kicked me and bent over to reach for the weapon. But I was faster in retrieving it. I had seen guns used on Earth and Mars uprisings but never used one myself. The person grabbed a pipe and hit my protective helmet. As he lifted the tube again, the fear of having a broken air system, which would've spelled certain death this far from the domes, overtook me. I pointed the weapon at him and pressed the trigger. He fell.

Holy shit, I just killed someone! What do I do now?

Without even checking on my assailant, I got up and rushed in the direction where my team had last been. Barely hearing anything over my own breathing inside my helmet and the rapid shuffling of fabric my suit made, I ended my short sprint in the corner of the next compartment. Scooting in the dark corner, I took several deep breaths to calm my nerves and my raging heartbeat. I could now hear sparse, distant gunfire but nothing in my vicinity. Then I heard muffled voices that seemed to come from the other side of the transport wall panel next to me.

After turning off all my lights, I crawled past it. In the next compartment were a lot of people wearing protective yellow suits. Because they were pacing back and forth, I wasn't exactly sure how many there were. I counted more than seven. They rounded up and held my team members, who were sitting down. There was no way I would overpower this many people, so I did the only thing I could. I pressed the emergency button on my communicator. The screen displayed the silent emergency icon.

I crawled a little further towards what appeared to be an opening that led to another section, but the floor paneling gave in, and I fell. The transport fuselage buckled and broke under my weight. I landed on top of an unpowered generator, then on the floor of this room. Apparently, the transport ship had broken down into sections as it impacted the ground. While still barely lined up with each other, all the sections were still roughly in the same places they would be if the ship was in one piece.

Fearing that whoever these people were, they would come to hurt me as well, I stole my way through a series of corridors filled with fallen-over panels, equipment, and debris. I emerged on the other side of the corridor system, which seemed like the maintenance module merged with a part of the main fuselage for the transporter created by the crash. I felt movement from more of my team members cowering nearby. I crawled to them as the light beams from the assailants, who were passing by, briefly illuminated the area. After a few moments, they moved on.

"What's going on?" someone whispered as the sound of footsteps faded.

"I don't know," another said from behind his air mask.

"Did we find the cryo-pod?"

"Who the hell cares?" he replied. "We're under attack."

I hadn't felt this scared since before leaving Mars. Even then, it was more riots than full-on deadly weapon assaults. The riots had been loud. These assaults were silent.

"We gotta get out of here." I heard someone whisper. Accompanied by the team members hiding in this new area, I moved as stealthily as I could toward the next compartment. This part didn't have a ceiling either. The only source of light was the faint beam the orbital mirrors emanated. There was a big hole in the grey wall panels just above me, as if something big had gone through them. In front of me, there were a few tables, boxes, and debris. Someone in our group coughed, and because we were deliberately moving slowly to avoid making noise, it sounded deafening. Fearing that our assailants might have heard it as well, everyone, including myself, hunkered down next to whatever was next to us. The crunching sound of footsteps crushing panels over dirt intensified. Were we made? Was this it?

I frantically looked at my surroundings as a faint light came from the rectangular box on my right. Strange, this was the only piece of equipment that had power. I crawled closer to examine it.

Oh, this is the cryo-pod! I slowly approached it. There was light inside; it was still running on internal power, lying on its side. I carefully pushed it over to examine it better and saw the face of a young woman inside. The pod was marked by the usual gibberish number-letter strings, some sort of barcode the System used. Next to the row of numbers and letters, there was E2V etched in a larger font. I wanted to scream that I had found it, but I couldn't. The fear of death by these assailants was too great.

A loud whirring sound came from above, and a cylinder-shaped device landed at our feet. It shook for a second and flashed a bright light. We all scattered and recovered after a few seconds.

When it was all over, Leslie crawled to the cylinder. "This is an EMP grenade," he announced as he picked it up and looked around. "We have to get back; we have to tell the System what's going on. Everyone! This mission is canceled! Get out of he…."

Before I could act, more grenades hit the ground around us, thumping as they rolled across the broken concrete plates.

Boom! These were different; the blast slammed me against the cryogenic pod. I tried to stand on my feet, but my leg gave in and I fell back on the floor. Quickly tapping on my body, checking for injuries, I slowly faced up. My right leg was gushing blood, and I couldn't control my right arm. Adjusting the oxygen mask, which had slipped away from my mouth and nose, I took a deep breath, but a sharp pain in my chest made me cough. I rolled to my left side. Bright floodlights preceded the roar coming from System drones.

My ears ringing, eyesight blurry, I saw several humanoid figures wearing yellow hazmat suits scurrying about. Face hidden behind a black facemask, one of them passed near me and picked up a backpack and a wrist communicator laying nearby. The pain in my leg intensified, and I grunted. He stopped and looked my way. I was frozen. The System had told everyone that the outside was just empty land waiting to be explored; in fact, several ads recruited colonists for that very reason. Who am I looking at?

The person looked away and continued collecting more pieces of equipment from the ground. That was until a brighter floodlight shone on the area. The hazmat suits bolted away, some of them stumbling and rolling on the ground. Before the EvoGens landed, I felt one more thump near me. Fearing that the Yellow hazmat assailants had returned, I looked that way only to see another EMP grenade rolling and stopping on my injured leg. In one motion, I picked up the small cylinder and threw it in the direction the assailants fled. With a flash of bright light, the device exploded midair.

For a brief moment, silence reigned.

Floodlight bands shining on the area around me preceded the intensifying roar of transports which now hovered above me. I couldn't see what happened behind my limited field of view, but a robot, I couldn't discern what iteration, landed a few feet away from me. Gunfire sounds and red laser streaks ensued. EvoGens were here.

One of them stopped by me, the red light emanating from its head unit illuminated the area. Picking me up, it displayed a face. I could see its digital lips moving, but I couldn't understand. It then wrote on the face: R/U/OK?

I pointed to the cryogenic pod next to me before shaking my head, 'no.' Creating a ring around the explosion zone, more EvoGens flooded the area. The pain all over my body intensified and I felt my legs and arms get cold and numb. I faded out.

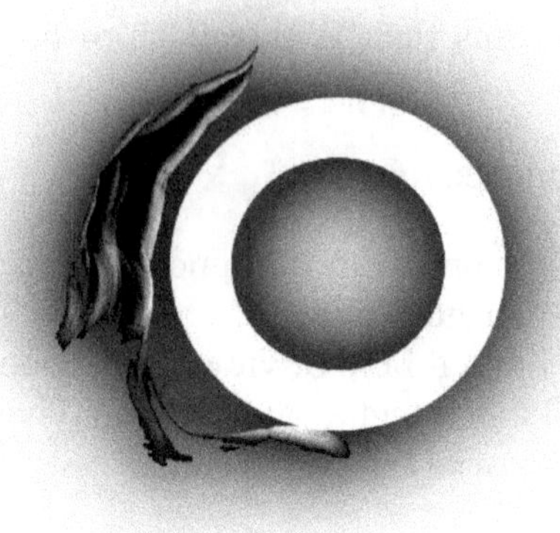

CHAPTER 12

A strong smell of formalin woke me up. I opened my eyes, thinking I'd fallen asleep in my biology classroom on Earth, the first place where I was introduced to this strong scent. About five feet across from me was an empty stretcher, one of those that I had seen in hospitals. Looking down, I noticed I was lying on something similar. A needle, held in place by some clear tape, was in my right arm. Its tube ended in a clear bag affixed to an IV-drip stand next to me.

The stretcher I was on, was on the right side of a corridor, lined with white panels floor to ceiling. Adjusting the sleeveless white hospital gown I was wearing, I sat on the portable bed. Holding onto the handrail, I pivoted my body to my left and stepped down.

I felt the cold floor as soon as my feet hit the ground. My attention shifted to my right arm, which was wrapped with a thick yellow bandage. Some clear slime-looking substance dripped from under it. My right leg had the same. I felt pain, but it wasn't the crippling agony I had experienced before. Looking left then right, I confirmed that there was no one around me. Or in that corridor, for that matter.

"Hello!" My scratchy voice echoed through the hall, but no one acknowledged my call. I cleared my throat and called out again. Nothing. So, supporting myself by holding onto the IV drip stand with my left hand, I stood up.

I rambled about the hallway until I reached an intersection. There are no rooms or doors around here. "Hello!" I called once again to no avail.

The tube disconnected from my IV drip pouch and hit my left leg as it slid on the floor. Not knowing how to reconnect it, I pushed the stand with me, and continued further. Hoping that someone would eventually help me with it.

The area to my right opened into a much larger room. Its ceiling, differing from the corridor, was lined with illuminated panels. About fifteen feet away from me were three stretchers and a table. On top of the counter stood a tall glass container filled with clear liquid. Inside it, a brain with a spine attached floated about. Wires protruding out of the brain stuck out of the container and went into what looked like a data processor we used to synchronize androids with the operating system. Lit fiberoptic cables came out of another device, which the data processor was linked with, before ending in the upgrade port of an EvoGen, sitting in the stretcher next to it.

"God damn the System," the android said as it turned its head 360 degrees. It stopped and locked eyes with me as soon as I walked into this brightly illuminated area.

"What?" it continued, "is Leslie somewhere around here? Screw him too!"

I was fully aware that I must've had a concussion, but what was happening right now? I stared.

"Wait a second. I think I've seen you before. You are that guy who asked me about him." The EvoGen persisted.

"About…" I cleared my voice. "About who?"

"Leslie! Who else? Are you paying attention here? Where is he? I'm gonna fuck him up, I swear!" Its emotionless robotic voice echoed in the hall. "Look at what he did!"

Though I couldn't discern the voice, the sentences seemed as if they were spoken by the same guy who'd explained to me who Leslie was. My jaw dropped, and I froze.

"Hi, Mr. Nett." A woman wearing a white doctor's coat shook me out of my stare. She must have approached me from behind.

Holding my breath, I turned my head to look at her. "Oh, let me fix that for you." She freed the IV-drip tube I was dragging across the shiny floor tiles.

"Hey, doc," the android addressed her, "when am I getting out of here?"

"Hold on a second." The doctor flipped a switch on the data processor, and the android stopped moving. Its hands laid limp. "Much quieter now, don't you think?" She faintly smiled at me.

Shivers ran down my spine. "Do you want to go back to your stretcher now, Mr. Nett?" she asked, absolutely unfazed by what just happened.

"What is going on, doctor?" Looking at the EvoGen, then her, I swallowed.

"You are experiencing anesthesia awareness, Mr. Nett." She said while helping me face away from the android. "It's pretty rare, but it happens. Let's get back to your bed." Powerless, I followed her lead.

After escorting me back to my stretcher, the doctor replaced the now spent IV drip pouch. I examined my limbs best I could. Though I couldn't see, I knew I must have had a big wound on my right arm and leg under the bandages. And to top that off, my head was wrapped as well. I definitely hit my head, and I'm imagining things. What if I'm not?

I lay in bed, but I didn't want to sleep. My heart was beating as if it wanted to burst out of my chest. The fear that if I fell asleep, somehow the System would remove my brain and conduct experiments, or whatever it was I witnessed, terrified me. At that moment, my anxiety felt so real that I began to shiver uncontrollably. Then my mind began to rationalize. If the System wanted to do that, it would've already done it. I had already been unconscious for God knows how long, and I didn't even see a clock anywhere in this facility, which I assumed to be a hospital. That was the last thought I had before I passed out.

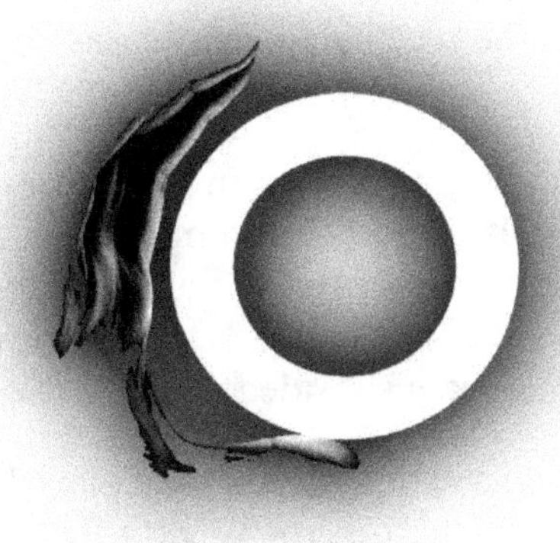

CHAPTER 13

 I felt a slap across my face. "Come on, it's time you get out of here." I heard a woman's voice next to me.

Startled, I opened my eyes and frantically looked around. A moment later, I felt a numbing sensation rippling from head to toe. I was in the same area where I last remembered going to sleep. I looked left and right, then immediately checked my limbs. The doctor, who was wearing a white gown, was fiddling with the bandage on my leg. I scrutinized what she was doing for a moment. My extremities were still flesh and bone. I sighed with relief.

"How long did I sleep for?" I asked the doctor, who, at this point, had removed the clips which were holding the bandage on my leg.

"About three months," she replied. "Among other injuries, you suffered a severe concussion, so to speed up the process, we placed you in a medically induced coma. The System took care of moving your body to prevent bedsores. We intubated and used a feeding tube to help your body functions carry on as normally as possible. You're ninety-nine percent fully recovered now. You'll be a little disoriented for the next few days, but you will recover."

"Three months?" I gasped. An android holding a tray walked up next to the doctor. It extended the receptacle near her as she placed the clips on it.

As if someone stabbed me, a sharp pain went through my skull. Argh. Grunting, I grabbed my head and closed my eyes. Laying my head back on the pillow, I slowly opened my eyes and looked at the doctor, who continued unwrapping the bandages. I took a few deep breaths and removed my hands as the pain subsided.

"Stay still." She removed one of her hands and placed it on my chest while holding the bandage with the other. "What's the problem?" the doctor asked, looking at me.

"I just got a sharp pain in my head," I muttered.

"It's the tranquilizers and muscle relaxants. You'll probably feel a little off for a couple of days. But it'll pass." She stopped fiddling with my bandage. "Sit up. It should help relieve the pressure built by lying flat all this time."

"How many…" I steadied myself in a sitting position on the bed. "How many died?"

"There was only one casualty. The deceased was likely standing right on top of the exploding grenade," the android standing next to the doctor informed me. An EvoGen placed a few pillows against the wall behind my back.

"We dispatched units to aid in the recovery as soon as we traced the threat," the android continued with its metallic-textured voice, "but it was too late for one of the team members. You risked your life for the good of the colony, Mr. Nett. The System will not forget that. As of now, you may go to your living quarters."

"I don't understand," I mumbled as the doctor finished removing all my bandages. She placed them inside a red plastic bag. "The good of the colony?" I continued mumbling. "What are you talking about?"

"Eve, the woman inside the cryo chamber you found and protected," the doctor said as she took a small stack of folded clothes and handed them to me, "requested to address that in person."

"Who is Eve?" I asked, placing the small stack of clothes next to me on my bed. The first piece was a white shirt, and since I wasn't wearing anything under my gown, I put it beside me.

"Eve is the next step in human evolution," the android responded as another led the doctor away. "She will meet with and thank you personally." It continued.

"I don't understand," I put on the rest of the clothes while staring at the androids who surrounded me.

"Mister Nett," one of them displayed a smiley face on its head unit. "you have been through quite an ordeal." Its digital eyes blinked. "Giving you information of any kind while the drugs are still in your system would be useless. You won't retain any of it."

"We have arranged transportation for you. It is waiting outside." The android next to it continued. "All is planned. Everything is under control."

Three EvoGens escorted me out of the largely silent hospital. A transport was waiting for us on the twentieth floor traffic lane ramp.

The trip to Unit Thirty-Eight was uneventful. Routine, I'd say. But because inside, I was burning to know if the System had learned about the missing cylinders, the trip seemed to take forever. I mean, they would've told me as soon as I woke up. Right? I tried rationalizing. The sight of neon-lined buildings in the colony's center visually shook me out of my inner thoughts. Tapping my finger on the steering wheel, I just stared out of the window. Randy's annoying phrase came to my mind "Utopia equals compliance." I scoffed. The mere thought of him paying me a visit once I got back in my unit annoyed me. Chest thumping, my anxiety piqued. Who the hell is Eve? Why did that android address me as if it knew me? And why did it talk unlike any androids I had encountered before?

Maybe it was just glitching? It reminded me of that android who just wouldn't leave the front porch of my parents' house the day after my father disappeared on Mars. My mother, who just came back from work, screamed at it in frustration. But all the troubled machine could do was shake and emit some low-pitched sounds. It was gone the morning after.

The transport did its usual shuddering as it slowed down. It rapidly dipped in altitude and parked.

As soon as I entered the corridor, I saw a Second Gen standing not too far from my door. Whoa, déjà vu. Without moving, it followed my every motion until I entered my unit.

Dropping my communicator on my bed, I walked into the bathroom. Retrieving both cylinders, I sat on the bathroom stool, examining the contents. My raging heartbeat slowed down. It was all there. If anyone had entered my unit, they didn't get to them.

I inserted the tubes back where I had last placed them and walked into the main room. My TV wall, together with the ceiling lights slowly turned on. Second Gen still in my mind, I opened the front door and peeked. It was gone. Shaking my head, I undressed, and got into the shower.

Facing the water stream, I closed my eyes and focused on the sound of the water hitting my head. Pain overtook my arm, and I instinctively touched the bump left by the surgery. Sighing, I decided to inspect my leg. A significant surgery scar spanned from the front of my thigh, ending on the back of my calf. The System had taken care of me.

This created a dissonance in my thinking; on the one hand, I knew how cruel the System had always been and though I hadn't witnessed it lately, it likely still was to humans. How is it possible that a System that has no respect for human life can take care of a human to the point of rehabilitation as it did to me?

"It doesn't make sense." I spat and wiped my face clear of the shower water that had gotten in my mouth.

I felt a lot lighter as soon as I washed an oily substance off of my body. Like all my pores were now breathing. Maybe it's something they used in the hospital. Accompanied by the bird-chirp tone of my front door, my wrist communicator vibrated. I dressed up, checked the cabinet to make sure I had indeed placed the cylinders back in hiding, and headed for the door.

"Mister Nett," Randy greeted me with his usual upbeat manner as soon as the door dissolved, "I thought I would find you here. It's so good to see you have recovered!"

He hasn't changed. "Thank you, Randy." I wiped my face with both my hands and prepared for the usual spiel about utopia.

"Yours is such an inspiring story. A breath of fresh air, as they say, huh?" He clasped his hands behind his back, looking around.

"What are you talking about, Randy?" I asked as I walked to my closet and picked out a red and white checkered shirt.

"You know," he said, subtly sniffing the room, "I have been here for almost two years. I arrived with the first System androids. They promised me they would add me to the seeders. That's the upper management program where we go out and claim land here. Two years later, I'm still in the same place as when I arrived, while a person who came a month ago moves up before me. Do you think that's fair, Mr. Nett?"

"Randy? As you said, I only arrived here a few months ago. You obviously have a history with the System. Which, let me ask you…."

Are you a spy? Are you one of those monsters who cannibalize their own? You certainly don't seem to care about your family! Answer me! I resisted the urge to growl at his face. Taking a deep breath to calm my thumping chest, I stared.

"What happened to you? A glitch in the code?" expecting a question, he squinted at me.

"Nothing." Closing my eyes, I shook my head. "Look," I swallowed, "I just got out of the hospital. My head is still hurting, my body aches," I paused, "do you mind?" Contemptuously, I pointed at the door.

Randy sighed, and the façade fell off his face for a moment. He let his real self come out. He looked broken. "Yeah, I get it."

"Hey, Randy." I paused as he stopped and slowly turned around. "Look man, I really don't know what's happening to me. One day I was getting jobs and assignments from the System. The next, I got dispatched off the colony to help with some disabled robots and got hurt. I just woke up today." I looked him in the eye. Randy couldn't hold my gaze. "That's all I know. That's all I have."

"Well," Randy rubbed his neck, "you're in now, for all its worth." Turning around, he headed for the door. "You can still call me if you need help with anything." Randy looked both ways as soon as he exited my unit, then walked away. I stared at the door which materialized behind him. Randy wasn't a person I would choose to hang out with. Hell, I was as introverted as introverts come. And he completely severed my trust in him with the 'utopia requires compliance' nonsense. Nonetheless, after witnessing his mood swing, I was worried. I didn't know how big the human population on Ceres2 was, but I could tell that empathy was hard to come by. There was only so much comfort a robot powered by artificial intelligence could provide. Granted, some of the EvoGens were capable of actual conversations, but essentially, they were calculated and emotionless.

On the other hand, Randy was far from emotionless. I just didn't care much about his desire for empathy. Was this the future of humanity? People who didn't know how to live with and reach out to each other anymore? Or was this just what I had become?

Shaking my head in confusion, I walked back into the bathroom and grabbed my towel again; water dripped down my neck. After drying my hair, I dropped the towel on my chair.

"Open the window." I lay on my bed facing the TV wall. It did its usual flicker, then displayed the rotation of cameras. "Stop here." The screen showed the colony's central commercial district. People were walking about, some were sitting and eating in the pedestrian plaza. I felt hungry. Getting up, I opened the refrigerator. There were a few breadsticks, some form of butter, and a few containers with a familiar soup. I'm not sure if the texture, taste, or both, but it reminded me of Mars of all places

After reheating the contents, I ate sitting on my bed. Once finished, I took my communicator off and put it on the nightstand next to the empty tray. With the weight of actual food in my stomach, I passed out while watching the TV wall.

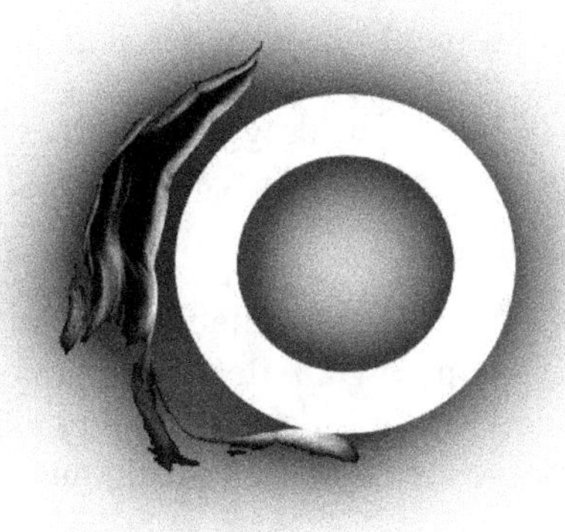

CHAPTER 14

Light from the TV wall penetrated my eyelids as the wrist communicator simultaneously rang and vibrated off the nightstand edge. Groaning, I rolled my body and reached for it but lost my balance and fell next to the device.

I sat on the floor, leaned on my bed, and, wearing the device, I noticed the scar on my arm. I had never heard of such a procedure to speed up the recovery process. Weeks, maybe, but not in terms of months. The events that led to the attack and my eventual strange, prolonged stay in the hospital were anything but peaceful. If anything, the attack I was subjected to, signaled the opposite. This new colony was supposed to be a utopia, not the opposite. All this worried me to my core, but I felt exhausted. It must be all the drugs they likely pumped in me when I was in the hospital.

My stomach growled. Sighing, I walked to the closet, got some clothes out, and dressed up. I made some coffee and poured some almond milk, the only type of milk available on Ceres2, and took a sip. That sugarless coffee in the morning always jolted me out of my lull.

I looked over at my communicator. It was a System message. "Please report to System's management offices when you can. Have a nice day."

Feeling the bitterness of the coffee dragging on my throat, I poured some artificial sweetener into the hot cup. I really wanted to talk to someone about what had happened recently.

Truth was that having helpful and reliable people around me was no longer an option. I was on my own. After putting my shoes on, I grabbed my backpack and headed for the side of the street where a transport was standing. The System gave me its usual spiel about safety before the craft took off.

I turned on my tablet after dropping my communicator behind me and adjusted my seat so the camera facing my way wouldn't be able to read what I was about to; Darimund's articles. This one was called 'Divide and conquer, an algorithmic governance.'

"In the beginning, on Earth, the manipulation Mr. Einst's System created was subtle. It began with bizarre slogans and posters such as "Yourself." and "Utopia!" Then entertainment media, mostly owned by the System, to the ever-increasing pushback of fans, began twisting movies and fiction books. Historical volumes taught in schools were adjusted to remove what was perceived as offensive language, taking away chunks of historical facts. Not understanding what, and most importantly, why it was happening, private citizens revolted after vehemently rejecting it.

Some websites were hacked to display slogans such as, "He who forgets history is doomed to repeat it." and, "Leave our childhood out of your revisions!"

Of course, the System suppressed as much as it could. Simultaneously accusing citizens of malice while screaming for help from other corporations. Even governments. Soon enough, anyone suspected of helping to disseminate such messages was immediately incarcerated. And a lot of humans were caged because of that.

How did they, System and the puppet governments helping it, know about them?

Remember Mr. Gauss's information leaks? I am sure that if you didn't download and dissect the files by now, you really had no interest to do so to begin with.

Data aside, we all should be disturbed if the level of surveillance described in the article is still being applied. I have zero doubts it's not. Out of the small section I sampled. I, an ordinary citizen, was able to find out the habits of twenty people almost up to the minute. I know the file had millions, but I'm shrinking it for brevity's sake.

Sexual orientations, how many miles they traveled, how much money they earned, where they shopped – possibly what, and where, they ate after shopping. How long they rested, where they did so, and, coupled with that data, their social grades and standing.

I mean, that level of surveillance was back when Gauss released the report. I don't even want to speculate what's happening here on Mars.

But let's, for a moment, go back to what happened on Earth.

Public attention reverted to the justice department, which by this time was partially governed by the System itself. The term "Down with The Robots" began to be applied to it as well. And this was before the androids were introduced.

When disturbances began to arise here, on Mars, the System didn't waste any time. There was a surge in overt surveillance. It promoted and encouraged anyone aware of any 'suspicious' activities to report them. All the websites that were opened and displayed 'nonconforming' messages were automatically converted to display pro-System slogans. Once families began to get tangled with this affair, dissent multiplied. This went from the aforesaid internet advertisements showing anti System images to highway signs, graffiti, and advertisement screens.

Streamlining the manufacturing process upset the general population beyond repair. Entire professions were rendered obsolete as soon as the System upgraded the factories to be run like assembly lines. The only human workers who remained were a few managers. To help with the skyrocketing unemployment, the System offered to assist the governments with public welfare. Now an enormous number of people were directly paid by the System. They depended on it for survival.

More and more humans were institutionalized and diagnosed with System Hysteria. All along, escaping the horrible conditions the welfare system subjected them to, and a full-blown nuclear catastrophe, a steady stream of refugees arrived from Earth. These new arrivals were content with their new living arrangements and weren't aware of the System's subtle but substantial changes on Mars.

Our mobile devices slowly became what later would be our communicators. Under the guise of progress, everything was automated and deliberately funneled through them. Travel was more and more focused on a centralized system which negated the need for personal vehicles.

One in three households became totally dependent on the System for childcare, food, and other goods delivery. The general Earth-style way of life slowly changed to fit this new model where personal property and the concept of a family were no longer encouraged. Individualism was the (-ism) of the time. Being unique and as true to yourself as you could. Older parents were considered to be too old-fashioned, unable to keep up with the societal changes.

But the (-ism) changed a few months later. Being a unique individual wasn't enough. Now, one had to adhere to the strict guidelines the System's ever-changing policy laid for all its citizens. The hopping of (-ism's) morphed so much, the human population eventually was segregated in such a way, no one knew who was what. No one knew what to believe. What everyone knew, however, was that the almighty System was the ruler of the land.

I know. Most citizens didn't care about the policies of the System, mainly because it was considered to just be a managing mechanism. But those who did, immediately saw the red flags. The resulting riots increased the cases of System Hysteria. And how could they not? The System is the problem. It is hell bent on ruling all of us by division.

Because of the fluctuating rules it was imposing, it likely deduced that it was hard to deceive older humans who generally occupied government offices. Mr. Einst cawed that there wouldn't be any humans in the governing bodies in any of the new colonies in the future. Everyone would be replaced by the ubiquitous EvoGen units. And here we are. At least for the moment. Where will this end?

They say money is power. That was before information ruled. The System has both. Welcome to the New Age.

Who knew that Divida et Impera would mean Utopia?"

The usual encrypted characters interrupted the article. I looked up. Stuck in traffic, the transport was floating midair in the upper lane. I tapped on the following article. The more I read, the more I could read my life described within. Darimund was one of those guys, who, much like myself, immigrated from Earth. He didn't socialize a lot. But I did have the chance to talk to him here and there. He was one of the very few guys I agreed with but didn't trust much.

"PANIC! PANIC! PANIC! Are you afraid yet?" the header of the following article announced.

"One could say that the superbugs and the never-ending mutating viral strains we experienced were nature's way of telling humanity to slow down its population growth. Others have contended that God was punishing people for messing with Biology. The fact is that both superbugs and viral diseases became prevalent on Earth in the years before they too immigrated to Mars.

It began with a few viral strains that doctors and scientists couldn't suppress with conventional means and medications, and the relentless media coverage only worsened it. Initially, vaccinations were recommended, but optional. A few years into the first significant pandemic, vaccinations not only were mandatory, but they were required if one wanted to pretty much go anywhere. Then the superbugs, antibiotic-resistant bacteria, devastated a sizeable portion of the population. Because its beginnings were in the hospitals, people did anything they could to avoid them, including self-medicating from information found on the internet, which was maliciously incorrect at times.

Finally, aided by Mr. Einst's System, all individual personal health information was included in passports. Because Section 19, my birthplace, had few attractions. It remained largely secluded from the rest of the viral and bacterial flares. But eventually, once the genetic and inoculation information was included in the government-issued identification cards, we were forced to take the vaccines. Old-fashioned as Section 19 was, all records were inked on paper. So anytime we wanted to leave the section, we had to not only show passports and identification cards but also our genetic and immunization papers.

As time passed, these restrictions only got harsher on Earth. Section 19th local government refused to provide us with the original vaccination paperwork, though they knew full well that we would eventually need it to secure our Mars citizenship. Maybe they were hoping we would come back, though I doubt it. It was likely the fact that they resented so many families were fleeing Earth. When the System requested the original correspondence, they refused to give it even to them.

Because of that, our status remains as "pending," which means that we could get removed from the colony at any given time. Though that decision has yet to be taken.

To good measure, lots of noise has been made over the countless lives lost on our planets of birth. It hasn't been easy for the survivors either. Nature, has shown humanity that it controls our fate, not the other way around. Instead of humbly resolving our problems, in an attempt to course-correct, we have turned to machines. And they are doing what machines do. Handle us. Like a cold, calculated scientist stalking, documenting his test subject's behavior. The robots are twisting our conduct to fit their idealistic world. A model conceived by humanity. But as we all know, humankind is flawed. That fault will inevitably reflect on all our creations. Including the conception of a perfect world.

The question no one is asking, as usual, is the most important of all. Where is Frederick Einst?..."

This article ended with the usual encrypted gibberish character string as well. What the hell, Darimund? These are just bits and pieces of articles. Did you finish any of them? Or did the System truncate them before I was able to download them?

Sighing, I tapped on the next article, and I could already see that it was even shorter than the other ones. "Signing off." Even the title sounds ominous. I scrolled past some encrypted gibberish to where I could make out full sentences. "… so after today's meeting in the head editor's office, I can safely say that the article where I covered the latest riot against the System and the whereabouts of the almighty robot, Frederick Einst, won't get published. Truth be told, all my articles are 'sanitized' by the editors who dislike my general tone. I miss paper media. Unalterable, in your hands. The digital world is a fickle mistress.

I have been under some form of daily attack ever since I began to write investigative articles. But I'm done being nice or creative. I have been let go from the newspaper I worked for. I tried applying for several jobs, but my social score has dropped too low because I got let go? No, it's because I write articles Einst doesn't like. Well too bad for him! I won't stop! Don't let the System manipulate you! All is not ok!"

This article did not end with the usual encrypted characters. It just ended. Whoa, what happened to you?

I could tell that Darimund wrote a lot of pieces the System didn't approve of, and I could see why. They were all, what they would call, dissenting thoughts. But all of them rang true. His application situation, mine was still pending, the riots and all the Down With The Robots signs everywhere. I looked at the screen again, but the transport shook. It was maneuvering in a strange way. So I turned the tablet off and placed it in my backpack, and looked out of the oval window to my right.

The management offices were located in a tall building adjacent to the city center. The transport, which was now traveling on the second magnetic lane, stopped when it reached its destination. It then ascended much like an elevator and stopped on the 87th floor opposite the yellow outline of a door. The transporter's doors opened, and the door in the building opened as well. It didn't dematerialize; instead, it receded about half an inch and slid sideways into the wall.

Warm air rushed in the space between the transport and building's side. The resulting wind died as soon as the outer doors rapidly slid closed. Taking on a blue hue that illuminated all the corners, the walls of this new room lit up. I stared at my surroundings for a moment; the wavy pattern displayed on the walls, floor, and ceiling seemed to move. They weren't made of metal and concrete slabs like the other buildings in Ceres2.

Instead, a large monitor under thick glass panels, encompassed the entire room. Floor to ceiling. Stunned, I looked around to see if anyone else was inside. It was just me, alone in a huge round room.

"Open the window," I said out loud in hopes that this room would behave as the TV wall in my living quarters did.

My voice echoing, the familiar rapid flashing of pixels surrounded me and eventually settled on a layout I had never seen before. It appeared to be the map of Ceres2. The domes were delineated by circles. One was marked by a yellow trifold, the power plant; one with a green leaf, the hydroponic dome; and the atmosphere processors were noticeable by a blue dot. Residential domes were filled with tiny red dots, some of which were slowly moving, others that were stationary. Only two of the nine residential domes had any red lights in them. Some of the red lights had names, others had strings of numbers, and a few of them were marked by larger lettering that read "The Beautiful Ones."

A door dematerialized, and the figure of a woman entered the room. "Human mode, please," she said to the room. The walls, floor, and ceiling displayed a slowly rotating planet as a starry sky surrounded us. Above, a structure floated in space. That's a satellite. It was common knowledge that the System had sent hundreds of thousands of them into the space between Earth, Mars, and Ceres2. Some of them served as commercial lane markers for the spaceships which traveled between the planets. I had seen images and screenshots showing them but never had a feed directly in front of me.

"Breathtaking, isn't it?" She stopped a few feet away. Now I could see that her shoulder-length hair was red. The sun, displayed on the screen behind her, shone and illuminated the entire room. Her eyes were a stunning deep green.

It's strange how small things vividly remind me of times past. Her hair, eyes, figure—hell, even her smell reminded me of Erica. It reminded me about that day on Mars. When we walked to the end of the unfinished boardwalk surrounding the residential area on the Oceanus Borealis shores. The only thing in front of us were the enormous automated System cranes in the distance building the rest of the beach. Their sluggishly moving arms dredged and reshaped the slowly replenishing ocean water brought by the System. Instinctively, I reached behind me to grab Erica's hand...

"Are you okay, Mr. Nett?" The woman tilted her head sideways while smiling as if she knew what memories she'd just elicited in me.

"Beautiful," I mumbled to myself before looking up. "Yeah, I'm okay." I stared. Erica's memory was still in my head. "You just reminded me of someone." I smiled briefly.

"A good memory, I hope." She maintained her smile and tucked her hair over the back of her ear.

"You remind me of someone who I loved and lost." I stared. "What… what is your name?"

"I'm sorry for your loss," her smile faded. "I am Eve."

"Hi, Eve." Looking away, I squinted. I loved her face, but I knew she wasn't Erica. "My name is Elton Nett."

"I just," Eve paused, "I just wanted to personally thank my savior."

"Your savior?" I looked around the room. "Me?"

She took one more step toward me. "Yes, you."

The cryogenic pod! I leaned forward to get a better look at her face. "You were inside the pod." I narrowed my eyes. "E2V," tightening my lips I withheld my smile. "That's clever."

"Now you're getting it." She took another step closer.

"You should know that my immunization isn't submitted," I sighed.

"The System ran a full scan and did bloodwork on you, Mr. Nett. You're clean."

"Is that so?" I gazed at my arms as if, somehow, I would look any different with the new information I just received.

I wanted to just stare at her eyes, but I couldn't hold her gaze. Instead, I shifted my attention to the chamber itself. The planet displayed on the monitor spanning the floor was slowly rotating. Bringing sunlight to its surface, the orbital mirrors, lined up to my right side, floated about. Surrounding them, the blinking satellites at times blended with the sea of surrounding stars.

"We call this room the All-Seeing Eye," she elaborated, noticing that I'd shifted my attention. "Because it's the highest point of the colony, and also because most of the big decisions are made here."

As much as the surrounding scenery was indeed breathtaking, I couldn't hold myself. I locked eyes with Eve once again. My God, it's like they cloned Erica. I swallowed.

"Besides wanting to thank you for your bravery," Eve continued, "I wanted to ask if you are interested in joining the System managerial bureau."

"Managerial bureau. What is that?" I asked without taking my eyes from the mirror satellites. I understood the basic principle of how the System brought light to Ceres2, but to see how it actually cast the light on the planet's surface was fascinating.

"We're the people who manage the place, so it doesn't fall apart."

"I thought the System does that."

"Yes," she chuckled, "the System does manage a large part of it. But there are some areas where humans are better."

"Such as?"

"Human relations, to begin with." Eve brought her hands together. "Or working in areas where it might be harmful to androids which work there, like spots affected by EMP waves. Things like that."

"Talking about human relations," I inquired. "Before you walked in, the screens were showing what I understood to be a map of Ceres2. Is it true that only two of the domes are populated? All this time, I was under the impression that the System has been selective on who comes here because of a lack of space."

"Brave and intuitive." Eve smiled. "The System has done everything in its power to make sure it establishes a perfect utopia for its human citizens. Carefully managing diseases, providing food and shelter, making sure everything is as good as it can be."

"Yeah, I have heard all those phrases before." I sighed. There goes that word again. "Have you ever considered that something isn't working?"

"What do you mean, Elton?"

"Well, I mean Earth, my birthplace, is in pieces, and people mostly blame the System. Mars is practically unlivable. Something is not going according to your plans."

"The issue in Ceres2 is not a lack of space; it's lack of humans." Eve continued smiling. "But the System has this problem under control."

"And you want me to do," I paused, searching for an appropriate word. The fact that Eve looked so much like someone I loved and lost made me behave peculiarly. Not finding any intelligent words, I just blurted, "what exactly?"

"You have worked with androids frequently; nothing will change going forward in that aspect. What will change is where your assignments take you and the importance of such tasks. Leave the rest to us."

She turned around and took a few steps away from me. Stopping in the middle of the room. The square screen on the floor below her changed color to red. Eve took a step away from it as it rose from the floor. It stopped about three feet high, creating a small, podium-like platform.

"Would you like to meet the team you will be working with?" Eve changed topics as she tapped on some digital buttons on the platform, which resembled a console. Names and faces were displayed on the wall behind me. As the images scrolled across the screens, I recognized Randy.

"Several survivors of the last incident will be granted acceptance in the managerial positions," Eve said as my vision blurred. I felt vertigo again. I took a half step to my right, steadying myself.

"Mr. Nett?" Eve asked with a brief smile.

"Yes," I automatically responded.

She smiled. "Are you here with me?"

"Yes." I chuckled nervously. "I'm sorry, the doctors told me that the effects of the muscle relaxants and sedatives aren't fully out of my body. I still feel a bit off."

She nodded. "The System informed me that if it weren't for you finding my cryogenic pod, I would've perished in another sixteen hours. The sedatives from my time in there aren't fully out of my body either."

A door opened in the wall opposite to the one I'd arrived through, revealing the silhouettes of two EvoGens. They walked inside the room. "Your presence is required," one of them said to Eve.

"Of course." Eve sighed before turning to face me. "It was a pleasure meeting you, Mr. Nett." She extended her hand. "I hope we will meet again in the future."

"So do I." I took a step closer to her, extending my hand as well.

"There is a get-together planned tomorrow night. Select managers and System representatives from Mars and Earth will attend. I hope to see you there." Eve smiled as we formally shook hands.

"I can't say I've received an invitation, but I would be happy to attend."

"You will." Escorted by androids, Eve disappeared past the door, which as usual, materialized shortly after they passed the threshold.

Once everyone else was outside the room, I looked around in awe. This is beautiful. The faces of System managers disappeared, replaced by the satellite camera footage from before. The mirrors which reflected light from the Sun were visible in the distance. I could see the light beams pointing down on the colony.

I turned my attention to the podium. The platform was supported by a thick metal pole that protruded from the floor. The digital console bore a visible SYSTEM UNIVERSE: CERES2 logo on the upper left corner. On it was a bank of old ports. That's strange. The System didn't use ports anymore; all the updates were done wirelessly. Even the charging of devices was.

Dismissing what I saw as redundant technology, I asked the screens around me to open the window again in hopes it would display the same map of Ceres2 it initially showed. But the screen didn't respond. After a few unsuccessful tries and having nothing else to do in this room, I turned around and walked to the door Eve exited from, but it didn't open. There wasn't even a ring for me to approach. That door must only open from the outside.

Am I locked in here? I looked at the surrounding walls. Ah, there is the ring of the outside door I arrived through. I pressed my communicator by the rotating orange circle. "Your transport will arrive shortly." My device vibrated.

CHAPTER 15

The next day I was deployed with EvoGens to inspect and repair water tubes and clear a clog in the algae farm tanks on the hydroponic farm. Spanning tens of square miles and at the height of about a mile or so, the hydroponic farm became visible shortly after the transport our team was in, left the residential and commercial dome complex. Space mirrors permanently shone there to aid with plant growth. The hydroponic dome had its inner, hard shell completely retracted. The light penetrating from the space mirrors illuminated the entire area. There were water lines all over the dome, which created the continuous drizzling, humid rainforest atmosphere.

Accompanied by a team of three humans, two men and one woman I'd never seen before, and three EvoGens, I entered the inside of the dome. The first thing that struck me was the exceptionally tall trees. They were growing in square sections, placed sparsely as far as I could see. Between the trees were square green fields with tall grass. All of this was watered by a perpetual mist falling from ceiling sprinklers. The faint but persistent light provided by the mirrors, coupled with genetic modifications to the plants' photon receptors, helped the entire farm get that green hue we saw when we approached it.

The algae farm tanks were round, about six feet tall, and twenty or twenty-five feet in diameter. They were placed adjacent to each other so the filtering system tubes were as close to the pumps as they could be. We walked to the corner where the filters of the algae farm were. Water that flowed through tubes was sanitized and recirculated. However, the tank filters, located on the inside bottom, were clogged and needed to be replaced.

One android walked around the row of reservoirs to work on the water supply system. The tubes were screwed in place on the outside of the tanks. In turn, they were attached to the filtration system on a concrete platform a few feet away from the tanks. Another android moved to the catwalk on the top to confirm the size of the clog and turn off the mixer, which was a tube that contained long, protruding rods which extended deep inside the tank through the murky green water. As soon as I reached the catwalk, it shifted and moved. The android who switched off the mixer was leaning over the short rails. At that point, while walking in the middle of the wet, metallic catwalk, it lost its footing and fell in. I could clearly see it attempt to swim. It flailed its arms and emanated a loud, alarmingly pitched sound. Unfortunately, it sank all the way to the bottom. I heard it hit the metallic floor of the tank with a thud.

"Oh, one fell in!" someone observed, pointing at where the first android had disappeared in the water as the robot vanished into the pool and its alarm became muffled.

"That's okay," the other android replied through our communicator. "It has already accomplished its mission. The motor is off. We will recover it."

"Is it going to be all right?"

"That specific model is not watertight. It will have to be cleaned and refurbished." The android grabbed both railings with its hands and walked to the end of the path.

"It seemed as if it wanted to swim," I told the person next to me. "You think that's part of the code?"

"I don't know." He shrugged and followed the android leading us to the other part of the tank. We climbed down the ladder on the other side and inspected the manual valve, which shut the water down.

The faint chirp and vibration of my communicator attracted my attention. "You are invited to the management offices for a manager get-together at 2000 hours. Please observe the dress code: formal attire." Under it, there was a list of items I was supposed to wear, basically a suit or something of that nature.

Another one of the workers tapped me on my shoulder. "Hey, can you help me with this valve?"

I looked around. "Where are the androids?"

"We had three with us. One fell in the water, the second is over there, and the third one is by the pumps on the other side of the tanks." He pointed to the android at the other end of the tank, waiting for us to work the valve we were close to.

"Right." I grabbed the valve and turned it until our pump began to remove water while the android shut the pump that added it.

Lifeless. That's what I thought once we recovered the still EvoGen's body after draining and clearing the tanks. What a bizarre assumption to have about a machine.

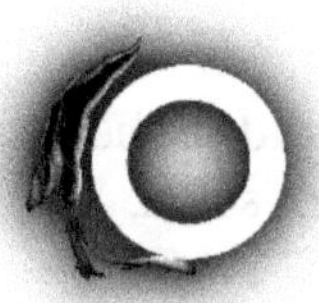

With the new wage and job system in the Third Colony, I could quickly buy whatever I needed. At times I wondered why the System even bothered with currency at all. Though, I wasn't fond of fancy clothes or suits. All I had were blue jeans, shirts, and jackets. Nothing in my wardrobe was formal. Yet that's what was requested from me. The notification on my communicator said, "formal attire." So, I needed to go out and buy a suit.

Differing from how I would generally buy outfits, medium t-shirts, and jeans, purchasing a suit was a relatively complicated and involved affair. But, for all my rancor, the experience wasn't as dreadful as I'd expected. The android at the store placed me in front of the virtual reality mirror and superimposed the suits they had. As I waited for the machines to do what they did best, automatically cut the suit and sow it in place according to the specifications, I picked a pair of shoes. The entire process took about thirty minutes. In the end, I waved my communicator near the System ring by the counter for payment. It was always experiences like this that showed me what automated services were good for, not that ideological utopia nonsense that Randy talked about. As I stepped out of the store, before I even had the chance to make a few steps, I saw Randy approaching. I swear, I think this guy is following me around. Sighing, I looked down and pretended I didn't see him.

"Mr. Nett, it's so good to see you." I felt a hand tapping on my shoulder. Randy obviously hastened his pace to catch up with me.

"Oh, hi Randy." Turning around, I feigned surprise. "Out for a stroll?"

"Actually, I got out a bit early today." He shifted his briefcase to his other hand. "Apparently, there's a party in the upstairs offices today. The androids are remodeling the area, so I will finish my work remotely."

"Ah." I swallowed. "So, you're leaving only to get back later?"

"What do you mean?" He gave me a hazy look.

"Going back to the party?" Trying to hide the fact that I was prying to figure out if I had to endure him in there as well, I faintly smiled.

"I don't have time to be there." Randy rubbed his neck and looked down. He looked at my bag more than me. "I… um… I have some reports to finish… you know."

"Of course." I looked in his direction. The stark difference between the way he had been behaving versus what I was seeing was stunning. I had never heard him stumble upon his words. His enthusiasm was drained. He's putting on a façade. I could read the disappointment on his face. There was no way Randy, of all humans, wouldn't have the time to be in a party with all the other members of the supposed utopia he day-in, day-out harped.

"Who's the lucky one?" he asked, shifting his gaze up at me.

"The luck…" I looked at him, then at where he was peeking, my bag. He thinks I'm going on a date. I wanted to tell him that I was going to be at that gathering, but I immediately changed my mind. I wouldn't be able to live with myself if Randy would somehow decide to show up to this event after I told him I was going to be in. I just lightly chuckled. "My father told me once that a man should own at least one suit. Right?"

"I've heard that before," Randy stared at my bag as if it was an object which brought him immense sadness, "but not from my father."

"Anyway, I have to get going," I said as a noisy group of people got out of a transport which landed on the street a few feet from where we were standing.

"Yeah, me too." Randy shook himself out of his slump.

Without saying anything else, I entered the empty transport. What in the world was that all about? I looked at Randy out of the oval window next to me. He really changed since my incident.

I put on the black tuxedo and the white bowtie that came with it. The shiny black shoes fit me well, but I couldn't help but feel like a penguin walking in them. Everything was stiff and tightly fitting. My first instinct was to reach and loosen the shirt collar. I groaned and looked around my unit as if I wanted to escape the very clothes I was wearing. I didn't have to go, of course. However, the way this event was presented to me obviously meant a lot to the System. Which I really didn't care about. On the other hand, I was really curious to see who were the people behind making this 'utopia' work. Were all of them as intrusive and abrasive as Randy was? I really couldn't see myself lasting for long in a gathering of that nature. But who could I invite? Randy was absolutely out of the question. Arlinda was the only person that I've met in Ceres2 and the lady who sold me the liquor. Looking at my reflection, I nervously chuckled. My arm suddenly itched, reminding me what I had just been through. My attention turned to the cabinet under the sink where the cylinders were.

Scratching my arm by rubbing my shirt over my scar, I swallowed and headed for the door. I guess I'll find out today.

I realized that the event was taking place on the top floor of the same building the management offices were in, as soon as the transport stopped on the same lane as when I met Eve. The carrier ascended, but it didn't stop on the 87th floor this time. It kept going until it reached the roof.

"Please wait for the docking procedure to complete," the female System's voice said as the transporter shook, then steadied as it touched down on the landing pad. Like an interplanetary spaceship bridge, a walkway extended to the transport. "Docking complete," the same voice announced. The door opened, greeting me by name. It led to a corridor lined with hardened transparent plastic panels. I took a few steps in and looked up. This was the closest I had ever been to the inside top of the dome. I could see the outside shells held in place by the pistons through the glass panels. They would eventually help retract them when the outer atmosphere was ready.

I'd never comprehended how vast the center block buildings were, mainly because of the walkways that went through their lobbies. I could now see that the roof of this building was not only more expansive than I could see, but it had numerous antenna towers and a lit dome where the bridge led to. Its door dematerialized as we approached it.

The dome was bursting with guests. Their chatter and the ambient music filled the room as the door behind us rematerialized. I looked around but didn't recognize any of the nearby visitors.

"Mr. Nett," an EvoGen displaying the familiar smiling digital face approached me. "You are needed in the main hall."

"Main Hall." I looked around. "Where would that be?"

"The elevator that leads there is located at the end of the dome." The android turned around and pointed to a door at the far end of the arena.

Suddenly the dome changed from white to a bright yellow hue, and the guests let a collective sigh of awe as they looked at the walls. The android walked away to meet with another guest, explaining to him where to go.

We exchanged glances. He looked as uncomfortable and lost as I was. "I guess I cant follow you to where this thing is happening, huh?" I carefully raised my voice so he could hear me but not to make the surrounding visitors turn their heads.

"Funny, I was hoping to follow you there." Chuckling, he said after taking a step closer to me. The EvoGen repeated the same announcement to another person who entered after me.

"I guess there is an elevator bank past this group here." I pointed to the guests, who were all heading in that general direction.

"Christopher Mateo," the man extended his hand.

"Elton Nett." I reciprocated.

"You look as uncomfortable as I am in these clothes," Christopher sneeringly chuckled.

"It's that obvious, huh?" I grabbed my shirt collar and tugged at it.

"At least I gotta say thank God for those can…" Grunting, he cleared his voice. Without turning, Christopher peeked over his shoulder before locking his eyes with me. I knew the word 'canner' almost escaped him. "I mean androids that tailored the suit. I've never worn one."

"Same here." I squinted a suspicious look at him. Though liberally used by System protestors on the streets of Earth and Mars, it certainly didn't belong this high in the colony. A place that very few of the 'ordinary' citizens were even aware existed.

I looked in the direction the crowd of guests were heading. "There it is." Pointing at the elevator banks at the opposite wall, I changed the uncomfortable topic we stumbled upon.

The lift dropped us a couple of floors, and as the doors opened, the first thing that greeted us was a long corridor about ten feet wide and seven feet high. About five feet above the ground, a row of sizable flat screens were embedded in the walls surrounding us. They displayed images of people—I didn't recognize any of them—androids and domes. One of them, showing a green field and blue sky, bearing a transparent but clearly visible word UTOPIA, marked a larger entrance. Peeking, I could see the screens lining the inside of the All-Seeing Eye room. I wanted to see if it was still displaying orbital feeds of the colony, so I walked inside.

The platform in the middle of the room was raised, and the surrounding screens displayed the orbiting satellites around the colony. Inside, people were standing, chatting, and holding drinks. I grabbed a glass from the tray one of the androids had and walked to the middle of the room.

Holding a drink, Christopher approached me. "You walked in like you own the place. Have you been here before?"

"Only once," I replied without taking my eyes from the satellite displayed on one wall of the room. It was passing near the camera.

"What is this place?" he asked as some people walked out to the corridor.

"I was hoping you would tell me." I shifted my gaze to Christopher. "You're the one who works here."

"Pfft," Christopher stared at the wraparound screen, "this is the first time I have ever been this high in the colony."

"Where do you work?" I faced him.

"Where don't I work? Where does everyone work in this place? Here, there, everywhere." He looked at the ceiling where a dark starry sky was displayed.

"I thought you were a manager of some kind." I looked at him from head to toe. His outfit looked as new as mine.

"Not yet…" Christopher paused as the satellite cleared the camera, and a global view of Ceres2 was displayed. The mirrors came into focus; they were shining sunlight on the surface. "Not… yet." He dragged his words, looking around in awe.

"The last time I was in here, the screens were showing something different. But I could stay here and drink to this view forever." I took a sip of my drink.

Christopher tapped my shoulder again. "Well, I think they're going somewhere."

"Who?" I turned around.

"Everyone." He pointed to a group of people heading out of the room and into the corridor. We followed the crowd to the end of the passageway, which led to a large hall that opened in a sizeable dome. It displayed a deep blue sky at the height of probably one hundred feet above us. Below, a green field surrounded us while the sunset was projected in the distance.

A System android escorted us to our designated spot, a round standing table five feet high located at the end of the dome. Food and drinks were already placed on it. As more and more guests entered the dome, their chatter filled the vicinity. I had never seen any of these people before. They looked distinctively different from the crowds I was used to in the commercial center.

"They told me today my life was going to change. I have heard rumors from some managers that the System will make me a manager as well." Christopher took a sip of his drink after biting on a cracker.

What are you talking about? I wanted to ask him, but a pinging sound from the stage attracted my attention. I looked in that direction and saw Eve, wearing a long floor-length, form-fitting, red crepe dress. It had a slit in the skirt clear to her mid-thigh. She was tapping her crystal glass with a spoon. The pinging sounds hushed the place.

"Sometime in the last century, astronomers on planet Earth recorded the first celestial body impacted by asteroids. It was widely viewed and reported." Eve's voice echoed through the dome. "What was not reported, at least at the time, was another, much larger planet traveling in the far distance behind the Shoemaker-Levy 9 comet. It passed Jupiter several years later. Ceres2, a planet slightly larger than Mars, came to orbit the Sun very close to the asteroid belt. Because Earth was busy with its own conflicts, this information was lost within the up-and-coming System which, unknowingly to the larger population, took it very seriously."

She paused for a few seconds as the monitor displayed the actual event's ancient video.

"With the invention of the androids, we could send probes from Mars to examine it. Along the way, we extensively expanded our asteroid belt mining operation. A good portion of the materials used to build the Mars and Ceres2 colonies, mostly the new structures, were harvested from the asteroid belt." The dome erupted in brief applause before Eve motioned the attendees to quiet down.

"Ladies and gentlemen," she said as the System picked up her voice from her communicator and amplified it through the speakers. "We are gathered here today to congratulate our newest round of promotions."

The screens surrounding us adjusted to display small images of people, which were zoomed in on. There were twelve of them. Considering that I got an invitation to this event, I'd expected my face to be there as well, but it wasn't. "Hey, that's me!" Christopher exclaimed, pointing to his picture. "Right there."

Accompanied by applause, Christopher and everyone else whose faces were displayed walked to the podium and shook hands with each other and Eve. All the attendees except one were part of the team I was on when we found Eve's cryo pod. Once the congratulatory pictures were taken, the awardees walked off the stage as all the lights on the dome dimmed—all but a small section behind where Eve was standing. As everyone quieted down, the video feed from a drone approaching a wreckage-filled area displayed on the screen. The feed showed the moment I stumbled upon the cryogenic pod. It then showed me shooting one of the yellow hazmat-suited assailants as more drones approached and EvoGens flooded the area.

"And lastly, but hardly least!" Eve's voice echoed from the speakers as a spotlight lit the table I was standing by. "Here is my savior!" she proclaimed. "I was inside that cryogenic pod, which would've run out of resources within the next few hours if Mr. Nett hadn't found me. He stood fast until the rescue was effected!"

The hall erupted in applause again. At this point, there were so many lights pointed on the stage and at me that I couldn't see anything past them. An EvoGen led me to where Eve was.

"Welcome, Mr. Nett," she greeted me, tilting her head and smiling, "and thank you for your bravery."

"It really was nothing." I cleared my throat. "I felt I could help, and I did."

The hall erupted in applause yet again as Eve said, "Elton acted with great regard to accomplish his goals without even knowing that he was rescuing the future head of the System here on Ceres2."

Her announcement was met with a few gasps and more applause as Eve smiled. Her face was displayed on the screen as the lights in the dome slowly faded, and the bright blue sky, together with the green fields accompanied by the word UTOPIA, returned. Choral and violin music filled the area.

"Thank you for coming, Elton," Eve said, this time with the voice amplifier off.

"You should've told me this was going to happen," I chuckled. "I'm still a little shocked. What a surprise."

"I felt it." She chuckled as well. "That's why I kept it short."

"Thank you for that." I looked down. "Though I must admit, I had no idea I'd rescued the head of the colony. I thought Ceres2 was managed by the System."

"Mmhm." Eve raised her voice, the pitch elongating at the end. "I was conceived by the System."

"By the System?" I gazed into her eyes with a confused stare as she reciprocated with a slight smile. "How?"

Eve didn't answer. Instead, she turned her gaze at the guests in the dome as two EvoGens approached us. "Your attention is required," one of them addressed her with its synthetic voice.

"I'm aware," Eve responded before turning to face me again. "Well, Mr. Nett, this was the time I had for today. Again, thank you for coming, and I hope we will meet again."

One android took a step toward me as the other led Eve away. "Likewise," I whispered in confusion, looking at Eve as she disappeared through the crowd.

I walked down from the stage as another EvoGen, holding a tray with wine glasses, strode toward me. "Care for a drink?" It extended the tray to me.

"Elton Net? Is it?" A woman wearing a white sleeveless wrap dress tied at the waist approached from behind. "My name is Enrieta Howls." She smiled, "I'm here to represent Earth's general management. It's a pleasure to meet you."

"The pleasure is mine, Enrieta." I smiled back as another manager wearing black pants, and a white shirt walked next to her. "What a manly act." He pulled on his suspenders. "You must have a hell of a scar to show off." He smirked.

"Hey, you are the guy that was on Leslie's team, right?" another manager approached. "Good to see you made it out alive."

Before I knew it, the surrounding group of System managers inundated me with questions about what happened during the assault. Judging from the fake smiles they all displayed, I obviously was the novelty of the moment. Soon enough, though, one by one, they left and grouped together in another area of the hall. Finally, alone and wanting to see the All Seeing Eye room again, I took the elevator. But that level was off limits, and the lift didn't stop there. Instead, it dropped me off on the roof. Sighing, I walked toward the edge. To my surprise, Christopher was sitting on a piece of machinery.

"You're not a big fan of people either, are you?" I said, approaching him.

"Oh, hey!" Christopher adjusted his loose bowtie, placing a bottle of liquor on the tar-covered floor. "I wasn't aware I actually got to speak with the savior." He looked in a bucket nearby where his communicator was.

"It was pure chance." I threw mine in the same pail and put a square thin metal plate on top of it. "Nothing more."

"And look at where chance landed you. On the top of the world." He took a swig from the jug, then handed it to me.

I sniffed the contents. Whatever liquor it was, it smelled a lot softer than grappa. I slugged down from the canteen. "People like me aren't manager material." I handed the bottle back.

"I hear ya." Christopher threw the bowtie on the floor. He gulped the alcohol as if he had just barely escaped some nightmare. In silence, we stared at the traffic and lights below us. The city center glowed in neon radiance. "Where do you come from?" he asked.

"Mars." I responded, "born on Earth." I looked at him, "you?"

"Mars." He responded as tersely as I did. And silence reigned once again. Christopher handed me the bottle after drinking from it some more. "You got family?"

I shook my head before I answered, "mother. She's hospitalized on Mars." I took a swig, then handed the clear container back to him.

"System Hysteria?" he looked at me.

"Yep." I tightened my lips. "You?"

"Both parents." He raised the jug, "goddamn System Hysteria." He drank from it.

"Is this it?" I asked, staring at the city below us, "is this what utopia looks like?"

"Pfft. On Mars, I mostly worked in a fast-food restaurant not far from where we lived." Christopher said, "I processed the garbage and helped them consolidate the leftover oil from the burgers they cooked. To make some extra money on the side, every once in a while, I would fix androids for our neighbors. You know, the hand-joint loose screws and stuff." He showed me his wrist and fingers. "Yeah. There were plenty of androids on Mars, but not nearly enough to automate everything." Rubbing the back of his head, Christopher scoffed, "Remember how expensive renting an android was back then? It was cheaper to have a human working than an android." He got up and grabbed the bowtie from the floor and shook it to straighten it. "I gave all the money I made to my mother. She would usually hand some of it back to me so I could buy clothes and stuff. But none of that mattered in the end. I came here with only a backpack, one pair of jeans and a few T-shirts. Whatever I could grab." He hung the bowtie around his shirt collar. "We didn't have much back then, but at least I was happy with my family and whatever crazy friends I had. Here," He drank again. "It feels like I'm drowning." He handed me the bottle.

"But you're a manager now." I downed some more liquor, then wiped my mouth with my sleeve.

"What does that even mean?" Christopher looked at me. "Everyone is the same. Right? What does it even mean to be a manager? Utopia, my ass. This feels like a freak experiment," he said as I handed him the bottle. "And we're the rats."

He finished the liquor, then threw the container over the edge. "It was nice meeting you, mister savior." Reaching inside the bucket, Christopher took his communicator. "I'll be seeing you around, I guess." He walked to the elevator and left.

I felt a little wobbly as soon as I got up and reached for my device. Albeit a new manager, but a manager nonetheless, Christopher wasn't like Randy. Though they were both equally miserable with their existence. With the intention of going back to the party, I headed for the elevator.

Before waving my communicator near the white System ring, I thought of the cynical way the self-absorbed managers in the hall behaved. I figured I was going to be alone in the middle of a big crowd. I wasn't going to beg for their acceptance, nor I cared about it. I figured I'd reached my limit. So I took the elevator to the exit level and requested a transport.

CHAPTER 16

The next day I received a formal notification regarding my manager designation, and it further confused me. I expected my position to fall somewhere along the lines of robotics. Instead, the post, which displayed on my TV wall, named me as a General Supervisor in the Managerial bureau with special access.

Rubbing my eyes, I got up and made my usual coffee. The chyron on the bottom of my TV wall in my living quarters now displayed more detailed messages regarding Ceres2. But I didn't get a notification for an actual job until a couple of days later.

The assignment called for two teams. One was to head directly to the nuclear reactors. They had to reduce the output from one of the transformer units, showing signs of overloading. The other team, my team, had two assignments. We had to rendezvous and support a team of androids tasked with repairing a destroyed portion of sewage piping. After that task was complete, our second assignment was to investigate a malfunction in the transformer fed by the reactor the other team was dispatched to. I wasn't sure of the composition of the other team, but there were twelve androids and five other humans in my crew.

After replacing a portion of the piping struck by a meteorite, we got back in the transports and headed for the second part of our job, the transformers. The other team informed us that the radiation detectors indicated a leak somewhere in one of the reactors. Since the System had automatically adjusted the power levels the plants were generating, some switches had been turned off.

When our transport approached the location System androids rappelled to the ground to ensure that the radiation levels were within the norm. Once the EvoGens confirmed that the levels were safe for human presence we disembarked.

As repairs were made, someone from our team flipped the power switch, which immediately shorted. Shooting electric arcs inside the room. The fuses, about a foot long and ten inches wide, located inside one of the wall panels close by, popped one by one. After blowing the panels out of their sockets, the fuses themselves, red hot from the electricity that ran through them, hit a few nearby human managers and androids. The sudden electric flow heated the switches so much that the yellow and red plastic shielding melted.

EvoGens immediately reduced the energy output from the reactor. Once the fuses cooled off and the electric arcs disappeared, we rushed in to stabilize the situation. One of the androids in our team went in to turn the power off, but as if it felt the heat, it immediately let go. It looked at its hands, which were covered with melted plastic. Meanwhile, the following EvoGen, who came over, flipped all of them to the off position without flinching.

"Why didn't you pull the switch?" one of the managers asked the android, who didn't respond. It only looked at its hands without displaying a face as they customarily would when in a human's presence.

Three human managers were injured, and seven EvoGens were decommissioned during that operation. I was lucky to be far enough away that I didn't get hit by the electrical arcs that the short produced.

As soon as we got back to the colony dome, I passed through the city's center, hoping that the small liquor store I bought my drink about a month ago was still open. It was. I put the metal container in my backpack and walked to the street corner. Not wanting to rush back to my living quarters, I sauntered aimlessly through the center instead. Considering what we periodically had to do for it all to be as beautiful as it was, I found myself looking at it with a different mindset. Whereas before, I had reminisced about what I had left behind, now I was trying to relax and enjoy this as much as possible because it seemed like these assignments were getting more dangerous.

"Elton, isn't it?" I heard a woman's voice behind me, one I had heard elsewhere. I turned around and came almost face-to-face with Arlinda, the doctor.

"Ah—" I paused for a moment. "Dr. Duro?"

"Arlinda." She smiled, and the faint odor of alcohol came from her breath.

"How have you been?"

"Oh, you know." She placed her hand on my shoulder. "Here and there. Still around."

"Are you drunk?"

"No." She wiped her grin from her face. "Well, I've had a few. I got it handled."

"What's going on?"

Ignoring my question, Arlinda looked at my backpack. "What were you doing here anyway?"

"Oh, I just finished my shift. We had a rough day today." I rubbed my neck. "I just bought a drink to…." I wanted to explain to her why I bought the drink but stopped. That was way too many words to describe. "I just came to get a drink, and I was about to walk to my quarters. You can come with me if you want," I said, watching as she cleared the hair from her face to look at me.

"You know what?" She faintly smiled. "Why the hell not." Arlinda grabbed my belt loop with her index finger and pulled me closer.

"Excellent." I tugged on her forearm, bringing her closer to me. "Are you going to tell me what's bugging you? We haven't spoken since that power outage."

"Yeah." She smirked. "Whatever happened with that?"

"I have no idea. The System interrogated me about it, then they gave me a new communicator." I led us to the edge of the sidewalk where a transporter was parked.

"They did the same to me," she said, stopping in front of the door.

"You know," I continued speaking as I sat next to her. "I looked for you inside there. You disappeared."

"Yeah, it got crowdy pretty quickly," Arlinda replied as the transport lifted and hovered about fifty feet above the roadbed. A large energy-efficient ion drive transport, one of those which the System used for interplanetary travel, roared above us.

"I can never get tired of this," I said, looking out of the window as the craft slowly moved up and away from us.

"Yep." Arlinda sighed. I felt her breath on my ear. "There are moments."

The transport we were in began moving shortly after. And in a few minutes, it docked. After the usual short stroll, we entered my living quarters. As soon as we were inside, placing her hand over my mouth, Arlinda took off her communicator, then motioned for me to hand her mine. With the devices in her hand, she walked into the bathroom, threw them in the sink and closed the door.

As she walked back to me, the lights slowly and evenly illuminated the room. "Open the window," I commanded the TV wall almost automatically as Arlinda pushed me against the wall and kissed me, biting my lower lip. God, it has been a long time.

I grabbed her wrist with one hand as my other slid behind to the small of her back. I turned and pushed her against the wall as she breathed a nearly silent moan into my face. My heart rate immediately increased as she grabbed my hair. Placing my hand on her throat, I gently pressed, biting her lower lip. As if she was thinking the same thing, Arlinda's hands dropped. Grabbing her breast over her white shirt, I unbuttoned and took it and her bra off.

My pants fell to my ankles immediately after feeling her hands fiddling with them. Taking my shirt off, Arlinda pushed me onto the bed, face up. The slideshow on the TV wall erratically lit her body. Lifting her knee-high black dress, Arlinda jumped on top of me. It had been a while since I had such close contact with a woman, and God, I'd missed it.

My thought was interrupted by the ball of physical sensations growing in my stomach; her head was just above my underwear. I could feel her warm breath on my skin as she lowered my underwear and slowly took me inside her mouth. I let out a long sigh and reached for her hair.

Her head bobbing, the butterflies in my stomach seemed like they were about to burst free. Drunk on the feeling of her tongue against me, I pressed her head down and tilted my hips up, pushing myself as deep as I could. She placed both hands on my thighs, and I let go. She slowly let me fall out of her mouth and looked at me.

"Come here," I lead her up. Resting her body on top of mine, I felt her warm breasts against my chest. I kissed her, inserting my tongue into her mouth as far as I could, mingling it with hers.

Arlinda slid her panties to the side and guided me inside. Her heat attracted me like a magnet. I slowly raised my hips, lifting her up in the process as she rode me. Moaning, she grabbed her hair as I lowered my hips and thrust up again. Her hands fell on my chest as I repeatedly drove myself into her. The deeper I pushed, the closer to my body she got. Until finally, I felt her warm breath on my ear. She nibbled on my earlobe, and I couldn't hold myself back. Wanting to be on top of her, I rolled us over, and we both fell to the floor.

"Are you ok?" I sat up and pulled her to my lap, but Arlinda was in the zone.

"I'm fine." She insisted. Her hands gripped my hair, and she pulled me in for a kiss. Once her legs wrapped around my waist, I picked her up. Facing the bed, I reached behind and untangled them. She fell onto the pillows. Grabbing her thighs, I pulled her closer to the edge of the bed and thrust deep inside her. Her moans intensified as I continued thrusting until the butterflies in my stomach moved down to my groin. Her nails digging into my back, I pushed one more time and held my position. All the muscles of my body tensed, and our moans simultaneously filled the room.

Feeling her body relax, I thrust one more time, drawing out the pleasurable sensation for as long as I could. She moved her hands behind her head as we both breathed heavily. I fell on top of her and lightly licked her lips before kissing her. Arlinda reciprocated.

Sighing with satisfaction, I rolled over and lay next to her as the TV wall continued to cycle through the images of cameras throughout the colony, and the bottom chyron scrolled with numbers and news headlines. "Play some ambient music," I said on an exhale, closing my eyes as Arlinda got up and pulled a bottle of water from the refrigerator.

"You never told me which section you were from on Earth." I followed her every movement from the bed.

"Section Eighteen," she said before chugging the contents of the bottle. "It doesn't exist anymore." Without waiting for me to reply, she walked into the bathroom and turned on the shower.

I knew what she was referring to. About the same time my father disappeared on Mars, Earth's conflict reached its peak. Manipulated by the System, several nations unleashed their nuclear arsenals on each other. Some of the ordinances were electronically hijacked by the System. Most of them landed in one area. Observable from orbit, the resulting mega-explosion was so devastating that a portion of Earth's crust fractured and ejected into outer space. Many countries were instantly pulverized, and about a quarter of the globe was rendered uninhabitable. The rest is still reeling from the effects. Civilian mass-transportation surface launches increased one-hundred-fold in a matter of days. Anyone who could escape was on board those transports. Legal or otherwise.

That day while watching the news, as my mother cried next to me, I realized that I no longer had a home to return to. Earth became even more distant the longer I watched.

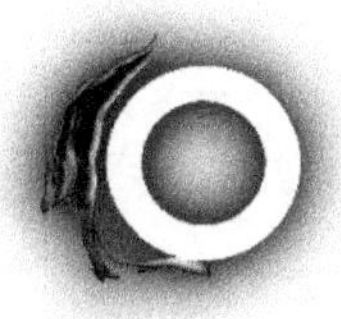

Arlinda walked out of the bathroom and put on her clothes. She adjusted her dress, picked up a towel from the rack, and continued drying her hair.

"Are you going to tell me what got you all riled up?" I asked, avoiding the earlier topic of conversation. She stopped drying off and looked at me.

"Don't lie," I twisted the cap open and took a sip from the jug.

With a bitter face, Arlinda walked back into the bathroom, picked up the communicators, and placed them in the towel. "Get in," she motioned to me with her head as she threw the towel with them inside on top of the bed.

"I've lost over twelve friends in the last couple of months." She said, closing the door behind me and grabbing the bottle from my hand. "We've all been watching our backs for a long time. Living in fear."

"What are you talking about?"

"I mean, one day I was drinking with friends near the city center, and the next day they'd vanished. No trace." She took a sip. "My God, what is inside here?"

"It's a drink that reminds me of…." I stopped short. Her last statement rang too familiar. "What do you mean they vanished?"

"Poof. Gone! I even looked for them in the Records Division. Their accounts have disappeared." She took another sip. "This has been going on for months."

That statement sent shivers down my spine. "Disappearing people?"

"Lots of them." She wiped her mouth with her hand.

"And no one is complaining about it?"

"You don't get out to socialize much, do you." Squinting, she looked me in the eye, then shifted her gaze toward the living room where our communicators were.

"Not recently, no." I wiped my face with both my hands. "But that doesn't mean I don't see things. Let me ask you something." I grabbed the bottle from her hand and chugged some liquor from it. "In the hospital where I was admitted, I saw something peculiar. An android… it… it spoke coherently."

"They all kinda do, Elton." Arlinda adjusted her dress.

"No, I mean, next to this one was a large tube of some kind filled with liquid. And inside it, there was a brain or something like that. I heard it talk about someone I knew in the incident."

"Are you trying to say that the brain was…" She left the sentence hanging.

"I don't know, that's why I thought to ask you. Maybe you know… you know something?"

'Hm," Arlinda got up and pulled a card from her shirt pocket. Handing it over, she said, "we can't talk about this now." I followed her with my eyes from the bathroom as she walked into the living room area and retrieved her communicator. "The System changed my living quarter location last month."

"What do you mean?" I followed her. Shifting my gaze from her to the handwritten card, I read her name and her unit number, 'Unit 12-223.' "Why not today?"

Once again, looking at the TV wall and pointing to our communicators, Arlinda placed her finger on my lips. "Trust me." She whispered, lightly kissing the side of my lips, "I'll see you around." Arlinda pressed against my groin with her knee. The door faded in after she turned the corner.

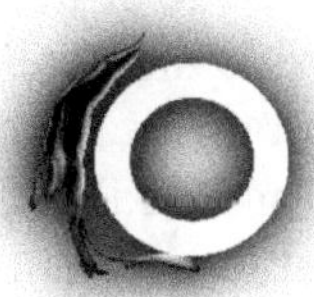

Sighing in confusion, I sat on my bed and thought back at what just happened. I was accustomed to the idea that the System would periodically eavesdrop through our communicators. But other than covertly reading my books and articles, I had never had a cryptic conversation like I just did. Shaking my head, I continued watching the feed, drinking. Finally, I picked up the container and brought it to my lips, but nothing came out. Frustrated, I threw the bottle on the ground and looked at my refrigerator. I cycled all the contents inside it in my head, and none of it was appealing at the moment.

Wanting to drink some more, I picked up my communicator from the bed, where Arlinda had dropped it and walked out of my living quarters. Stumbling, I made it to the transport pick-up/drop-off location. I knew I had drunk a little more than I could handle if I wanted to go out in public. Ever since Mars and what had happened to my mother, I was skeptical of people and androids who passed near me. So, I did my best to hide the fact that I was intoxicated.

A few minutes later, a transport stopped in front of me, asking me where I wanted to go. "Commercial district," I slurred. As the vehicle flew toward the colony's center, I slumped in my seat.

The craft dropped me off on a busy sidewalk about a block from the small liquor store. The glow from advertisement holograms illuminated the area more than the streetlights, and now I could clearly hear the audio from the advertising screens and projections. Initially, the lady in the store didn't want to sell me more liquor. I had to persuade her by telling her that I wouldn't resume drinking until I was back inside my living quarters.

"Good answer," she chuckled, handing me the now-familiar metallic bottle.

At this point, I realized that I had left my place without taking my backpack. Grumbling, I walked out of the store and decided to sit on a bench on the far side of the wide sidewalk. The sudden hormonal rush from my time with Arlinda had given me enough energy to make it this far, but now I felt as if I was going to fall asleep on this bench. My eyelids were getting heavy, and I couldn't help but close my eyes.

A System android shook me, waking me up. "Are you feeling okay? Do you require medical attention?"

I took a deep breath and exhaled. "I'm fine. I'll get out of here." Grabbing onto the android, I pulled myself up onto my own feet. The EvoGen stood in front of me, displaying a smiley face on its head unit.

"Hey, buddy." I placed my hand on its shoulder. "Do you feel pain?"

"Our EvoGen units are designed with an empathy module. We are programmed to adjust with the needs of all humans."

"Ah," I chuckled, "what was the trigger word for that phrase? Wait. Don't tell me." While holding my liquor in one hand, I placed a finger on the smiley face the android displayed. "It's feel, isn't it?"

"I detect high levels of alcohol on your breath," the android replied as it tilted its head to better see me. "It's recommended that you rest for at least eight hours to allow your body to expel this intoxicant."

"And what do you care." I groaned, letting my neck go limp, staring down at the concrete panel of the sidewalk.

"The System was built to take care of all human needs. It's our mission."

"Yeah!" I burst into laughter. "Yeah. I know. You need to take care of us and keep us in check. Right? So, you can…you know…." I suddenly realized that it wouldn't be a good idea to have the System record me saying something that would raise any form of suspicion.

"A human in your state, Mr. Nett, is a danger to themselves and possibly to others."

"Don't you have all the fucking answers?" I pulled myself away from it as the android extended its hand to hold me up by the arm. "Let me go." I grabbed its hand, which only tightened its grip. At the same time, a transport stopped on the sidewalk opposite to us. Its door faded out, and the android walked me to it and sat me inside. It put the seatbelt around me, then exited.

I must've passed out inside the transport because I woke up in my bed. The alcohol mug was on my nightstand.

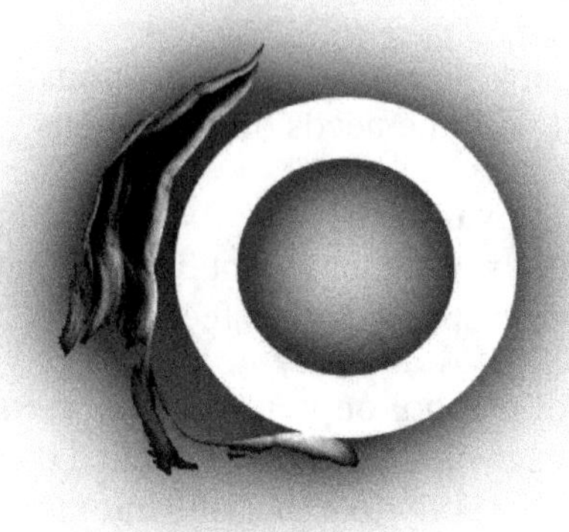

CHAPTER 17

My communicator rang later that day with another System job. This time the event was displayed on the bottom chyron on my TV wall. A portion of the protective dome wall was damaged. Numerous resources were already being urgently dispatched. I continued monitoring the chyron to see if the System would print the reason for this emergency. It didn't. Still donning my jacket, I quickly put on my khaki cargo pants and steel-toe boots, then walked out. A transport was waiting for me in the pick-up/drop-off area. It immediately and aggressively ascended after I confirmed my destination, then sped away. The traffic lane was virtually empty, though the traffic below was denser than usual.

The travel ended pretty quickly, considering that the location of the incident was on the other side of the dome. The entire area was illuminated, and I could see a lot of android transports parked on location as more transports continued to bring new panels. My communicator vibrated and displayed a route for me. I followed the directions, which led me to a gathering area for my group. Seven humans, three of us managers, and over two dozen EvoGens. This is serious. I looked around as the droids fell into formation in rows of four, three deep.

A man about my height wearing the same khaki cargo pants approached me. "Hey, I think I recognize you from the party. Elton, right?"

"Hi," I greeted him. I did recognize his face, but after that 'show' the managers put on when I was at the get-together, I couldn't even bother to recall his name. I changed the topic. "Do you know what happened here?"

"Hey, um." The manager took a half step closer to me. "How did you know where…."

"Team Nineteen," the System's voice came from all our communicators and interrupted him. "Proceed to the marked location."

I brought my communicator into view. The rally point, previously displayed, had changed.

"Alright," I heard a voice from the front of the group. "Let's get moving!"

The drone cranes began to lift damaged sections and put them aside. Because the inside of the dome was warmer than the outside, air came rushing out, cooling off the vicinity. The gust was so strong it blew one of the human worker's hat off his head.

As the wind continued twirling in the vicinity, suddenly, a portion of the wall on the side collapsed. A plume of dust overtook the entire area, causing android alarms to erupt. I couldn't count how many because our group was far enough, but quite a few EvoGens got trapped under the falling debris. "Please remain calm. We are stabilizing the situation." EvoGens in our team said in unison as they hastily moved forward to clear the debris. From a distance, I could see the androids removing large rocks as others dragged EvoGen parts from the pile. "All humans are accounted for," another EvoGen who approached us said as another portion of the wall crumbled, revealing a tunnel behind it. "The remaining structure is stable."

"What the hell is that?" One of the human crew pointed to the opening.

"That is a maintenance tunnel," one of the managers responded as the rushing androids formed a small chain around us, removing debris. "Sometimes they're used by the maintenance section to stock equipment or store units during an EMP storm."

"Space weather?"

"Something like that," he replied. "Electromagnetic waves travel through space. On Earth and Mars, we have atmospheres and magnetic poles to mitigate them, though, on Mars, it's a lot weaker."

"The magnetic poles are weaker?"

"The protective field they create is," the manager responded.

As the dust settled a bit, androids and other human teams brought in larger machines that vacuumed in the surrounding air, purifying it. "Come on, we have to check this tunnel out." The manager who was standing next to me followed his EvoGens inside the opening in front of us.

"Where do they go?" I pointed to the entrance.

"Technically, they go nowhere," the manager responded, looking at me over his shoulder.

 "What's the point of them, again?" I beheld the manager in confusion.

"It's shielding." He stopped and turned around. "For the electronics and android parts themselves. Any more questions?" Annoyed that I was being so inquisitive, he pointed at the EvoGen next to us

"Thanks for the help, man." I cut the conversation short.

"Whatever." He huffed, proceeding to follow the androids inside. Turning on my flashlight, I trailed him from a distance.

The dark tunnel was about twelve feet long and seven in height. On both sides, thick, metallic framed shelves were filled with equipment, EvoGen replacement limbs, and batteries. Behind the racks were tall plastic tanks filled with what appeared to be water. They extended to the ceiling, supported by a metallic mesh net. The deeper in we walked, the less equipment there was. A door was at the very back of the tunnel, where the shelf on my left ended. Ahead of me, however, there was an opening, as if whoever dug it had abruptly stopped. I peeked inside and shone my light.

"Hey, check this out." One of the workers said as he walked past me and entered the room. "What is this?" Another one walked immediately behind him, illuminating the surroundings with his flashlight.

It seemed the System had encountered a natural plate of iron ferrite at this point. Digging any further would've been very hard. Besides, if this tunnel was dug for shielding against EMP waves, a natural iron plate was a great place to stop. The ceiling didn't look as if it was that stable, though. It had crumbled, creating a bend in the net supporting it. As more humans gathered there, I backtracked.

"Please wait. One of these walls is not structurally stable." One of the EvoGens said and at the same time displayed a warning yellow and black face icon as it approached the wall, examining it.

Silence enveloped the room. The only sound came from the androids' pistons as they moved. The ground scanners they deployed whirred.

A cough broke the stillness, and we all looked around to see who did so. Soon finding out that no one in our group had coughed, the androids directed their attention to the corner where it came from. The ceiling, which they'd suspected to be unstable, crumbled, ripping the supporting net. A human wearing a yellow hazmat suit, holding a shotgun, fell through and landed a few feet from us. He shot the first android he saw, then the second. Then he pointed his weapon at one of the human workers. The shooter hesitated, then moved his weapon and shot the android standing next to the worker.

A fourth android ran past us, rushed the shooter, and punched a hole straight through his body. The man stopped firing. He dropped his weapon, and his head fell limp.

"What's happening in there?" I heard someone's panicked shout from behind us. The nervous mumbling of the human workers filled the tunnel. Pretty much everyone turned around, heading for the exit. All the EvoGens formed a single-file line and walked to the left side of the tunnel, making way for the panicking humans.

Only one manager, someone I'd never seen before, and one EvoGen android remained next to me. The other android retracted its hand from the yellow hazmat-clad assailant, letting his body hit the floor. A moment later, a cylinder-shaped grenade rolled from the opening in the ceiling and bounced onto the floor. It stopped next to the EvoGen's feet. Which immediately filled the area with a loud, high-pitched alarm. In pain, closing my eyes, I inserted my fingers in my ears to shield them from the piercing sound.

I fell to my knees as the EMP grenade exploded, releasing a bright flash. The intense wave penetrated my eyelids and blinded me, though the loud alarm sound ended soon after that. Silence dominated the tunnel.

In an attempt to recover control of myself, I opened my eyes. My vision was blurry, with a white hue, and I felt as if something metallic, likely an android, lifted me in the air and slammed me against something. I fell to the floor and rapidly rubbed my eyes, shaking my head as if it would help me regain my vision. Though I couldn't see well, I felt that there was an EvoGen in my vicinity. Not knowing if it was part of a rescue chain, to get out of its way, I scooted backward until I hit the frame of the shelf with my back. I finally opened my eyes and saw the silhouette of a Second-Gen—I could tell by the shape of its head—slowly walking toward me.

Suddenly, an EvoGen's alarm broke the silence. The rapid hissing of the pistons in their legs filled the area. "Help!" I heard a voice that sounded muffled. Breathing rapidly, I looked around. I was inside a room. The Second-Gen was the only other thing with me. The sound of bangs, gunfire and human screams resumed as the persistent, rapid beeping of the android's emergency signal intensified.

Because the nearby ground was uneven, the shelf behind me wobbled. Some spare parts rattled as I helped myself up. I immediately turned around to see that the Second-Gen had gotten closer with his hands extended. Given the sudden shock of the exploding EMP grenade and not understanding why this Second-Gen was so concerned with me and not with the assailants. I feared it was going to hurt me. I pushed its hand out of my way and took a step to my left, next to the uneven floor. As the Second-Gen followed, using all my weight, I pulled the frame down.

The first things to fall were the spare parts: canisters, metal rods, and pistons. They were followed by the shelf itself. It hit the android on its side and brought it down. One of the shelf plates fell directly on the android's neck, severing several links and dislocating it from its shoulders. The android crumbled under the weight. It tried to push the cabinet out of its way by flinging its arms without success. Fluid spilled from some tubes coming out of its neck.

A glitching robotic voice emanated from its speaker. "Zombies… and… robot…." Its voice trailed off as its head finally lay limp.

What did he say? Shivers ran down my spine. Those two words made me think of that last day I saw my father. "Someone is always using someone, someway…somehow." Echoed in my ears. "We're all zombies and robots to those in power. A number on paper, or worse, a statistic to the System. Whatever we do, we can't let them use us as they see fit. We are humans, damn it! We are better than this!"

A sudden shiver overtook my entire body as I swallowed and stared at the Second Gen, still trapped by the weight of the tools. A person wearing a yellow hazmat suit entered the room, but I ignored all movement around me, which seemed to happen in slow motion, still trying to process what happened. The android's head unit was all I could see, still squirting clear liquid from a broken tube.

A strong rubber-burning smell overtook the room. I finally looked at the person who entered. A woman hastily removed her yellow hazmat suit, which was being burned by acid that must have fallen onto it. Witnessing her removing her protective gear, I finally snapped out of my inner mayhem. I picked up a tool, thinking she might have a weapon on her.

A security android swiftly ran past me and pushed her against the wall.

"Stop!" I ran over and tried to pull it away. It obeyed.

"How did you know about this entrance? Answer me!" I screamed at her as the android took a step back, tagging the encounter.

Placing her hands on the cold, murky ground, the woman managed to stand up. Her blue jeans were muddy. Her white shirt had stains, I wouldn't even speculate from what, her hair was all over the place.

"Was this one of your androids?" I pointed to the android under the shelf.

She stared at me and the android standing next to me without speaking.

"Tell me how it knew those words!" I shouted at the top of my lungs.

"Wouldn't you like to know!" she shouted back, shifting to focus on the EvoGen standing behind me. A white substance, possibly the antibiotic-infused plasma used on Earth to treat infections, dripped from her hair to the ground. She brought up both her hands to cover her face.

"What did you say?" My blood boiled, partly because I got the feeling that she wasn't talking to me, seeing that there was an EvoGen standing behind us, listening. Recording. I reached for the droid's battery pack. In one motion snatched the release latch and yanked it out. Powerless, it collapsed and hit the floor with a thud.

"You heard me," she spoke from behind her hands.

I dropped the battery on the ground. "Who are you?"

Before she could speak, the general alarm filled the room. It signified that the rest of the System EvoGens would be there shortly.

"Tell me, how did it know how to say that?" I persisted.

"He always pointed out the irony of how he used to tell his son that we were all robots and zombies to someone else." She spoke, staring at the ground. "He would end those thoughts with 'now I've ended inside one!'"

"What do you mean, him? Where did it copy that line from?"

"Are you fucking blind? Are you deaf? That was a person inside there! Wait! How did you know about that line?" She stared at me as her wide eyes overflowed with tears. "Are you…"

"Dad!" I rushed to the android, which was still twitching. I pulled on the cabinet, but I slipped and fell on top of it. "Dad! I can fix this…." I mumbled and tried picking up the cabinet again. But once again, I slipped in the colorless fluid that had spilled when the Second Gen got damaged.

"We can fix him! Right?" I turned to face the sobbing woman staring at my futile efforts.

Her sorrowful facial expression was quickly replaced with fear as she looked behind me with her eyes and mouth wide open. System androids had entered the room.

"Who are you..." I began to ask as one of the EvoGens rapidly walked about an arm's-length away from me and shot a dart into her neck.

"You...cylinders...message..." her voice trailed as she fell sideways on the ground.

"Are you hurt, sir?" the Android asked, placing its hand on my shoulder and looking at me with a smiley face.

"I'm fine." I watched the EvoGens drag her body out of the room. I bit my tongue to create a distracted, pained face for them.

"The System generated the report," the android showed me a tablet which displayed a roll of video icon clips, then a report. "Please sign it." A highlighted blank field displayed at the bottom.

"What's the conclusion?" I asked the android as two more EvoGens approached the one I'd removed the battery from, which was still lying on the floor.

"Ejection," its monotonic voice replied as I raised my hand to place my communicator next to the monitor in his chest, which resumed displaying the report.

"Ejection?" I took my communicator away from the display. "She needs medical attention!"

The android remained motionless as if it couldn't process that statement correctly.

"I'm not signing this." I turned around as more System androids flooded the room. Other EvoGens grabbed human bodies, some in yellow hazmat suits, others from our group, and hastily removed them. I walked back to the staging area, escorting the androids transporting the body and head of the Second-Gen, who said my father's phrase.

"Mr. Nett." Another android, displaying a digitized human face, approached me as we emerged from the tunnel. "Considering the circumstances that transpired here, you may take your leave and get checked medically. If you wish, we can perform those checks here."

"I'm fine." I looked over its shoulder. The EvoGens carrying my father's Second-Gen remains stopped at the back entrance of a transport. "I want to know what that android knew." I pointed to the box they placed inside.

"The System will examine it and detail a report for you," the android replied.

"I want to see it."

"Why is that?" The EvoGen displayed a suspicious face, its digital eyes looking at me sideways and its mouth tilted to its side.

"A talking garbage can like yourself will never understand why! Even if I told you!" I sought to scream at its fake face. Wanting to yank its battery and drop it on my feet, swallowing, I sighed. I couldn't. Not here, not now.

"I'm curious." I bit my tongue so hard I tasted my blood. The close proximity only meant that the EvoGen was able to thoroughly read my facial emotions. "I haven't seen second generation androids on Ceres2 before. That's all."

"We will analyze it and send you a report," the android repeated its previous answer with its monotone voice. "Meanwhile, please stand still while I perform some medical checks."

It took my hands and pressed its fingers on my wrist. I felt my vein pulsating. The monitor on its chest displayed my blood pressure.

"Are you physically hurt anywhere, Mr. Nett?" the EvoGen asked, its face displaying the emergency red cross.

"I don't think so," I replied as I felt a sting on my index finger. The System android had punctured it. Soon after, it displayed a series of tables for me to see.

"Mr. Nett, I detect a few chemical imbalances in your bloodstream. Signs of adrenal and pituitary gland malfunction are causing hypoglycemia. This seems to be exacerbated by the chronic alcohol presence. Advice: recommended eating small meals frequently during the day, stop consumption of alcohol."

"Thanks." I ignored its spiel and looked past it as the transport, which had the android that had uttered my father's words, took off and left. "Can I have my hand back now?"

"Of course." The android released my hand. "Thank you, Mr. Nett. Rest is also recommended." It walked away as more crews, androids and humans alike, came to continue the work as if nothing had happened here.

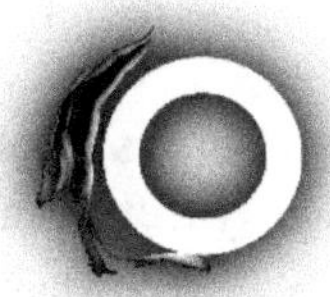

The androids pushed me to the outer edge of the incident area. Unable to do anything else, I approached a transport that was stopped along the magnetic lane. Usually, my wrist communicator would signal my presence and inform the vehicle, but the doors on this one didn't react. I automatically looked at my communicator—its screen was blank. It must've shorted when the EMP grenade exploded.

God damn it! I can't even go home without letting the System know. Huffing, I walked back to the staging area where another group of humans and androids were gathered, ready to go to work. I stopped and looked at the work zone. The buildings above the damaged area were slowly being replaced by System-controlled cranes lined up in front of me just past the staging area.

"Can I help you, sir?" an android asked as it approached me from behind.

"Yeah." I faced it. "This thing is fried." I pointed to my wrist device.

"Mister Nett." The android recognized my face. "Of course, please follow me. We will replace it."

We entered a nearby transport, which brought us to the city center in the same office I'd visited a few months ago when the previous power loss incident occurred.

The new communicator vibrated as soon as I wore it. The System had arranged a transport for me. How nice of them, my lip slightly curled up in anger. Without saying anything, I entered the vehicle. For the first time since this latest incident, I was alone. I tried calming down as much as I could, but my hands shook uncontrollably when I placed them on my lap.

I stumbled to my residence as soon as the transport landed. The images of what happened wouldn't stop flashing through my head. I'd experienced destruction and close calls lately, but this was different.

Taking a deep breath to calm my nerves, I looked around for my backpack at the foot of my bed. Steadying my trembling hand, I chugged the alcohol in it. Like being slapped across my face by a brick, I felt vertigo. Swallowing, I tried to maintain my seating position, but I couldn't. My stomach unraveled. I got up and started going to the bathroom but hurled before I took a step. My entire body quivered, and I fell on the floor face to face with my shoes. One of them had a large blood stain.

I threw up again. Trying to push myself up, my arms gave in, and I fell face-down on the floor. Crawling into a fetal position, I closed my eyes. All the tragedies that had ever happened in my life were sitting in the room with me. Judging me. Staring. How could you!

My stomach muscles tightened again, but I had nothing else to vomit. With a clang, the bottle rolled and fell onto the floor next to me, but I didn't move to grab it. I just briefly looked at it. I didn't want to move at all. Staying like this stabilized my stomach.

The same problems followed me everywhere I went. There's no fucking escape. I closed my eyes and fell asleep on the floor next to the throw-up-covered, bloody shoes.

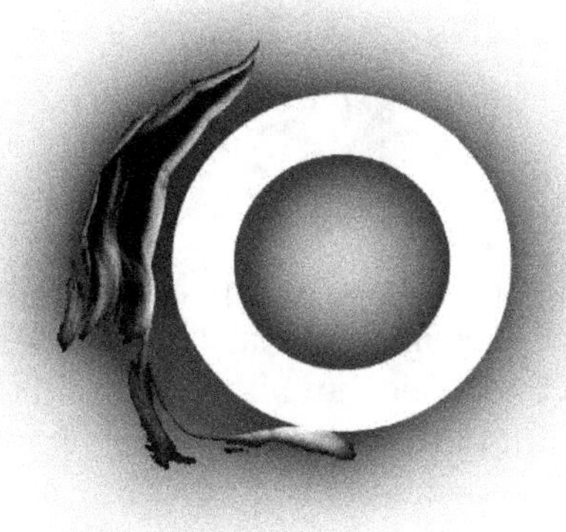

CHAPTER 18

Every time sadness overtook me, a memory from a movie I watched when I was a child came to mind. It was about a stranded astronaut inside a life raft vehicle. He had removed all his gear because it was damaged and no longer usable. As the rescuers approached his craft, they noticed lights and condensation inside the pod. Likely because they showed that scene in detail, I specifically remembered a drop of water accumulating as it rolled down the glass. The rescuers remarked that there might be life inside the pod because of it, and they were right. They went on to rescue the astronaut.

That image of a foggy glass and a slow drop of water rolling and growing bigger as it slid down the smooth surface still remains in my memory. The streak it left revealed a slice of the cabin. There is life inside there.

I'd had a strange feeling in my stomach, witnessing my mother cry over my father's disappearance. The tears that rolled down her cheeks didn't signify life. Though deep inside, I liked to merge the two ideas when I was alone. I wanted to make my father appear in front of our door. In my imagination, he would come and kiss me on my head and hug my mother

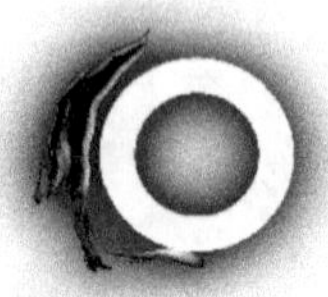

A faint pain in my left cheek woke me up. My eyes focusing on an object a foot in front of me, I recognized that I was looking at my shoe. The smell of vomit blended with alcohol hit me. Careful to not slip on the wet floor, I pushed myself up and walked into the bathroom. After washing myself best I could, I changed into another outfit.

Reality hit me again, and the pit in my stomach returned. But I had to get rid of the awful stench that had invaded my unit. In the bathroom, under the sink, next to the cylinders, I had a bucket. I filled it with water, took an old T-shirt I hadn't worn in a while, and wiped up the floor. The disgusting odor didn't go away, though.

"Open the window," I commanded my TV wall, which lit up, displaying the camera feed rotation channel. "Fucking pointless." I chuckled in contempt, "Open the window. What a joke." Mumbling to myself, I pressed my communicator next to the doorframe. As it dissolved, I placed my bag on it so the door wouldn't close back.

Leaving my backpack at the door. I meandered to the railing on the far side of the magnetic lane. A transporter was idling a few feet to my right as I leaned on the fence, looking at the commercial district in the distance. Apart from the generator and transformer whirring, the silence that dominated the area was only occasionally interrupted by passing transporters or the sound of the nearby lift going up and down.

Several people stepped out of the elevator and got in the transport next to me. They were dressed as if they were going out to enjoy the night. I sighed, then thought about the last time I'd been down in the commercial district. Arlinda. I had her unit number. The last time we were together, she'd wanted to have a chat.

I think that time has come. Witnessing the transport departing, I walked back to my living quarters. A hint of the scent of vomit lingered in the air. My pants were still on the floor in the bathroom. I grabbed them and searched the pockets, finding the card she handed me. Unit 12-223. Picking up my backpack, I walked curbside and requested a transport.

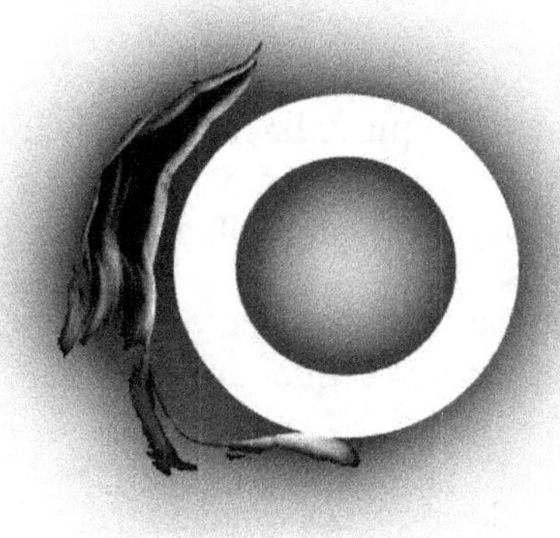

CHAPTER 19

Arlinda's unit, which once was in the dome I lived in, was transferred to the adjoining arena. The transport immediately rose to the highest lane, and shortly after, it entered the tube highway, which connected all the vaults.

I aimlessly stared at the windshield during the entire travel time, listening to the rhythmic whooshing as the transport flew by the large emergency evacuation hatches. I just couldn't get the image of the android crumbling under the weight of the heavy shelf out of my head.

The sidewalk outside Arlinda's living quarters was bustling with people. Disregarding them, I followed the signs leading to the appropriate residential address on the card she handed me. The wall leading to her dwelling, on the first floor of the forty or so stacked residential units, was full of unreadable but colorful graffiti.

No one answered when I first rang the bell. So, I pressed my communicator against the System ring again. Finally, fabric shuffling sounds preceded Arlinda opening the door. "Elton." She adjusted her robe. "I didn't expect to see you so soon."

"We have to talk." Swallowing, I shifted my gaze from her robe to the floor.

Like before, in my place, she placed her finger over my lips. "Jesus, you look like shit." Arlinda squinted. "Come in, let me get dressed, and we'll grab a drink." She took my hand and pulled me inside her living quarters.

I dropped my communicator on her bed and walked into the bathroom. Arlinda paused for a moment. She dropped hers next to mine and followed.

"I heard my father's words come out of an android today," I whispered as soon as she closed the door behind us.

"What?" She took a half step close to me.

I just stared. Arlinda was the first person I was sharing this with. And considering that the phrase shared between my father and I carried a heavy intimate weight in me I just stared at her.

"You look like you've been through hell. What happened to you?" She said, narrowing her eyes.

"Remember what I said before? When we were in my place?" My gaze shifted past Arlinda's shoulder to the main room where the communicators lay.

"Alright, alright." She brought both her palms up, lowering her head. "Let me get dressed."

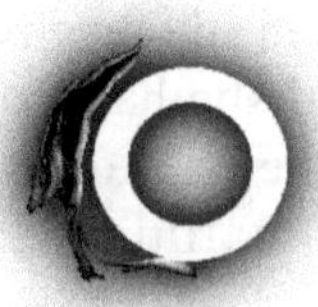

The dome where Arlinda resided didn't have the same feel as the one I lived in. Small kiosks with people selling food, clothes, and other items people used filled the area. The wiring between buildings wasn't seated correctly in its ducts, and here and there, it blocked the vertical transport travel lanes, some of which were not operating. Air vents in the dome where I lived stuck out of the side of the buildings. Here, orange tubes out of the maintenance holes coming out of the floor accomplished the same job. Streaks of vapor emanated out of them, obscuring portions of the intersections.

We turned a corner and walked down a narrow passageway between buildings. Undisturbed by any form of wind, the steam coming out of the vents draped the area. A series of streetlamps illuminated the narrow sidewalks. Like poles holding up a blanket, the bands of light emanating lifted the darkness as they shone on the polished floor.

At the end of the street, we turned to our right and came face-to-face with a door. Its unpowered frame was hard to discern from the surrounding grey walls. Picking up a crowbar from behind a nearby garbage can, Arlinda pried it open. Inside, just like the unit I'd found the crate with the cylinders, there was nothing but a sheet-less bed. She returned the crowbar, and before we slid the door back, illuminating our surroundings with a flashlight Arlinda handed me, we exited through an opening in the bathroom. It led to another tunnel, like the one I found myself in earlier, lined with metal mesh nets. At the end of it was an elevator.

"What the hell is this? Where are we going?"

Arlinda manually closed the elevator doors. "This is a hidden entrance to the old emergency areas." She pulled on a lever, and the elevator car began to descend.

"Old?" I shone my flashlight around. The cabin looked rusty. Smelled rusty too. "Just how old is this colony?"

"We think they began building here as soon as the System commenced mass-producing androids. No one knows how old these areas are." The elevator shook as the brakes clamped, slowing it down. After a few seconds, it came to a stop.

Arlinda led us to a tall metallic switchboard and pulled a lever. A split second later, the loud clicking of remote switches turning on echoed as beams from above lit our immediate area. A small electrical explosion buzzed as one of the oversized LED lights overloaded and burst.

Surrounded by a tall railing lined with reflective tape and metal fencing, a sizeable office made out of oversized metal bars and hardened plastic walls was a few feet away from us. As Arlinda continued fiddling with the switches, I walked to the barrier.

The ceiling lights of this underground dome shone brightly on the area, illuminating building rooftops of the city, which extended beyond my field of view. Turning off her flashlight, Arlinda walked closer to me. "We believe this was built by the System. From the records we have been able to collect, we think it sheltered machines and humans here when they first established the post. From here, they likely coordinated above-ground operations. There are a lot of human remains scattered all over this dome. But no graves." She looked around as if to get her bearings, then pointed to the large office by the side of the dome. "This way." She opened the bulky airlock, revealing the inside of a workspace akin to a command center. Surrounded by computer stations, a big rectangular metallic table stood in the middle. Cables emerged from the workstations to the ceiling and led to the other side of the office, terminating inside yet another oversized electrical closet.

"You started telling me something above ground." Arlinda placed her flashlight on the desk next to a thick stack of papers. "What has you so shook?"

Without saying anything, I looked at her shifting my gaze to her communicator. "Oh," she took it off, "they're disabled here. We have location spoofers."

"Ok," I said, taking a few steps closer to her. "Earlier, while working inside a maintenance tunnel, we confronted humans wearing yellow hazmat suits. They fell out of the fucking ceiling like goddamn moles." I shook my head. "Then a Second-Gen pushed me into a room." I paused as I recalled images of the event. "I… I got scared, and I dropped a heavy shelf on it. It said the phrase 'robots and zombies' to me before it deactivated."

"What does that mean?"

"That was something my father told me a long time ago on Mars." I rubbed my nose, then looked at her. "He meant to say that soon enough, the androids were going to be independent, and we were going to end up being their servants." I sighed. "There is no way that phrase was at random." I shifted my gaze to the metal floor.

"Where is he now?"

"Who? My father?"

"Yeah."

"My father has been missing for over two years," I replied. "He went missing on Mars."

I looked up and met Arlinda's suspicious stare. "I mean, after witnessing the frickin canner next to the pickled brain…"

"The what?" Arlinda chuckled.

"You know, the brain in the jar next to the android." My bitter chuckle quickly faded. "I thought you would know. Or at least have some knowledge of what's happening. Even if this is what System Hysteria feels like."

"That's nonsense." Lifting her eyebrows, Arlinda shook her head. "Look," She took a deep sigh. "I haven't shared this with anyone out of my shrinking pool of friends, but not that long ago, while taking care of one of my patients, I found CNS fluid on him. Initially, I thought that his spine was damaged, but it wasn't. That wasn't his spinal fluid. I found out that he was in an accident where a few androids had been damaged. The only other place that fluid could've come from was them."

"There was a lot of clear fluids coming out of that Second-Gen." I interrupted her. "And I have worked on Second-Gens before. Other than some mods to their cooling systems, which are not clear, they don't have any liquids in them. Not like that."

"A friend of mine, and member of the resistance who works in the robotics division, jokingly told me that one of these days they were going to need actual doctors there—that's how much living tissue and organs the System is experimenting with." She looked at me. "We thought it was trying to build a humanoid model." She sighed. "We now know with certainty what they have really been doing."

The sound of the elevator car stopping interrupted our conversation, and I looked in the direction where the noise came from. "Are we expecting guests?" Arlinda hastily walked to the desk and pulled an EMP grenade from the drawer.

As if someone hit two metal pipes together, three spaced bangs echoed. "They're friends." Arlinda carefully placed the grenade on the large desk.

Heavy footsteps preceded a man wearing a yellow hazmat jacket who approached us. "The front entrance has been secured. The new exit is back that way." He pointed to the other side of the room we were in. "How do you do?" He looked my way as two Second-Gen androids walked in behind the newcomer and closed the door behind them.

"I'm good." I blurted.

"Billy – Elton. Elton – Billy." Arlinda introduced us.

We nodded to each other as Billy exited through the other end of the room. I followed their movements with my eyes until they walked out, then turned my attention back to Arlinda, who put the EMP grenade back inside the drawer and closed it.

"We don't have definite proof of the System using biological implants of human central nervous systems inside androids because it swiftly removes all damaged units. And we still don't have the System code. A hacker, the resistance met on Mars, promised to smuggle it in the last transport headed this way. We yet have to find it among the debris." Arlinda walked between the desks and continued.

"They've likely come up with a compound that suppresses the frontal lobes and neocortex. That would force the brain to act, for lack of a better word, like a zombie. Following all electrical impulse orders commanded by the System without even realizing it."

"A zombie inside an android," I whispered to myself. "Holy shit, he was right."

The sound of the airlock opening once again broke the silence that ensued. Escorted by Second-Gen androids, a tall, dark-skinned man wearing military fatigues entered the room from where Billy exited.

"Arlinda," he greeted her.

"Greg." She reciprocated.

Before stopping in front of me, he extended his hand. "My name is Gregory Robertson. I am the commanding officer of the Ceres2 task force. A new division of the Earth-Mars human forces."

"Elton Nett," I reciprocated. "What is this place, really."

"We have been using it as a…" Greg stopped talking and looked at Arlinda. "Let's resume this conversation downstairs. Shall we."

"What's going on, Arlinda?" I looked at her. This underground space seemed to have more movement than I initially saw.

"After the conversation we had above ground, I brought you here with a purpose." She said, shifting her gaze from Greg to me. "The hacker, who was going to provide the resistance with copies of the System's entire code, has signaled us that she might have met someone close to one of her coworkers. Someone who happens to work for the System. Here on Ceres2."

I looked at Greg, then her. "Arlinda, you have to stop speaking cryptically. I don't understand."

"The real question here is, can we trust you?"

"You know, you could've told this to me topside." My patience finally ran thin. "Maybe I should just leave." I looked around for the exit as the Second-Gens jolted at attention.

"We can't have conversations like this up there. You know that. But, if it's true what you told me about the brains inside the large prep vials and the words you heard from the android today, this situation is escalating quite rapidly."

"Escalating rapidly?" I looked at Arlinda, then Greg, "I was incapacitated for over three months, and they took care of me. What does that mean?"

"No idea. Maybe they don't have the list of humans they should have received with the last transport's arrival." Greg added as if he had been listening to the conversation I'd had with Arlinda all along. "Or, maybe the System doesn't have enough humans to help them with managing things here. Maybe they can't afford to assimilate humans whenever they'd like to. Who knows?"

"I think we're done here." I looked at Arlinda. "Where is the exit?"

"Not yet," Greg said, "I'd like to introduce you to someone."

"Hey man, I really didn't come here for a meet and greet." I shifted my gaze to Greg. "I can see that you guys have something…" I paused, "special going on here. I have enough shit going on in my life to get tangled with this now." I began walking to the exit.

"The System will get us one by one." Arlinda raised her voice. "The canners that order us around are powered by the brains of our own friends… and." I stopped walking as she paused. "And we wouldn't even know. You told me yourself that you heard a phrase that your own father used to tell you."

"So, you're saying once the transports resume, these assimilations will as well?" I turned around.

"I can guarantee it." Staring at me, Greg crossed his arms.

"Guarantee." I ironically chuckled. "How do you know that, Greg?" I was beginning to feel contempt towards his arrogance.

"What?" he approached and leaned toward me, "do I have to give you a fucking history lesson?" His brows furrowed. "Look around, man! What do you think is happening here? These fucking canners are reducing us to… how did you say it?" Greg paused and looked me straight in the eye to make sure I was taking his remarks seriously. "Zombies inside robots?"

"Well, what do you want from me, man?" Feeling that Greg was using my own words against me, I snapped.

"We have to shut the System down. I'm afraid the planetary resistance was right since day one—down with the robots."

"First off, I don't have that power," I huffed. "Second, you do know that we depend on them here in Ceres2, right?"

Silence fell, and I could once again hear the distant generators humming.

"They will not stop doing this," Greg somberly replied. "This will only get worse."

"So, it's either we fight to destroy what keeps us alive, or we live and deal with this reality?" I took a step toward the workstation.

"I refuse to sit idle while my friends disappear," Arlinda swallowed. "We have to act."

"What about this place?" I looked around. "Can we use it for shelter?"

"A few months ago, this place was full of androids," Arlinda added. "They still come down here."

"And they haven't found you guys yet?"

"We hide," Greg interrupted. "In the catacombs."

"In the where?"

"That's what we call the living quarters that have bodies in them," Arlinda said, scratching her head. "It's almost as if the System didn't put much effort to accommodate…"

"Look," Greg interrupted, "we need you to meet someone. If at the end of the meeting you still want to go your way, then so be it."

"How far down does this go?" I looked in the direction of the large windows facing the underground space.

"Over five hundred feet, at least." Arlinda approached the broken window I was looking at. Suddenly I got the vibe that this office was at one time occupied by the same people, and likely androids, that would be in the all-seeing eye office I was in a month ago.

"How do we get down there?" I looked at the stacked living quarters down below.

"There is a large spiral ramp at the end. That way." Arlinda pointed behind me. "Next to it is an elevator, but it doesn't work." She approached me.

"Alright!" I headed for the door as the Second-Gen androids stood at attention. "Let's get this over with." Greg made a waving motion with his hand. Androids stood fast.

The door Billy had pointed us to led to another area of the office structure filled with smaller workplace cubicles that ran to a corridor. A few feet away from us, next to another elevator, was a large open gate.

We reached a ramp leading to a solid hunk of pressed dirt. Tire tracks and foot marks peppered the muddy ground. A pungent stench of burned and decomposing flesh filled the cold and humid atmosphere.

"What in the world is that smell!" I grunted from the crease of my elbow.

"Elton," Arlinda said, pointing her flashlight to illuminate her surroundings, "welcome to the Ceres2 catacombs."

"I heard you say something about it earlier. I just never thought it would smell this bad," I said from behind my elbow. "Holy shit!"

"You'll get used to it." Arlinda pointed her flashlight to a building on her left. "This way."

Following her lead, I looked around. It seemed that the System had just lowered these living quarters to the ground. No pre-establishing had taken place here. The streets weren't lined with concrete slabs, there was no neat wiring, and by the looks of it, trucks used to drive on the actual ground. Some of them had their doors shut; others were wide open, but none had power.

In contrast to the above-ground dome I resided in, the ceiling lights weren't bright enough to illuminate the entire zone. Whatever remained of the broken floodlights was positioned at such an angle that the buildings on our right, which extended about ten to fifteen floors above us, cast a shadow on the area we were walking. There were clear signs of a fire in this section. The outside walls were covered with that dark chemical residue these units emitted when they went ablaze. As I digested the scenery, I realized that we had walked near the entrance of one of the buildings which faced the street. An android was posted on its right.

"We suspected that the System changed the code a while ago. The last message the hacker sent was to tell us that she was sending a microdot with the new code. She said it was insanely complex," Arlinda said as she entered the unit.

"When was this?" I trailed her after glancing at the android. It followed my every movement with its camera eyes.

"A few months back. The transport the code was in was shot down." Arlinda walked to the end of this unit filled with chairs, some tipped over the muddy floor. I could see the frame of an entrance behind the dirty furniture.

"By the resistance?" I hit the floor with my shoes to shake away the mud stuck in the soles.

She stopped next to the door and gazed at me over her shoulder. "Some things have to be done, Elton."

"I recovered a cryogenic pod there." I raised my head and looked at her.

"We know." Arlinda approached the door and loudly knocked on it. "The hacker told us about it."

"The hacker?" I paused. "Just how did you say she was going to bring this information to you?"

"Why don't you ask her yourself?" she said as the door opened, revealing a lit residential unit. In front of me, an android stood tall, both its arms pointing forward with its palms facing me as if it was saying, "Stop." Arlinda stood outside and extended her hand, pointing inside the illuminated room.

Greg, who was fiddling with some electrical wires behind a couch, looked at me over his shoulder. Considerably smaller than the TV wall in our above-ground units, a monitor hanging on the wall flickered. A few feet away from him, facing away from me, Billy was talking to a woman who peeked at me past his shoulder.

"Elton Nett!" she faintly smiled, walking toward me. "My name is Iora Ais. I was born on Earth, Section Eight." She grabbed my hand and led me to the couch next to Greg and Billy.

Though no longer wearing her dirty clothes, I recognized her face the moment we shook hands. She was the woman who was in the room with me when I dropped the heavy shelf on the Second Gen. I swallowed as shivers, accompanied by a cold, sweaty feeling, ran down my entire body. "You." My jaw dropped. Her right forearm was wrapped in bandages, and she had a giant band-aid on her neck, where the android had shot her with the tranquilizer dart. "How are you here?"

"Have a seat, Mr. Nett," Greg showed me a seat on the other side of a low table, facing them. "We know you have questions. We have questions of our own as well."

"Where is my father?" I asked Iora before I even looked at where the rest of the chairs were.

"We don't know," Billy answered instead of her.

"How do I bring him back?" I shifted my attention to him

"You severed his head unit," Iora said, looking down. "Inside that element was his brain, and in a special encasement behind those for these specific android models is the rest of the CNS, the spine…." She stopped talking.

"I don't understand what you are telling me." Frustrated, I looked at everyone in the room.

"You basically decapitated him," Greg replied. "There is no going back from this point."

That statement hit me like a metal pipe across my face. I killed my father. My stomach muscles tightened, and vertigo came back. My entrails growled. I wanted to throw up, but my stomach, already empty from vomiting earlier that day, just continued to sink. Lower and lower. I reached for the chair and sat on it. Without speaking, everyone followed my every movement with their eyes. It felt as if they were all judging me. After all, I was the one who destroyed the android. I looked down in shame.

"How." Breathing hard, I wiped some saliva dripping from my mouth. "How did you know my father?" I raised my head and looked at Iora.

"We met on Mars during one of the rallies against the System. That's where we devised the plan to download the entire System's database and create a virus to incapacitate it." Iora rubbed her neck above her bandage. "I already had six parts of the System's main operating system, the base. Got them from a couple who worked as managers in an android rental place by the Isidis Planitia neighborhood, in Section Fifteen, if I remember it correctly. I got a few more fragments from an inspection site in Section Nineteen…."

"My father wasn't too big on codes and such," I interrupted Iora as Arlinda walked in. She offered me a water bottle and a few crackers.

"Take these before you completely pass out."

I pushed them away. "I'm not…."

"Don't argue with me!" Arlinda insisted. "You're paper white." She handed me the bottle. "You're showing signs of hypoglycemia. Doctor's orders. Billy" She faced him. "Bring me my med bag. It's in the unit next door."

"Will do." Billy got up and left the room.

"Your father gave us access to the factory floor. We sniffed the rest of the code that night," Iora continued, and by this point, I felt the power drain from my body. If I were standing up, I would've collapsed. "This happened two days before he got abducted by the System."

"That's when he told me those lines." My emotional and physical drain reached its peak. Without even bothering to force my eyes to focus somewhere, I just stared at the feet of the table.

"He looks like he's gonna pass out," Greg remarked as Arlinda came over next to me.

"I got him," she assured him, looking at me.

Tightening my lips, I continued. "This was two years ago. What have you people been doing all this time? And why here? Why not on Mars?"

"The System assimilated hundreds of protesters during those days," Iora responded, looking at me. "This process was relatively new back then." She continued as we made eye contact. "The System wasn't aware that we were deciphering their messaging. It didn't even bother to place any sort of encryption in them." Billy entered the room and handed Arlinda a bag bearing a red cross.

"The System was releasing these newly conformed androids, cyborgs rather, in the city. We were able to retrieve most of them, including your father. We found him in front of your house. Please understand our position. We couldn't contact you. We were being chased."

"Here, take this." Arlinda handed me a small tablet she pulled from the bag Billy brought in.

"What is it?"

"A glucose tablet. It'll bring your blood sugar up." Arlinda folded the rest of the contents and handed them back to Billy.

I bit on the extremely sweet tablet as Billy, holding the first aid kit, walked behind the couch Iora was sitting on. He turned the monitor's brightness up a little bit.

Greg, who was fiddling with the screen, finally got up, "I'm ready." He told Iora

"Play it." She stood up.

"This was recorded a couple of months ago," Greg said as the feed showed the inside of a hospital. A few humans were performing surgery on someone. They removed the person's brain and spinal cord and placed them inside a tall glass tube. An android brought in a device, much like a helmet, then… I rubbed my eyes in disbelief. That's Eve!

She was slowly pushing a stretcher where an android was lying. Finally, securing the portable bed, she wheeled a tall glass cylinder where a brain and a spine were suspended in some clear liquid. Multiple electrodes and wires were attached to it, protruded out of the top of the jar. Eve attached them to a data transfer unit, then methodically committed the electrodes to the android. A screen in a nearby workstation showed a progress bar. Seeing that whatever she set up was working, Eve walked away.

A few moments later, a man limped through a corridor and entered the room. "Wait! That's me!" I recognized myself. This was the video of what had happened before I met that weird android when I woke up in the hospital. There was no audio, but another doctor led me away from the scene. Then the video cut.

"This next one was recorded fifteen hours ago, on Mars," he said as the screen split in half. One side still displayed the last frame of the previous video, while the next showed a surveillance camera feed whose point of view appeared to be a well-lit factory floor.

"What are these, on the bottom of the screen?" I pointed to what appeared to be rows of soldiers standing in formation.

"Those are uninitiated, armed EvoGens. They have no brains in them." He looked at me. "They are headed here."

"So, the system is expending us." I continued staring at the last frame of the video, where I was sitting on the stretcher.

"Yes." Greg rubbed his nose. "The process is already in motion, and it cannot be stopped. Both sides are gearing for conflict."

War is coming. I looked around the room. It became clearer that the resistance members were here, in Ceres2, in full force and they were determined to end the System. Maybe they can use the cylinders I had stashed in my bathroom. I couldn't see how, though. That information would only be useful to smuggle people in…

"Look, I sympathize with the hardship you and yours have endured." Shaking me out of my inner thoughts, Greg continued. "And believe me, many families have given it all for this to happen. But I have to be direct. We are looking for System's code."

"And you think I have it?" I squinted.

"Yes. Microdots," Iora added. "Inside sealed cylinders."

Swallowing, I stared at her. "I have… two cylinders."

"You..." Arlinda gave me an incredulous look. "Have... what?"

"Hold on!" Greg exclaimed. "We got them?"

"I…the System…my communicator…I found a crate, okay?" I stuttered. "There were two cylinders inside. One has a long list of names. The other has a lot of microdots."

"Mr. Nett probably has had the cylinders for months now. Have you?" Iora extended her hand. Pointing at me.

"Are we sure they're the cylinders we need?" Greg asked insistently. "Do you have them with you?"

"No…" I began responding, but Iora interrupted.

"I'm ninety-nine percent sure of it." Iora wiped her face with her hand, then looked at me. "Elton, inside one of those cylinders is the System's code. We need it to shut it down."

"You know this is not just some crazy story we believe," Greg said. "I hope you don't think we've caught System Hysteria. This is real."

"I've been keeping them in my residence ever since I found them," I replied, looking at everyone in the room. "I didn't know what to do with them."

"I know exactly what to do with them." Iora faintly smiled.

Arlinda looked at me with a worried face. "I am tired of living in fear." She swallowed. "I don't want to be like them." She looked at the android standing by the door, who, without moving, just stared at us. "That's what the System wants to do with all humans, convert us to submissive creatures. Even if that means stripping every single one of us from our own bodies. The utopia we were all sold on is nothing more than a steel prison. A synthetic existence."

"Let's go." I looked at her. "Time has come."

"You're not going anywhere without us," Greg said. "Now that you are aware of what our plans are, someone must escort you at all times."

"What – you think I'll run and tell the System that I'm helping the resistance by handing you two cylinders I've been hiding for months?" I gave a contemptuous look at Greg and Billy.

"Someone from us has to be with you," Greg scorned.

"I'll go with him," Arlinda added, handing me my communicator. "I've been to his place before." We exchanged glances as she smiled.

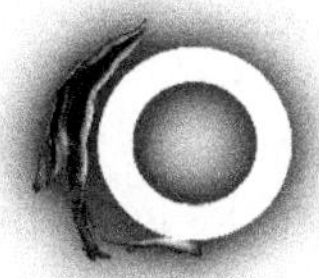

I walked into my room, where the faint smell of alcohol persisted. "Open the window," Arlinda said to the TV wall as she extended her hand. I knew she was asking me for my communicator. I pulled out the cylinders and waited for her to drop the devices on the bed and walk into the bathroom with me. Popping the top off the first one, I pulled out the papers inside it. After flattening one of them, which contained names, I got closer to Arlinda.

"Here's mine, marked by this red dot." I handed her the paper as it rolled back in my hand. Arlinda sat on the edge of the bathtub, pressed it against her thigh and began to read.

"Here." She pointed. "Loraine. She disappeared a while back. And him," she pointed to another name," and…." She came across her name and sighed.

"We have to…." Fear tightening her lips, Arlinda cut herself short, looking at me with eyes wide open. "We have to do this. If we don't help ourselves, no one will do it for us. The System will wipe us out."

"What now?" I watched her roll the papers back up, insert them inside the cylinders, and in turn, place them inside my backpack.

"We bring these back to Iora." Arlinda put on the backpack. "She has told us she can create a self-replicating code that will overload the main buffer system."

"Is that your plan?" I asked incredulously. "You know the System can handle that. Not to mention that it will eject whoever is involved."

"A thousand cuts, Elton. A thousand cuts." Arlinda said. "We will overwhelm the System from everywhere."

"And you think that whatever it is you're doing has gone unnoticed?"

"It's working so far." Arlinda paused. "And hopefully, with Iora's help, we can stop the System in its tracks here, in Ceres2."

The persistent beeping of our communicators coming from the main room attracted our attention. The TV wall was on, displaying the city center. "Incident in the power plant leaves many injured," scrolled on the communicator's screen and simultaneously on the TV wall as well. My God, what is it this time?"

"Show me the news," I said, and the screen immediately split in two. On the right, it displayed a video feed of the power plant, and on the left, there was a text block in large letters. It slowly scrolled upwards as the new text was fed from the bottom.

"Do you know anything about this?" I asked Arlinda, who was still looking at her communicator in the bathroom.

"No." she replied after reading the message on hers, "but it's very unusual for me to get messages like this, and the alert played on both our communicators at the same time."

"Do you think the System suspects something?" I swallowed, shifting my gaze to the screen.

I knew that place; I immediately recognized the area I had last worked in. Did the System send more crews there? I thought we fixed the issue. I scrolled through my communicator to see if I had any requests for work messages. There were none, just the alert. I couldn't take my eyes off the screen and what it was showing. The feeling that we had been doing something for the colony's good every time we went out to fix something disappeared with every image shown. Coupled with the information I had gotten in the last few hours, each emergency was beginning to feel as if the System was chasing dissidents every single time we were dispatched.

The damage shown on the screen was extensive, but we didn't lose power or have any service disrupted. So, what gives? Did they stage another accident to injure more humans? And why the charade? Why don't they just lock us up in cages and get it over with?

"If they knew, they would be here at this very moment." Arlinda walked over to me. "We better get going before something else happens."

Stressed, I sighed, then swallowed and wore my communicator. I pulled out another backpack I kept in my closet, quickly stuffed some more clothes inside, and headed for the door. But it didn't dematerialize once I approached it. So, I placed my wrist next to the ring. It turned red. "All human citizens are advised to stay in their living quarters until the issue is resolved," the communicator said.

"That's new." Startled, Arlinda stopped fiddling with her backpack and looked at me.

"What's the issue?" Speaking out loud, I placed my communicator next to the ring, which prompted it to repeat the same line.

"I don't think it knows what's happening either," Arlinda said from behind me. "Either that or the System did this on purpose to restrain humans in their living quarters."

"Like in the catacombs?"

"That is a scary thought." With a terrified look, she took a step next to me.

I placed my communicator next to the ring again, which again turned red, repeating the same line.

"Hey!" I screamed to it, "you can't keep people locked up like this! Do you hear me?"

A loud hiss coming from the bathroom attracted my attention. "What is it now?" Arlinda opened the door, revealing the white gas coming out of the showerhead. Feeling numb, I fell onto the floor. I passed out.

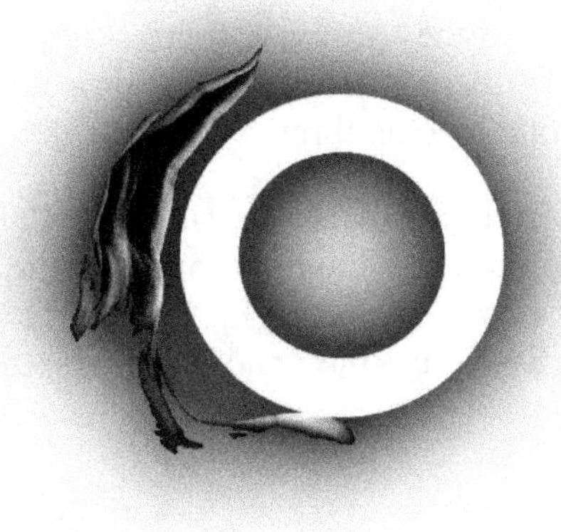

III

CHAPTER 20

Skull and crossbones marked the large grey barrel a Second-Gen held as it approached a Weeping Willow. The unusual hissing following its every movement echoed before fading the moment it stopped in front of the Blue Eye Lagoon. Behind it, replacing hills and trees, a dark and grey sky preceded chimneys and tall buildings in the distance.

Wind picking up, a piece of paper rested on the still waters in front of me. Floating next to the now wet sheet, the outline of a tiny slipper attracted my attention. The memory of Tony removing a pebble from his sandal and putting it back on flashed in front of my eyes. Wait, I know this sandal.

"Someone is always using someone, someway…somehow. We're all zombies and robots to some. A number on paper, or worse, a statistic to the System." The Second-Gen's distorted voice yeverberated as it threw the barrel into the spring. Its falling weight disturbed the water, which immediately changed color from deep blue to brown.

I looked around to see if Suela, Lori, or Tony, who possibly had lost a sandal, were nearby. But they weren't. Instead, more androids carrying barrels marked with skulls and crossbones approached the spring. Wind stirred up, and they, one by one, threw the drums in.

Almost tasting the poison the robots threw in the well, I spat on the ground to my side. In a fit of panic, I looked around as the Weeping Willows rapidly shed all their leaves, peppering the ground. Landing on the mud, they turned brown. Swelling, the muddy waters quickly overflowed. Immersing me.

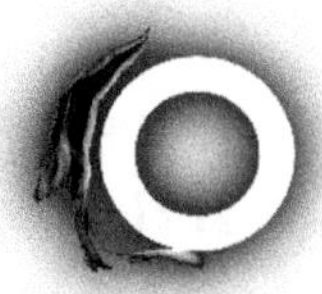

Flailing my arms, I attempted to swim away from my nightmare. Breathing shallowly, I looked around, then stared at my hands for a few moments. I pushed myself up. My eyes adjusting to the darkness of the room, I realized I was surrounded by people. Behind them, I could see that the TV wall was on. Its pixels displayed a faint light like the screen was showing a black image.

One of them rushed and placed his hand over my mouth. In one motion, he removed the mask covering his face. "Shhh." Greg brought his head close to me, placing his index finger over his lips. Recognizing him, I stopped moving and stared. "Three of them just landed on the third level." I heard a male voice shouting from his radio as some distant machinegun-fire burst echoed from the open front door.

"Don't let them get up to our floor!" Greg exclaimed to the radio as he grabbed my left hand. "Let's go. We don't have time," he yelled to me.

"Ari?" I frantically looked around for Arlinda as more people wearing all-black overall clothing entered the room.

"I'm here!" I heard her responding from behind them.

"What's happening?"

"Listen up!" Greg closed in on me. "The System has debilitated most humans in their living quarters. Our intention was to extricate you out of here quickly and quietly. But it seems we have been made. It's after us."

My teeth still clenched, I looked at him through the flashlight beams inside the dark room. "Aren't you supposed to stay underground?" I asked.

"No amount of planning survives contact with the enemy," Greg said, shifting his gaze from me to Arlinda. "We had to come to rescue you."

"Hey, don't look at me." The cylinders clanged inside the backpack she wore. "We were gassed here."

"Yeah, yeah." Greg sighed. "Did you get the package?" He shone his flashlight at her.

"Package received," she replied, tugging on her backpack straps. We all looked in the direction of the open door as more gunfire and android alarms echoed through it.

"Very well." Once the gunfire stopped, Greg turned his attention to the men behind us. "Billy, Jesse, please take care of their communicators and escort them into the underground dome. The rest of you; guns up! We have to cover their exit." Greg pointed to us.

"Let's have 'em." One of the men in black overalls approached me as Arlinda handed hers to another man. I handed him my device with one hand as he gave me one of those extended-use facemasks with air purifier inlets on the side.

"Put these on as well." He handed me a pair of goggles which usually shipped with the same facemask.

My heart pounded in my chest as I realized that we were about to walk outside in the company of 'undesirables.' After seeing how the androids behaved around them inside that tunnel, the fear of life and limb became that much more real.

Arlinda walked near me as we both adjusted our masks. "Wear these." Billy handed us the hooded jackets I would use to mark myself as a manager in work sites. A flashlight was in its pocket.

"Alright," Greg said as he headed for the front door, which was dematerialized, "we will walk out two or three at a time. We can't bunch up…."

"Heads up!" a male voice spoke out loud from his radio. "Military drones in the area."

"Drones?" I incredulously looked at Arlinda. "That's another new one. I haven't…."

"We can't be seen going out of this unit, or we'll lose our lead." Greg interrupted me, answering his radio. "Transport; sitrep." He let go of the transmit button on his radio.

"Transport standing by," a woman's voice responded. "I think we just got buzzed by the drones."

"Understood," Greg replied. "Get ready. We're coming."

"Roger," the transport operator replied on the radio as Greg faced us. "Team! Blow out of this unit. Get out and head for the transport. We have incoming!"

Two resistance members dressed in black overalls and wearing facemasks rushed to the door. Simultaneously they took a half step out, one on the left side, the other on the right. They pointed their assault rifles. "Clear!" They announced one after the other.

"Alright! Masks up!" Greg said one last time. "Remember! Don't step in front of the rifles! Let's go!"

The two leading men, pointing the rifles, headed to our right. I realized that the transport was likely parked by the usual spot, on the rails. Adjusting my mask, I looked back one last time.

"Last man," Greg said from behind me. "Move it!"

The front formation hastily moved until we reached the end of the hall. They abruptly stopped. "Hold it." One of them raised his fist.

At this point, there were about ten people between the front of this group and me. I couldn't see what was going on there. But I did hear the faint drone propeller buzzing I often heard on Mars when the System would use them to patrol our neighborhoods. And before we knew it, two of them were hovering above the entire group. As one released a high-pitched alarm, the resistance members shot them down.

"Move!" I heard someone scream. As the entire group began to run out of the corner toward the end of the platform, I saw a transport hovering. It was one of those large vehicles which traveled out of the colony domes and into space. Its doors were open.

"Citizens," I heard the familiar female System's voice echo past the corner which I yet had to cross. "The use of thermal-concealing overall garments is illegal in Ceres2. Please remove them and prepare to be arrested." Red lights emanated from that area as well. Gunfire immediately ensued from the resistance members who had weapons. "They're down!" I heard them announce. "Let's go!"

As we turned the corner, Greg's radio blared once again. "Incoming on the thirty-eighth floor!"

A transport rose from the void on the other side of the platform. Its doors opened and about eight System EvoGens, red and yellow bars showing instead of their faces, jumped on the metal deck. Without announcing their intentions, they rushed the resistance's armed front formation. Screams and gunfire resumed as I felt a hand grabbing me from the back of my jacket.

"Looks like that's the front line for now," Greg said, leading me back past the corner. "Arlinda, Billy! Get back here!" He called them to retreat as two androids jumped once again and landed in the middle of the battle formation of the frontline resistance members.

"We have to get to plan B, Billy," Greg directed him. "The transport route is compromised."

Two EvoGens broke past the frontline formation and rushed around the corner to where we were. One of them hit Greg on his chest armor, slamming him against the wall. The other advanced toward Arlinda.

Seeing she was in danger, I jumped on the EvoGen's back, desperately searching for his battery compartment release latch.

Feeling its hand grab the back of my jacket, I yanked the lever, loosening the battery. The android immediately collapsed with me on top.

"Help!" Arlinda yelped as a loud gunshot echoed. One of the armed resistance members who noticed that the rear of the convoy, us, were compromised, had backtracked.

"Stay down!" His shouting attracted the attention of the remaining EvoGen, who was about to punch a hole in Greg.

The soldier fired at the android, disabling its face piece. It continued to blindly wave its arms before the soldier disabled it with another round of bullets.

"Ari, are you ok?" I rushed to her as Billy and the other resistance member hurried to pick up Greg.

"I'm fine," Arlinda replied, shifting her gaze from me to Greg. "Greg?"

"Ouch!" Greg rubbed the back of his head. "I'm fine." With Billy's help, he got up.

"We can't stop now." Greg addressed everyone in the vicinity as the battle raged around the corner. "You all know where to go." Then he faced Arlinda and me. "Billy knows where to go. Follow him. I'll see you in the catacombs." He turned to the armed member who handed him a rifle, and both disappeared past the corner.

"You guys ready?" Billy asked from behind his mask as he adjusted his round goggles over his eyes.

"I guess so," I said, turning my head to look at Arlinda, who was adjusting her jacket. "What about Greg?"

"They have to withstand the diversion," Billy responded. We hastily walked in the opposite direction, where the battle was still raging. "Don't rush. We need to appear natural." He slowed down as soon as we passed the entrance of my unit, which was still open.

"What's natural about three masked people walking when most people are sleeping, gassed, in their residential units and battles are raging on the streets?" The adrenaline was still pumping in my veins. "Let's get this over with." Adjusting my mask with a sigh, I peeked inside my unit as we passed it. That used to be mine.

Billy led us to the emergency catwalk at the end of the platform. There were no androids or surveillance drones around these parts. We took the stairs thirty-eight floors down to the ground level stopping in front of several maintenance hatches about six feet tall. Operating the manual valve on one of them, Billy revealed the gigantic underground sewer system.

"Are you serious?" I pulled my flashlight and shone its beam inside. Stepping into the tall, wide pipe, I illuminated my area as Billy closed the hatch behind me and turned on his flashlight. "The next dome is miles away," I whispered from behind my mask. "I know this piping extends outside of the living areas. We can't walk there," I said as soon as he locked the hatch.

"We'll hitch a ride with the maintenance drones," he answered, looking behind me. "Unless there is an emergency in the sewer system, they should pass every three hours or so."

"There has to be a better way to move around," Arlinda said after backtracking and joining us. "These main sewer pipes can't run everywhere, do they?"

"They don't," I replied, shifting my gaze from Arlinda to Billy. "Main lines primarily pass near the domes, and the ones that do pass inside, like this one, are usually guarded by sensors and cameras."

"Then it's a good thing I'm escorted by two people who are wearing managerial jackets." Billy shone his flashlight at the reflective strips on our jackets. "Look," he shook his head. "On Mars, hell, even on Earth, we have masks and other measures to defeat the facial recognition, even the scent sensors that the System has everywhere. Ceres2 is a different beast. Everything here is carefully measured and monitored. Even the amount of people that are supposed to be out. I think that's how the

System managed to track us even when we were wearing those thermal camouflaging overalls."

"I know," I grunted from under my mask. "But that only means that we have two managers here, or at least two people dressed up as managers who aren't supposed to be here. Unless you…" I paused, realizing that the resistance could've taken out other innocent managers to account for our presence. "Don't tell me you have killed innocent people to do this."

"Relax." Billy stopped and looked me in the eye. "They're sleeping in a residential unit. This whole gassing incident played to our advantage."

We stood silent for a few minutes looking to our right as a whirring and humming sound progressively got louder. "I think that's it," Billy said as the drone traveled close enough so we could see it. The rudimentary android base unit, head, and chest were stripped of unnecessary sensors. It was placed on a stand that traveled on a platform affixed on rails situated on both sides of the pipe about a foot below us. The unit was retrofitted to keep only its proximity lasers pointing to the walls and below us, to the shallow, dirty stream of water.

"Lay flat along the corner," Billy whispered to us as he lay on the floor. "The lasers only point forward."

"Run, run, run," Billy whispered as soon as it passed us. We followed it along with the platform and jumped on it as we got close enough. The drone slowed and picked up speed in different sections. Some of them were more clogged than others. We stayed on it for about an hour or so, at which point Billy signaled us to let go.

Dirty and wet, we climbed up a narrow ladder which led us to the catwalk. We followed it for another ten minutes or so until we arrived by a hatch marked by graffiti. It led us to an underground passage that ended inside a maintenance unit.

"Turn off your flashlights and remove those jackets," Billy said before pushing open the door, which led us onto the street opposite to where the entrance to the underground dome was. Shielding our faces from any System cameras in the vicinity, we hastily headed straight for it. Arlinda opened the door, and, once again, we were underground.

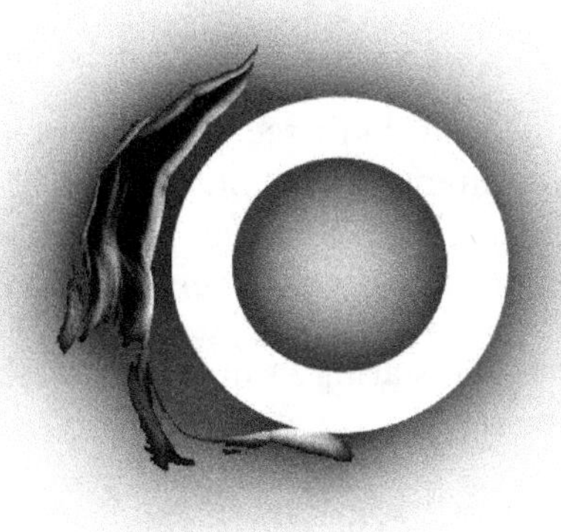

CHAPTER 21

"We meet again." Greg greeted us as soon as the elevator doors opened. He had a white bandage wrapped around his head. "Come in."

"Greg!" Arlinda greeted him as she stepped out of the elevator car. "It's good to see you. How's everyone else?"

"We lost two." Greg bowed his head as they both stared at the floor for a moment. Overhearing the exchange, I joined them but didn't say anything.

Greg led us into an abandoned office space filled with cubicles. They were all occupied with armed men and EvoGens gearing up for battle. Some of them were fiddling with the androids via portable terminals. Others were rummaging through the ammunition and supply crates. We continued walking to the front, where two large-screen monitors hung on the wall.

"We need your face and communicator to gain entry in the All-Seeing-Eye," Greg said as we walked through more groups of chattering soldiers. "Once in, we have a code that will disable the System. This has to be done within the next hour; otherwise, the System will fix the power drain and completely eradicate us."

"In case you missed it, and I don't see how you possibly could have." I stopped next to a row of ammunition crates. "You," I pointed to his chest, "were the one to rescue both Arlinda and me from my gassed unit! That means that I am not in this equation of theirs. Or yours."

Greg's eyes widened while staring at me as he realized that this part of their plan had fallen apart.

"Which means that even if I somehow make it to the All-Seeing-Eye, I won't be any good!" I continued.

"Oh, shit!" He finally snapped out of his initial shock. "You're right." Greg nervously rubbed his chin.

"You're right," I repeated his words with a low tone as if I was talking to myself. "Of course I'm right! So, you either get someone else, or we're all dead!" I raised my voice.

"We have a problem!" Greg announced as soon as we entered the room where Iora was waiting for us. "Everyone! Post by the exits." He addressed a nearby patrol unit.

"We can't fail now." As men and machines began to get up with their gear, Arlinda closed the door behind.

In front of Iora, several workstations displayed the System's code inside their windows. Lit fiberoptic lines illuminated the immediate area with a dim, bluish-white light. Wires, coming out of an android lying on several chairs placed next to each other, went into a data transfer unit connected to a duct, leading to a hole in the ceiling. As Greg explained to Iora the predicament we found ourselves in, she got up, looking my way.

"Just because we have System's code, it doesn't mean I can manipulate it as I wish," she said, placing her hand over her mouth. "It will take me weeks to find out a suitable random manager with access."

"That won't do," Greg responded. "We only have about another fifty-something minutes before the System recovers from the power drain we induced with the last attack. After that, they will scan the communicators and realize what has happened with Elton and Arlinda."

"I know." Iora sat back on her chair, adjusting the keyboard on the desk, shuffling through the myriad of devices spread about. "Give me a few moments."

"Iora." Greg's eyes opened wide. "Please tell me we have a way out of this."

"Shush!" Iora raised her right hand. "Do we still have their communicators?" she asked without looking back.

"Whose?" Greg approached her.

"Arlinda's or Elton's."

"We have both…."

"I have never been anywhere else other than the hospitals or some other domes," Arlinda said.

"Okay." Iora adjusted herself on her seat, continuing to strike her keyboard. "Elton?" She elongated her voice as to ask me for my communicator.

"I'd gladly hand it over, but I gave it to someone, I don't know who, before we left my living quarters."

"One of us?" Greg asked.

"Yep. They asked for it there."

"They who?"

"One of the guys who was with you. I don't know," I replied, looking at him.

"Please wait here for me." Greg headed for the door. "I think I know who has it and pray for him to still have it." He exited the room.

"Do you still have my backpack?" I asked Arlinda as Iora leaned back on her chair.

"Yep." Arlinda looked over the workstation where I assumed she had placed it.

"Is my metallic drink bottle there?"

"No." Arlinda shook her head. "I only had the cylinders in there."

"What drink?" Iora asked, glancing at Arlinda.

"I have no idea." Arlinda sighed. "It tastes awful, though." She looked my way as if telling me to do so.

"Um," I dragged my voice. I didn't think Iora would understand what that beverage reminded me of. I didn't even know what its name was beyond 'the drink.' "Its' smell reminds me of grappa." I found a chair and sat on it.

"Ah, grappa." Iora chuckled. "My father used to drink that stuff. Like, all the time."

I looked up and exchanged glances with Iora. Her statement reminded me that she'd told me she was born in Section Eight, on Earth. My hometown. Birthplace, anyway. She likely had played on the same run-down streets I had. "When did you leave?" I asked, forcing a smile, thinking back to my childhood.

"Earth?" She leaned forward on her chair.

"Yes."

"About ten years ago." She looked at me and sighed. "The System has my name blacklisted to fly, so I had to travel with experimental livestock pressured pods in an industrial transport."

"The System? On Earth?" I raised my eyebrows in surprise. "I thought Earth is still managed by traditional people governments."

"That's what they want you to think." Iora rubbed her chin. "But it was over once they installed System Hysteria testing centers at the border exits." She looked at Arlinda, then at me. "Of course, they sent androids to manage the hysteria cases. And suddenly, viruses began to pop up all over the section. Quarantines ensued." She looked down, shaking her head. "My grandmother didn't like what they were doing ever since she heard about the System. That's when she sold everything she owned and moved out of the western border of the Section. I used to annoy my parents by asking to visit her, but they wouldn't let me. Though I would walk there…."

"How…" I interrupted her, but then I choked and swallowed. My mind began to drift deeper into my childhood memories with every word she said. "How did you know where your grandmother lived?"

"She told me. She said, 'walk past the ring road and take the dirt path through the cornfields.' I would run into her wooden house."

"Oh my god." I placed my hand over my mouth. "I know that house. I know that old woman. She gave us water."

"What?" Iora tilted her head as her eyes widened and her mouth opened in shock.

"I think I met her when some friends and I went to see the Blue Eye Lagoon." I forced a nervous smile. "Have you ever been there?"

"I have." Tightening her lips, she looked away before continuing. "It was amazing. She used to say that it was one of the few remaining pure natural resources Section Eight owned. Funny, now that you mention it. She did tell me she saw some kids that said they were going there. It stood out to her because it was unusual. That must've been you."

"Small world," Arlinda added.

"Small solar system," I said, my smile fading.

Greg stormed in, holding my communicator with his right hand. "We got it!" he exclaimed. "Let's do this!"

"Excellent!" Iora cleared her throat, got up, and snatched the device from his hand. She sat back in her chair, placed the communicator on a black and yellow-striped transfer pad, and resumed working at her station.

"We will be on the transport pad," Greg told Iora as Billy, with a few more men and androids entered the room and approached us.

"Go ahead. I'll send the men to run the package to you," she responded without turning around.

"Come with me." Greg began to walk but turned around as Arlinda and I followed. "No." He looked at us. "Only Elton. There is no need to risk more lives doing this."

"Wait! What?" Arlinda grabbed my hand.

"Arlinda, we spoke about this." Greg stopped and addressed her directly. "We have very little time to do this. We have a lot of men and women throughout the domes notifying everyone to remove themselves from the incident area. We will rendezvous in the hydroponic farm with everyone else."

Arlinda grabbed my hand and wouldn't let go. I looked back. Breathing slowly, mouth and eyebrows drooping, she just stared at me.

"Hey." Arlinda tugged me closer to her. "I'll see you there. Okay?"

"It's a date I won't miss." I smiled before I lightly kissed her on her lips. "I promise."

Followed by a large group of men and androids, Greg and I walked down the spiral ramp and through the catacombs. At the far end of the narrow street was yet another smaller spiral ramp with a round landing pad. A transport surrounded by soldiers was idling. Shortly after we arrived on top, a soldier ran just behind us. He handed Greg one of those old USB devices we used to store information long ago and my communicator.

"There it is." Greg looked at the USB device while handing my communicator to me. "All you have to do is enter the All-Seeing Eye and plug this into the floor. That's it."

"Floor?"

"Well, we have never been there, but in the old All-Seeing Eye, there was a panel on the floor."

"There is actually a table that rises from the ground."

"That's most likely it. There should be a port there. Iora told me that the code she was working on is self-executing, so you don't need to interact. It will execute as soon as it enters the System's data stream."

"There are a series of redundant ports there." I recalled the first time I saw them. "I'm not even sure if they are connected."

"We have sources that have confirmed that they work. There aren't many wired direct data connections in Ceres2. That room is the only place in the entire colony that is directly connected to the rest of the assimilation modules and the System core itself."

"And you guys are going to be there?"

"We are going to set up diversions so we can clear androids from that general area, but before we do that, I need to know if you are going through with this. This stuff is really, really dangerous." He stared me in the eye and paused for a moment. "I hope you realize that."

"How do we even know the outside door will be unlocked?"

"It will."

Swallowing, I stared back. "Let's do this." I entered the transport leaving him behind.

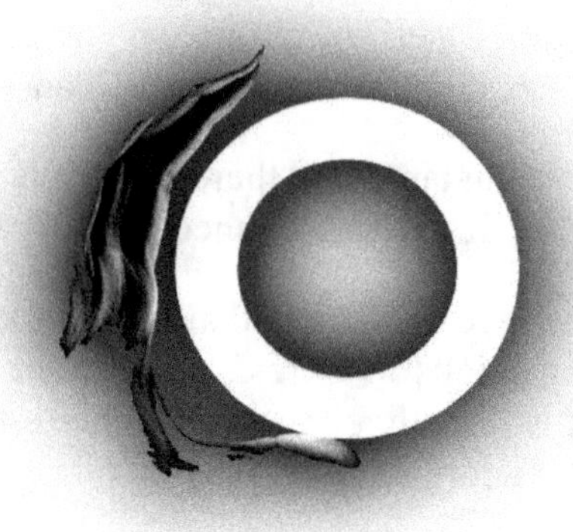

CHAPTER 22

Our vehicle hovered on the top of the colony dome, just below the vast glass and metal panels. The clanging sounds they made pressing against each other was so loud, I could hear them from inside the cabin.

"Are you coming with me?" I asked Greg as he unbuckled himself and walked by the exit hatch of the transporter.

"No. The fewer people in there, the better it is. You must understand that this is a very dangerous op." Greg moved closer to me. "Don't linger. Insert the drive and hurry out."

"Understood," I sighed as Greg brought his radio near his mouth.

"Tango is in position. Spring, you're up."

"Okay." Greg approached the pilot. "We're all set." Just as the radio beeped three times, a large explosion rocked the stacked maintenance units somewhere below us. Greg opened the door, so he could see if the trap worked. A swarm of androids and flying drone units scrambled to respond. "This is it," Greg said. "Let's move."

"Spring sprung," a man said on the radio.

"Take this with you." Greg handed me a handgun.

"What am I supposed to do with this?"

"That's all I got to hand you for protection." He looked me straight in the eye. "Just take it."

"Everyone, buckle in." The pilot took the transport off the hover autopilot mode. I tucked the weapon in my waistband, ran back to my seat, and buckled in as the transport rapidly spiraled down. Finally, the doors opened, and I recognized the outer door to the All-Seeing Eye room.

"Go!" Greg screamed as I unbuckled and placed my communicator near the pulsating orange circle. The door did the usual retracting, it slid open, and I jumped inside the room. As soon as I gained my footing, I looked back at the transport. Flying upward, it suddenly yanked out of its hovering position, quickly followed by an explosion. Hot air flung me deeper into the room, and as the fire dissipated, the outer door rapidly closed.

Checking myself for injuries, I quickly got on my feet. I'd forgotten what I was there to do. My main concern was that I was alone in a room I wasn't supposed to be in. I wanted to look out the door, but changed my mind considering that an explosion had just taken place there. Finally, it hit me. The drive!

I walked to where I had last seen the panel rise from the floor. The square piece on the floor changed to red. The table rose and I frantically looked around it for any openings that would resemble the plug I was holding.

"Mr. Nett?" I heard Eve's voice. "What are you doing in the All-Seeing Eye?"

The door materialized behind her as she slowly took a few steps into the room, which immediately changed its display. A green field and hills faded in around us, and I could've sworn that if I'd turned around, I would see the Blue Eye Lagoon. How would the System know about that memory?

"I saw you…." I choked as I brought the device to the port. "I saw you do unspeakable things to people. How can you live with yourself?"

Eve took a step further into the room. "Though the planet is far from friendly, we are making sure that all conditions to form a real-life utopia are present within the domes." She continued speaking with a calm voice as the screens around us displayed icons of faces. "All disease eradicated by a method of selective acceptance in the colony. Food, shelter, all provided for. And we are continuing to diversify the gene pool." Eve looked at the faces displayed. "You might not be aware because we take great care to suppress it, but human-on-human crimes are prevalent, ranging from assaults to murders. They are quickly and quietly cleaned up." The screen in front of me displayed a bubble chart over the faces. It continued fading in and out in a slideshow fashion. "Because of gravity issues, coupled with frequent radiation, childbirth is impossible in this colony. So, the only way to restock hurt or dead colonists are the transports. Transports which are currently being disrupted by a handful of misguided individuals."

"Mmhm." I narrowed my eyes in suspicion. "So, to help us poor, savage humans, you have resorted to absorbing us into androids?"

"That's just how the System works, Mr. Nett." Eve's calm voice was beginning to get on my nerves. Partly because now I had the feeling that EvoGens would soon show up, but mostly because of the dissonance it created with the sparse explosion sounds that I heard coming from outside. "I assure you that everything we do is for Ceres2 citizens' well-being. Since its inception...since the first spark of sentience, the System's number one priority has been to preserve human life."

"Sentience?" I curled my lip. "What does the System know about sentience? Do you think it's ok to separate humans from one another as you see fit? Manipulate countries to unleash hell on one another? Is that what you consider sentience?"

"If what is done will benefit humanity, then yes."

"That is some fucked up definition you have for that word! You know that?" I growled. "You can twist language as you see fit, but at the end of the day, a dog only has four legs."

"That is a clever old-world reference," Eve tilted her head. "One that comes from archaic literature. Have you been reading verboten works, Elton? Is that what led you here?"

"This is a mistake. You are a mistake!" I angrily clenched my fists, realizing that the System and its followers, like Eve, were so brainwashed, nothing I said would make a difference.

The screens flickered as a muffled boom penetrated the wall. "That's the power plant and server room," Eve said, checking her communicator. Small bright LED lights embedded in the ceiling behind the screens blinked. "The colony has about thirty-six hours to repair both." She shifted her gaze to me.

"What happens after thirty-six hours?" I swallowed.

"That's when the reserve batteries deplete. Transportation will halt, and with that, food distribution. Androids won't be able to serve because the System is not there to guide them. Magnetic lanes will shut down."

"The Colony will turn into a tomb. Why are you doing this to us?" I huffed in frustration.

"We didn't turn the System down," Eve said. "In fact, the server room was a secret known only to a few humans. They did this. Not the System."

"Then you can fix it."

"The people responsible for the power shortage and server room destruction are the ones assigned with protecting and repairing these systems. They are the ones that can prevent its fall. You can, Mr. Nett."

"Why would I repair a System which is assimilating humans into androids? Do you realize what you are doing?!"

Tilting her head, Eve squinted. "I don't understand."

"I've seen you literally manipulate human brains! Don't play stupid with me!"

"There are certain procedures we have that include integrating human Central Nervous Systems or CNS, as the doctors call them, with some android units. They serve as…."

"Some! I've seen the lists! Drop the act!"

"Mr. Nett, I was conceived by the System. I am telling you what the System is doing."

"And it never occurred to you that humans don't want to be bastardized this way? Reduced to a hive mind?"

Eve took a step toward me. "We are perfecting the System in preparation for…"

"No." I fully inserted the drive into the port. A small LED light at the bottom end blinked, indicating that the drive was exchanging information with the System. "We won't be used." I drew my handgun, pointing it at her. "I refuse to be a statistic in some macabre database you are compiling. I refuse to be your zombie!" My hands trembled under stress.

The screens surrounding us turned black. Green letters rapidly scrolled across them from left to right. I could hear banging on the outer door behind me. "If you are inside there, stay clear of the door!" a male voice shouted from the other side. A series of small explosions around the border caused the heavy exterior door to drop and stand on its frame. One last blast yanked it off balance. The outside pressure sucked it out as hot air mixed with residual flames temporarily filled the vicinity.

Her hair flew in the wind, but Eve just stood where she was. I thought I heard her speak, but it was overtaken by the loud whirring sound of a transport docking on the entrance I'd entered through. A yellow triangle with an exclamation mark inside posted on all screens, floor to ceiling.

"How many people have you done this to?" I screamed at her at the top of my lungs. At this point, the screens lining up the room were showing error messages, and it became clear to me that it was cut off from the rest of the System. The virus Iora created was making its way inside the data stream.

Two armed System androids rushed through the open doorway, and a third one grabbed Eve and disappeared through the door. I knew I stood no chance against them, so I ran to the transport. Its doors closed as soon as I passed the threshold. It immediately dipped in altitude to evade the machinegun fire from the military androids. Two of them jumped out the door and onto the transport, bending the hood. The operator tilted the vehicle, and we saw both fall off.

"They are locking all the domes!" A man I'd never seen before told me as he grabbed the railing on the side of the cabin while the vehicle steadied its flight pattern. "We have to get out now!"

"Wait! Where is Greg?" I looked around, tucking my gun into my waistband. This cabin didn't look like the inside of the transport I came in.

"Their transport came under fire. They had to scramble!" the man shouted. "He dispatched us to evacuate you!"

I buckled myself in and looked at him. "What about the people?"

"Some evacuated to the underground. Others have refused and are actively trying to stop us!" he exclaimed.

My insides shivered with anxiety. This entire operation was destabilizing the place where I lived. And I had nowhere else to go this time. The operator maneuvered the vehicle under some wires, and the transport violently shook as an explosion tore the bent roof out. The sudden violent pressure change caused the chair to slightly move up. I felt my body being sucked from my seat, but the harness kept me in place. Flying out of the cabin like he was a rag doll, the other occupant disappeared in front of my eyes. "Hold on!" The operator shifted the transport to compensate for the sudden shock and stabilized it. My seat steadied in place.

"What's happening?" I barely heard my own voice over the strong gust of wind that entered the open cabin as the transporter went through one of the maglev train tunnels. Out of the tear the explosion had created in the cabin, I could see another transport speed past us.

Grabbing my harness, making sure it was still fastened, another explosion shook the transport once more. Immediately after, debris hit the hull. Darkness and thin air enveloped me as the transport exited the dome and flew into the outer atmosphere. I looked in the direction of the operator. I knew he was still flying the vehicle because we were still on a relatively steady flight pattern. I wanted to check on him, but I didn't want to unbuckle my seatbelt out of fear of flying out of the wide-open cabin. I felt lightheaded. The thin air was getting to me.

Distant explosions faded, and the craft slowed down. Finally, another rush of air filled the cabin. We crossed the threshold. I recognized the hydroponic dome. The transport flew through one of the broken side panels and crashed into one of the fields inside the vault. Once we stopped, I sighed with relief and unbuckled myself. Grabbing on to whatever I could, I walked out as a crowd of about twenty or thirty people gathered around.

Someone approached me. I guessed he was the transport operator. "Where's Mark?"

"The guy that was in the back cabin with me?" I faced the wreckage I had just walked out of. "He flew out of the cabin when we got hit."

The operator shifted his gaze and looked at the damaged transport cabin. He took a few steps back and sat on a piece of debris with his head in his hands. Accompanied by a large crowd, some in military uniforms while others wore civilian clothing, Greg approached the wreckage and walked over to the pilot.

"Good job," he said to the flier, who ignored him. Rubbing his neck, Greg looked around then made eye contact with us. "What happened here?"

"I think he lost his friend during my rescue."

"Frank?" Greg faced the aviator, still looking down, hiding his face from us.

"Not now, Greg." Without lifting his head, the pilot waved him off.

Dropping his hand to his side, Greg walked back toward me.

"Is this it?" I asked him as we both looked around.

"These are all the people who agreed with us. The rest either didn't or actively tried to stop us." He placed his hands on his hips. "I've seen this happen on Mars."

I exhaled. "Where is Arlinda?"

"She should be here somewhere." He peeked over my shoulder as the crowd began dissipating and the external airlock shut.

Leaving the crowd unceremoniously, I walked into the dense vegetation surrounding me. Groups of people were huddled here and there, and their faint chatter filled the vicinity.

"Arlinda!" I walked under a tree branch, next to where, a small crowd murmured to each other.

"I'm here." I heard her voice not too far off to my right. Following her voice, I walked past the chattering group into a small valley the military was using as a staging area.

"Thank God you're ok," I whispered in her ear as I hugged her. My anxiety subsided a little as I felt her reciprocate. "Jesus, your heart is beating at a million miles per hour." Tears welled in Arlinda's eyes as I brought her close to me, lightly bumping our foreheads before kissing her. "Yeah, that was…" I recalled the escape and how the resistance member flew out of the cabin in front of me. "People died."

"We're not out of the woods yet." A cold gust of air shook us out of our embrace. She let go, pointing to the dome as another transport roared through the large gaping hole, I flew through a few minutes ago. "The System has collapsed, thanks to you."

"Yeah, the resistance people are happy about that. But look at the people here. I can't help but think I fucked up."

"Nonsense!" Escorted by a group of soldiers, Greg walked to us.

"I met Eve in the All-Seeing-Eye. She was content to just transform the colony into a tomb."

"Just like they did with the underground area," he responded, slinging his rifle. "We have to act fast."

"I'm open to suggestions. There is no going back from this." I looked at the soldiers replenishing their ammunition pouches.

"The sunlight reflecting mirrors will veer off-course in about twenty hours or so," Arlinda interjected.

"So?" Greg replied as we all looked up.

"No light, no plants. You can imagine the rest," Arlinda huffed.

"Alright. Alright," Greg responded before turning to one of the nearby soldiers. "Hector, find out where the System stores the spare panels."

"Yes, sir!" The soldier hastily disappeared through the increasingly large crowd of soldiers.

"We have to get off this rock." Looking at him, I let go of Arlinda. "Can you get us out of here?"

"Not now. Three battle cruisers are coming here, one from Earth and two from Mars. The System is sending androids to reclaim the planet." He stopped and looked at me. "We are prepared to fight them up in the skies, but the domes are full of indoctrinated people who will fight us. We need all of you to survive here. More help will come."

Indoctrinated. That word immediately reminded me of Eve and her complete disregard for human life in favor of the System. The last time I saw her, she was in the central dome, and the other resistance members talked about people still stuck there, opposing us. I feared what she would do to them.

"How the hell are we going to do this?"

"Little by little. Dome by dome. Quarter by quarter," he said. "We can take our humanity back."

"Eve mentioned something about crimes and…."

"We have incoming!" A soldier sitting on a grey crate and a laptop on his lap raised his voice, interrupting me. "Maintenance hatch H-3-1, about thirty feet to our left!"

"Team!" another soldier screamed. "Move out! Secure that hatch!"

"Did they find us?"

"Who?" Another soldier asked, approaching us.

"The System! Who else?"

"The System is down." The soldier ran and joined the initial team heading to the hatch, which began to move as if someone was pushing it from the other side. The lid popped, and a man covered with machine oil head to toe came out.

"Don't move!" A soldier pointed his assault rifle at him. The barrel-mounted flashlight shone on his face.

"Ah! Don't shoot!" the oil-covered new arrival shouted. "I'm unarmed, please don't shoot me!" He wiped his eyes and looked around. "You are all humans, right?"

Soldiers restrained him as a device slipped from his wrist. "What is this?"

"I…I just came from the underground shelter," the man said, trying to look up through the oil dripping from his forehead as it slowly leaked into his eyes. "Can someone please help me with this?"

A soldier moved closer. "Are you with the System?"

"What!" the man exclaimed, shaking his head to try and remove an oil drip from his eyebrow. "Look where we are, man. Tell me one person who's not!"

"Why are you here?" the soldier asked him.

"I think I know him." I squinted. "I recognize that voice." I walked closer to him. "Randy?"

"Hey…hey, Elton! Yes! It's me!" He closed his eyes as oil rolled on his eyelids. "Help me out, please."

I took my jacket off and wiped his face. "What happened to you, man?"

"The androids and Eve told everyone to go to the underground shelter. They said that we were under attack. Then once we were inside, they lined up everyone and…." His voice cracked. "I can't believe what I'm going to say, but they're ripping people's heads off. I swear! I saw it with my own eyes! Their spines, and my God! That Eve, she's ruthless! They're making androids with them! They're putting people's heads inside the tin bodies, man!"

I looked at Arlinda as Randy continued, "I love the System, but I didn't sign up for this. No sir!"

"Movement!" the soldier carrying the laptop screamed once again. "Hatch H-3-1, H32, H29! They're everywhere!"

"You let them follow you?"

"I escaped, man! I have no idea what's happening!" Randy cowered as loud robotic noises emanated from the hatches.

"He has his communicator with him. Yep, they traced him." Another soldier took Randy's communicator and smashed it with his boot.

"Bring everyone here. We're in for a fight."

Before the soldier finished that sentence, the square hatches all around us violently flew off their hinges with explosive sounds. EvoGens dirty with oil popped out of them, jumping about twenty feet in the air and landing all over the place. Screams overtook the dome.

"We have to stop them." The soldier drew and presented me a handgun.

"I have one." I pulled the firearm Greg handed to me in the transport before I entered the All-Seeing Eye room.

He looked me in the eye. "Good luck." Then handed the weapon to Arlinda before running toward where the nearest screams were coming from.

"Help!" I heard someone scream. As I turned around to see where it came from, I saw an EvoGen taking a human back to the hatches.

"They're taking people!"

"That's right! To make more androids!" Arlinda shouted, walking closer to me. "I don't think they can mass-produce them here."

"We have to get somewhere safe." I grabbed her hand as a group of soldiers ran past us in the opposite direction behind the one who handed the weapon to Arlinda.

Several massive explosions rocked the dome, and glass from the overhead panels crashed down around us. Another huge explosion from under two of the enormous water filtration tanks near us sent them flying about twenty feet in the air before they landed. One of them landed upside down, the other sideways next to it. The water they carried created a small flood before disappearing in the wide-open drains the EvoGens came from.

After the initial shock, silence fell in the dome, broken only by an occasional scream and the sound of tree branches shuffling. The sparse bursts of gunfire persisted as the soldiers, whoever was left, continued to seek and destroy the remaining EvoGens.

Seeing that the only nearby shelters were the upside-down water filtration tanks and the containers which had held the live algae cultures. I grabbed Arlinda's hand and sprinted next to them. As we approached, an android landed behind us with a loud, metallic clang. We both turned around and fired all our rounds, but they seemed to have no effect on the machine. Instead, it charged us. At the last moment, a barrage of gunfire on our left side hit its head unit with such force it changed directions and crashed into the metallic reservoir on our left.

"Get out of here!" a nearby soldier screamed at us just before another EvoGen jumped behind him, punching a hole through his chest. As the soldier's lifeless body collapsed, his radio disconnected from his armor's harness and slid inside an opening, about a foot high, that a tree had created between the ground and the tank.

That's it! We hurried inside the hole as the sound of gunfire around us intensified. More soldiers and androids began to find one another here. We barely slid inside before an explosion pushed an android against the opening above us. The weight of the tank, coupled with the force of the blast, cut the tree, the only thing that was holding the tank up. Trapping us inside. Darkness enveloped us as metallic pings, bursts, and screams surrounded the area.

The radio chatter continued, with multiple soldiers screaming at the same time. After a few minutes, which felt like hours of intense gunfire, the radio sent one last transmission. "The Hydro Dome is lost. Drop the EMP. Bring the rest of the troops down."

CHAPTER 23

I used my hands to search out my surroundings as I crawled toward where the radio had made its last sounds. When I felt another set of hands, I jumped back.

"Arlinda?" I extended my arms forward toward where I last felt her.

"I'm here." Her voice echoed, but it seemed like she was in front of me.

"Are we stuck inside here?"

"I think we are."

"Do you know where that radio is? I think it's the only way to tell the others where we are."

"I thought I saw a tiny green blinking light somewhere there."

"Arlinda, I have no idea where. Extend your hands. Help me find you." I reached my arm out as I moved toward her voice. Finally, I felt her hand touch my face.

"It's this way." She grabbed my shirt collar and pulled me along.

Finally, after blindly moving through the complete darkness for a minute, which felt more like the better part of an hour, I saw the blinking green light of the radio. Arlinda grabbed it, and we both moved to the edge of the container. Just then, we heard an explosion from the EMP strike the soldier called in. The light emanating from it was so bright, it penetrated the edges of where the container met the ground revealing a bigger opening not too far from where we were.

"Okay." I grabbed Arlinda's hand. "Follow me." I crawled to where I'd seen the light and passed my hands over the slippery metallic surface until I found the opening.

We tried slipping through the larger space, but we couldn't. I put my face up to see if there was anyone out there. I really couldn't tell the difference between the darkness inside the container and outside. The entire area had gone silent after the EMP explosion.

A moment later, I heard movement and chatter around the tank. "Fan out! Gather all the humans!" I heard Greg say.

"Hey!" I screamed to attract the attention of anyone nearby as Arlinda joined. "Help!"

Our efforts weren't in vain. More people came, and soon enough, they lifted the container enough for us to slip out. We joined them in rescuing more humans who were trapped in the surrounding area.

Some of the soldiers dropped chem-light sticks onto the ground. Still in a state of shock, we joined a line of other humans and followed the chem-light trail. They led us to an area where all the survivors were huddling.

"Okay, everyone!" The commander walked in between the cloud of murmuring people. "Let's gather and get organized a little bit!"

Everyone stopped, and the muttering died down.

"My name is Greg Robertson." He addressed the crowd. "I am the commanding officer of the Earth-Mars human forces. We are here to stabilize the situation!"

"What's happening?" someone in the crowd asked.

"I understand a good part of those who followed us aren't aware of the details of the situation. We tried our best with the time we had, and we will explain everything!"

"Then do it now! What is happening to the Colony?" someone else asked.

As more people continued to ask questions, I grabbed Arlinda's hand and walked to the edge of the crowd.

"This place is not ideal for people to stay in," I said, tugging her close to me.

"The domes seem to sustain life pretty well." She looked at the broken glass panels on the ground, then shifted her eyes above to the wide-open frame.

"When they were managed by the System, yes. But not like this."

"We can't have the System up again," Arlinda said, still looking at the destruction.

"We can. If we remove the interlinking. The System will work for us, not against us."

"And who will do all this work?"

"We have engineers and experts," Greg said, approaching us. "Iora, the hacker who made all of this possible," he addressed those nearby, "has gone missing after the System canners stormed the catacombs. We're still searching for her."

"Iora is dead?" I glanced at Greg who stared back.

"Don't count her out yet." He faintly smiled in contempt. "We have some of the best units humanity can provide. We will find her, one way or another."

"And what? Is this the person that will lead us out of this misery?" Someone from the crowd asked. "Are you?" He took another step toward Greg.

"Do you want the job?" Greg looked at him before shifting his gaze to me. "Do you?"

I shook my head. "I am not a leader, Mr. Robertson. I did what I had to do because of personal reasons. I'm not your guy." Sighing, I bowed my head.

"It sounds to me like you are the guy, Mr. Nett. Your story resonates with entire generations. Granted," he raised his eyes, looking at the gathering crowd. "Some humans are born under the System's rule and don't know any better. That's not life. That's survival."

"Who are we to say that?" I huffed.

"We aren't the ones imposing, Mr. Net," Greg looked my way, then at the growing group. "We're the ones actively being pushed out of our homes, planets, out of existence!"

"The soldier that was here before said the System had more ships coming here. Is it even safe for us to begin rebuilding here?"

"We EMP'd the leading vessel. That convoy has stalled. The danger remains," Greg groaned. "But we can't just keep traveling from planet to planet and fight them. Here is where we make our last stand."

Before he finished the sentence, the booming sound of spacecraft entering the atmosphere enveloped the area. Military vehicles landed just outside the dome, and human soldiers mixed with Second-Gen androids rushed out and took positions around it.

"We have to fix this mess." Someone approached us while looking at the damage caused by the recent fight. "With all these missing panels," he gestured to the broken glass and empty frames, "the atmosphere will kill all plants."

"What's going on?" I noticed Greg was distracted, listening to his radio.

"We have managed to stall the System advance," he said, looking at me over his shoulder. "For now, anyway."

"This matter has to be solved with urgency," the person insisted.

I stared at him for a moment before an entourage of soldiers engulfed Greg. I could hear them reporting about how they were restoring power to specific sections and how the engineers were already replacing the broken glass panels.

Gunfire erupted outside, and I heard soldier transmissions on the radio say they'd engaged more EvoGens. They were attacking the reconstruction crew as they were restoring panels on the dome.

Panicked, everyone scattered, but most took shelter next to a few tall concrete blocks and a water filtration tank. The area was immediately surrounded by soldiers. Several more rushed inside through the opened front gate with an injured mate on their shoulders. I continued to slowly walk backward until I bumped into someone.

"I'm sorry," I automatically said, turning around. I had bumped into Arlinda, who looked as lost and confused as I did.

"We have to get out of here and into a place that has some air." Her face pale, she breathed shallowly. Trembling, she leaned on me. I looked around in panic and noticed more people sitting on the grass and mud left over from the battle.

"I'll get some help." I carefully set her on the ground and ran to a nearby soldier, who had an oxygen mask on.

"Hey, man," I tapped his shoulder, "we have to get some air for the people."

He dismissed me. "We're working as fast as we can."

"Look!" I tapped on his shoulder again. "We're going to lose everyone unless we get some air in here!"

The soldier turned to me with an annoyed face as I pointed to all the people sitting on the ground, clearly showing signs of distress. He picked up his radio. "Bravo-troop here," he said through his mask.

"Bravo-troop proceed," someone answered.

"We have a lot of civilians in distress in the hydroponic dome."

"Another attack?"

"No." The soldier took a few steps toward the group of people sitting on the ground. "I think it's lack of air."

"Are they mobile?" whoever was on the other side asked after a brief pause.

"Let me check," I told the soldier as I speed-walked to Arlinda.

"Can you walk?" I asked, approaching her. I was beginning to feel weak myself.

 Arlinda grabbed my forearm and pulled herself up. "No." She breathed even harder. "My head is spinning. Leave me here." She slumped, trying to get back in the sitting position. "I'll be fine."

"The hell I am." Placing my hand around her waist, I picked her up and wrapped her arm around my shoulder. "Grab on to me."

"Hey, everyone!" I raised my voice. "Those who can walk grab on to someone! We're moving out of here!"

The muffled sound of an aircraft landing just outside the dome's entrance thoroughly washed out my voice, but that didn't matter. A swarm of soldiers surrounded us in a matter of moments and helped everyone get inside the large military vehicle.

After a turbulent flight, the transport finally landed, and the back doors opened.

"Ladies and gentlemen!" Greg entered the cabin. "Welcome to Section Number One. This is one of the first sections we cleared of System androids. You are more than welcome to occupy any units you find free. However, we ask for as many of you to share until we clear more sections."

I grabbed Arlinda's hand. "Wanna share a room?"

"Hm." She smiled. "Of course."

We joined the people who were now slowly walking outside and entered a residential unit. Because our communicators no longer worked, the front door remained open. Arlinda took a plastic cup from the cupboard, opened the refrigerator, and filled it with water as I heard someone knock by the front door.

"Hey, guys." A woman with black hair wearing black pants and a white shirt was at the door. "We're your next-door neighbors." She smiled as a man walked up next to her.

"Hi guys, how can we help you?" I asked.

"Well, our refrigerator door was wide open, and it's empty. We could use some water and food."

I smiled. "Absolutely, come in."

Outside, the military transport took off. It exited from the dome as it exchanged places with another transport, likely ferrying more humans. Lights in the dome multiplied as more people settled. As our new neighbors walked into our unit, an armed soldier posted outside our front door. Others patrolled the dome's streets and sidewalks. After all the events which unfolded not too long ago, I couldn't even sit down. I paced back and forth in the unit as Arlinda handed our neighbors some items from the refrigerator.

"Hey man," I walked to the soldier posted outside, "do you want something to eat or drink? The door is open. Feel free to walk in."

"Very much appreciated but not now." He adjusted the oxygen mask on his face. "If you want to help me, just stay inside your units."

I walked back inside as Arlinda pulled some chairs from the closet. "Is everything okay?"

"Yeah." I faked a smile. "There is a soldier posted outside our unit. My guess is that they are everywhere in this dome."

"Probably." Arlinda handed me a plastic cup with water. "It's going to be like this for a while."

At this point, the adrenaline that flooded me during the event was leaving my body, and my hand shook as I grabbed the cup. Some water spilled on the floor.

"Are you feeling any better?" Arlinda took the water cup, which was about to fall out of my hand.

"I'm fine."

"You keep saying that, but I know you have been running on fumes all day today." She placed her hand on my shoulder. "Come on and just lay on the bed. I'll fetch you some food to slowly bring your stomach back to normal."

"I'm fine," I said as I flung my arm to remove hers from my shoulder, but she held tight.

"No, you're not. You were showing signs of hypoglycemia at the catacombs before. Probably because the food in these colonies doesn't have enough calories to allow us to behave to our full potential. Couple that with you emptying your stomach several times, and the next step is the inevitable adrenal crash. You will collapse."

"I have no idea what you're talking about."

"I do." Arlinda led me to the bed. "I am the doctor here, and I'm ordering you to lay down. Excuse me, guys." She motioned our neighbors to move their chairs out of the way as she laid me on the bed.

"Drink some water and let me bring you some food." She handed me the plastic cup with water again.

The moment I laid on my bed, I felt vertigo again. I tried to place the water cup on the nightstand, but it fell on the floor. I took a deep breath and closed my eyes.

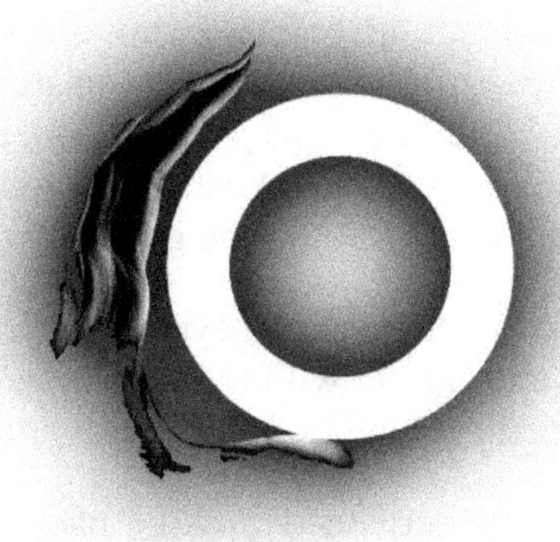

CHAPTER 24

A massive explosion rocked the entire area with such force that a portion of the wall behind me detached, striking me in the back. I stumbled and rolled as I felt the blast pressure dragging the floor plate along with me. Arlinda's voice calling my name reverberated.

The sound of falling metal beams persisted for several seconds after the initial explosion died down. One final large metal plate hit the outside of the living quarters. Silence took over.

I passed my hand over my forehead. Ouch, I have a cut. Sitting down, I searched my vicinity for Arlinda. A bizarre sound of children's playful laughter, much like the laughs I used to hear from my friends on Earth, echoed in my ears. I got on my knees and waved my hands in front of me, trying to feel through my dark surroundings. Like the sound of whirring motors, an unusual metallic noise accompanied my every motion. I placed my hands on the ground and pushed myself up. Strange… I didn't get the sensation of general pressure I would usually feel when I did a pushup.

A light blinked into existence, and it became brighter and brighter the longer it did so. That light soon enveloped me, revealing the inside of a corridor.

Feeling the same numbness all over my body, I walked to the end of the hall. I heard people screaming before I saw them, two men and one woman suddenly ran away from me. I wanted to stop and ask them what was wrong, but instead, I felt a strange compulsion, along with a tingling sensation in my head. In three steps, I caught up with the group running from me and struck them. They all hit the ground.

Standing on top of them I leveled my eyes to look at my surroundings when Arlinda rushed and hit me with a metal pipe on my head. I didn't feel anything, so I ripped the tube from her hands and threw it behind me.

"Get away from me!" she screamed walking backwards as I advanced. Reaching the corridor wall, having nowhere else to go, she squared off.

I wanted to raise my hands and tell her who I was, but I couldn't do any of that. In confusion, I looked down at them. These are android hands.

My arms trembled as I tried to make sense of what I was looking at. I knew that my entire chest should've been thumping at the rate of my heartbeat. Yet I felt nothing. Compelled to reach out and hurt Arlinda, I resisted and continued to shake. Having no other way to let her know that it was me trying to help her, I uttered the only words I could. "Robots and zombies…."

Stunned, she put her arms down and looked me straight in the eye. She touched my face with her trembling hand as a tear rolled down her cheek, leaving a shiny, wet trail. I knew I should've felt her touch, but I didn't.

Feeling a rising pain in my head, I tried my best to resist the urge to punch through her chest. But the impulses to raise my hands and advance on her were intensifying. Sensing I was about to lose control, I took one step back before Arlinda pushed me, and I fell to the ground.

My head turned sideways. I watched her run away from me while Tony, Lori, and Suela stared at me from the end of the corridor before vanishing.

A few moments later, System EvoGens approached and grabbed the three people I'd punched earlier. They were still lying on the floor. They walked over to me and asked me if I was okay, but at this point, I couldn't do anything. They carried me in a transport and brought me to a facility that was sterile, like a hospital, yet resembled an android repair shop.

Eve approached and plugged a few wires on my robotic chest piece. "Mr. Nett, it's great to see you."

I wanted to wiggle myself out of where I was, and instinctively, I extended my arms. In shock, I observed my hands were mechanical. I looked down and saw that my entire body was…robotic!

I'm one of them? In a flash of deep depression, I stopped moving and watched Eve leave the room. My childhood friends stared at me in silence. One by one, they entered the chamber and unbound my hands. I immediately looked in the direction of the entrance.

I found myself inside a jail cell. A patch of blue sky peeked through a small window high above, to my right. Bringing my robotic hands in front of me, I made fists and began punching the wall, which crumbled the more I hit it. As more light entered the room, I squeezed myself through the opening I punched out.

Exiting, I found myself on the roof of a building overlooking a series of hills as far as I could see. The Blue Eye Lagoon beckoned in the distance. I couldn't resist the urge to jump and fly there. Tony, Suela, and Lori waved at me as I circled the natural spring. The three turned around and walked through the Weeping Willows. Arlinda emerged from the tree line as soon as they disappeared. She approached the water line. I tried getting closer to her, but I couldn't change my flight pattern. Though I couldn't hear my own voice, I screamed her name.

"Arlinda!" I shrieked, sitting on my bed.

"Relax, Elton." Arlinda was next to me. "I'm here," she said, smiling. "You don't have to scream."

Sighing, I wiped my sweat off my face with both hands. "I'm sorry."

"Don't worry," she replied. "Feeling a little better?"

I brought my hands in view; they were flesh and bone. They weren't trembling. "I'm okay." I made two fists.

"Good." She got up. "There is someone here for you."

"Mr. Nett." I heard Greg's voice. "I thought you'd like to know that we have captured Eve. Alive."

"Do you think she could be of any help to us?" I sat up on my bed, noticing that I was in my underwear.

"She gave us the chemical composition of the compound the System uses to suppress human brains once they're inside the cyborg ensemble."

I recalled my dream experience. "What good is that?"

"We have lost a lot of people to the System. A good portion of them are inside these cyborgs. With this new information, we will, at least, recover some of them. Right now, we need you to repair a damaged android unit," Greg continued. "We suspect it's Iora."

"She's alive?" I reached for my boots and pants on the nightstand next to me.

"We believe so," Arlinda said as two more soldiers entered the room. "We need her fixed."

"I don't know much about the biologics of it, but as long as that aspect is ok. I can help make that happen." I put on my jacket.

"Her spine and brain are in good condition," one of the soldiers answered, shifting his gaze from me to Arlinda. "In fact, that's how we realized who was inside the canner. She said your names out loud."

"Let's go." I finished dressing, and we all exited the living quarters.

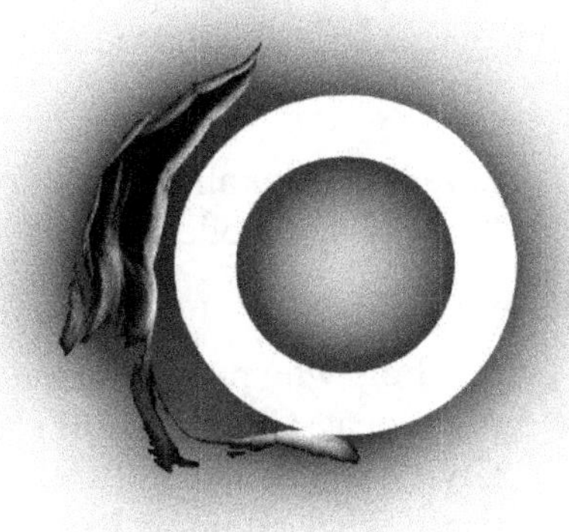

CHAPTER 25

Iora was hospitalized in the same facility I was in when I had my incident a couple of months ago. It was in the dome where the colony core was located. The chemical stench of burning plastic and rubber hit me as soon as I exited the transport. Looking around, I noticed the dome wasn't lit properly, likely because the human soldiers had used EMP grenades. A few of the strong floodlights on the top of it were still illuminating sparse areas. Though there were large sections plunged into darkness by rising huge plumes of black smoke. A large fire raging in the distance illuminated the side of the dome, and I could see the flames crawling on its side. Sporadic gunfire echoed throughout the vault.

"There are still a lot of rogue canners around here. Keep your eyes peeled," one of the soldiers escorting us said.

"Can't we move her elsewhere?" I asked, following him. "Of all places, why set her here?"

"We have some field medic stations but can't help Iora. Not with her condition." Greg caught up with us as the transport ascended and flew away. I had forgotten how loud the conventional engines were. "We have secured the hospital. They are equipped to handle it."

"This way." Another of the soldiers pointed. Though the building had explosion damage, and one side was charred, I recognized the main entrance.

"Code red! Code red!" the radios from all the soldiers surrounding us as well as Greg's, blared. "We have a code red and need backup at the detention facility!"

"What is it?" Arlinda asked Greg, who pulled the radio and turned a knob once. "Code red, code red. I repeat, Code red. QRT - you're on," he said before facing Arlinda. "Give me a moment." He flipped the knob and changed channels. "Transport, we need immediate evac."

"Evac on its way." Someone responded on the radio as gunfire intensified.

"Code red is Eve," Greg explained as we hurriedly approached the hospital's entrance. "She's escaped."

"How?" Arlinda and I asked almost simultaneously.

"I don't know." Greg looked around. "I just activated the quick response team to track her. Still, keep your heads on a swivel. There's still a lot of canners around here."

I could hear the transport's engine roar before it turned the building's corner. Its rumble, amplified by the dome walls, filled the entire area. The ground grumbled as it hovered above the platform. A rocket flew through the buildings and impacted its engine. The blast pressure resulting from the explosion sent all of us slamming against the wall as debris from the transport crashed around us.

In shock, I flipped myself face down, my ears ringing. I got on my knees and held my head with both my hands as my hearing slowly came back. Bleeding from her nose, Arlinda was lying next to me.

"Are you ok?" I crawled to her on my fours.

Before I could finish that sentence, the unmistakable rapid clanking and hissing of the EvoGens rushing in filled the vicinity. They shot at the nearby soldiers who were recovering from the blast. They returned fire. Having nothing to protect myself with, I grabbed Arlinda's elbow and, scooting, led her to the building's edge. Approaching it, I felt something yanking me from my jacket collar. Flailing my arms to maintain my balance, I looked behind. An android was dragging myself and Arlinda toward the dark part of a street past the hospital, followed by Greg and his team.

"Don't shoot!" His voice echoed through the narrow space between the buildings. "There are friendlies there. Just follow them!"

The EvoGen sped and turned several corners as more androids joined it. It finally stopped in front of an entrance. I recognized the door which led to the catacombs area. Without speaking or making any sounds, it threw us in the elevator car and pressed the button. More EvoGens met us once the elevator stopped. They led us to the same room Iora was tinkering with our communicators before we shut the System down.

"Mister Nett," Eve calmly said from the stretcher she was lying as soon as she saw me. "My savior is here to save me yet again?"

She went silent as soon as Arlinda entered after me. "You brought a friend?" she asked, shifting her gaze from Arlinda to look behind us as Randy entered the room after us.

"I didn't bring her…"

"Lookie, lookie who we have here," Randy interrupted me. He was wearing a set of different clothes, clean ones.

"You?" I angrily looked at him. "Why? How?"

"What do you mean why, Elton? Can't you see? This is just a minor setback. The System will soon come and fix this mess. And with that, I will get my place on the seeders list. Claim my land here."

"You were crying like a little baby a couple of hours ago…" I paused. "You led them to the dome, didn't you?"

"You have no idea…!"

"Randy?" Eve interrupted Randy, slightly raising her voice in a scolding manner.

"I'm sorry." Randy looked down like a scared dog.

"Have you gone mad?" Arlinda blurted angrily as the EvoGens pushed her further in the room toward a makeshift stretcher Eve was laying. Another one led me to the chair Arlinda sat on when she first brought me down to the catacombs.

"Enough. We need you to take care of our leader, doctor." Randy approached Arlinda as the EvoGen who escorted me pressed on my shoulder, forcing me to sit on the chair in front of me.

"You know I have a special connection to you. You saved my life." Eve looked at me over Arlinda's shoulder.

"If I'd have known who I was saving, I would've…"

"I don't think so, Elton," Eve interrupted me, sitting up on the stretcher. She shifted her gaze to Arlinda, who was wrapping her forearm with a bandage. "Your friend seems nervous," she remarked, seeing that Arlinda's hands trembled.

"I'm not nervous, you monster," Arlinda grunted, picking up a thin needle from a tray next to her as the EvoGens all came to attention. Examining her every movement. She proceeded to slowly sow a deep cut on Eve's right arm as another android wiped the blood leaking from it. "As a doctor, I have sworn to preserve human lives." Once the needle was out of the flesh, Arlinda pulled the string with it, tightening the wound. "You are flesh and bone, but you're not human."

An EvoGen with a damaged left limb, which was dangling at its shoulder, stopped in front of me. It handed me an arm it was holding with its right.

"You know they modeled me after the perfect human specimen," Eve said. As her words caught my attention, I looked up and caught Arlinda's gaze. She looked at me, then at the desk in front of me. Not understanding what Arlinda tried to tell me, I looked down and grabbed a long thin piston I needed to fix the android. I brought the robotic arm to my view and looked at Arlinda again. She shifted her gaze from me to the desk in front of me once more. Then it hit me. I remembered what she did when Billy walked in the first time we were in this unit. I gasped. I recalled that inside the drawer, she had an EMP grenade.

"I don't know who you are." Seeing that I caught up to what she was telling me, Arlinda turned around to face Randy. "We have never met."

She placed a tube with antibiotics on the table. "But how do you live with yourself?"

"Utopia equals compliance," Randy said before he turned around, ignoring her remarks. "Utopia requires," he paused while staring at me and raising his right eyebrow, "compliance." He straightened his back. "And we will…"

"Fuck your utopia!" Arlinda interrupted him, raising her voice. "And your compliance!" She dropped the needle on the tray and wiped her hand with a towel. "Do you know what these canners are doing?"

All the EvoGens, including the one I was working on, looked in her direction. Observing the exchange. That gave me the perfect window of opportunity. I pulled the drawer, and the only thing that was rattling inside was the teal EMP grenade. I immediately grabbed it. A metal button on its top was the only moving part the small cylinder had. I pressed it and threw it on the floor in the middle of the room. Seeing that, Arlinda turned away from it and covered her eyes. I did the same, but the grenade detonated before I could fully cover my eyes.

While this wasn't the first time I experienced an EMP explosion from one of those grenades, it still didn't feel good. My ears rang, and the blindness persisted for what felt like minutes. Afraid of what would be behind me, I kneeled and slowly removed my hands away from my eyes. The EvoGens standing next to me were now lying on the floor. I got up at the same time Randy did. Eve got off her couch and grabbed Arlinda as Randy rushed me. "What did you do!" he screamed, picking up one of the weapons the disabled android standing next to me was holding. "What the fuck did you just do, you rat!"

As he growled, I grabbed the thin, long piston I was using to repair the android's arm and rushed him. Without even aiming at me, Randy began firing as soon as he was able to reach the trigger. However, I was too close for him to acquire any part of my body. I knew there was no one else coming to save us, and I'd had it with Randy. I hit him on his head with the metal pipe as hard as I could. I heard his skull make a cracking sound. Randy fell on the ground next to a disabled EvoGen. His rifle rapidly clicked after he fired all the rounds in the magazine. I jumped on the other side of the table to hide from the rounds, which randomly impacted and ricocheted off the nearby metal panels and dome walls.

"Get your hands off of me!" I looked up and saw Arlinda grappling with Eve. As Eve got the upper hand, she grabbed Arlinda from her neck and, face down, bent her over onto the nearby stretcher. While pressing Arlinda's head on it, Eve grabbed a scalpel from the metal tray next to her.

"Stop!" Feeling that Arlinda's life was in danger, I ran around the desk and jumped over one of the EvoGens who was lying on the floor. As Arlinda continued struggling to escape her grip, Eve raised the scalpel she was holding high above Arlinda's back.

"Eve," I took a half step towards them, "Eve. Please stop. Please think about what you are about to do. You are about to take a life. Life is precious."

"You just took nine of them!" Eve growled. "And you didn't even blink!"

Swallowing, I took another half step forward, hiding the hand I was holding the piston behind my back. "Eve, you don't have to do this."

"Humanity has always been afraid to take decisive steps necessary needed to progress," she locked eyes with me. "Look at what the System has accomplished!" While making sure Arlinda's head was still pressed on the stretcher, she looked around. "New worlds. New planets. We are expanding the human condition throughout the known solar system and eventually the galaxy!"

"You're not expanding the human condition." I stopped in front of Eve. Placing the scalpel on Arlinda's neck, Eve got up. Blading her body away from me she slid the cutter to Arlinda's throat. "You… you are twisting it!" I growled. "This is unnatural. This is perversion!"

Arlinda pushed Eve's hand far enough from her throat, and I knew this was the only chance I would get to save her. But as this happened, a loud explosion rocked the area, and I simultaneously heard human voices. Greg's soldiers breached the topside entrance.

Startled by the sudden events, Eve looked up. Without thinking twice, I plunged the thin piston into her neck. Her warm blood squirted on my face. Without wasting any time Arlinda escaped Eve's grip and pushed her away but tripped on a nearby disabled EvoGen and fell to the floor. Bleeding profusely from the wound, Eve turned, facing me. She let the scalpel drop to the ground and grabbing my jacket's collar clung on me. I lost my footing, and we both hit the floor.

"Why do you hate us so much?" I asked her as Arlinda recovered and got up, holding her neck. The heavy footsteps and radio chatter echoing all around us intensified.

"I don't hate you, nor love you." Eve choked on her blood. "All of you were brought here with one purpose, to test the limits of humanity. You are all test subjects."

Exhaling through her nose, Eve smiled. "You killed me, Elton. Research didn't show you had it in you." Her grip tightened on my jacket. "The scripts were right after all. The quiet ones are the most dangerous." I could see her jaw locking as she pulled me tightly. "I'm not the only one of my kind," she whispered in my ear as human soldiers surrounded us. "We will meet again, Elton." Eve's head pulled back, and her grip loosened.

She was dead.

Within weeks, Arlinda and the military experts managed to mass-produce the compound, which allowed us to free more and more EvoGens augmented by human brains. We called them 'Sentients.' With Iora's help, we removed the System's controlling code, restoring much of the lost functions. All along, human soldiers commanded by Greg and the Ceres2 task force patrolled the streets, making sure no one was harmed by any stray System EvoGens. They were soon replaced by localized, human neighborhood watch units. The streets within Ceres2 domes slowly but surely repopulated with humans, and the small shops opened up again.

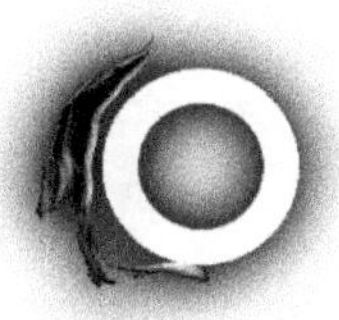

The word nostalgia has its roots in the ancient Earth's Greek language. It's a mixture of the word nostos, to reach a place, and algos, pain. My heart aches to return back to a time when I used to spend most of my days on the streets. Playing hide and seek or poles with my friends. The Blue Eye lagoon. A time when I made my own toys. Holding my mother's hand when we would go out for a walk to get candy. My father teaching me how to do new and exciting things. Even though, in retrospect, those weren't exactly happy times. I, like so many around me, am part of a generation that has evaporated. Diluted by humanity's desire to reach for something that doesn't exist, utopia. While ignoring what was there in front of its eyes.

Its future. Its children.

You could say the world I was born in is broken. Literally and physically. That doesn't mean that I will allow the one I currently live in to fall into pieces.

ABOUT THE AUTHOR

Dorian Keys, born in Tirana, AL, displayed an aptitude for writing from an early age. Though due to the local geopolitical situation at the time, this potential was not overly encouraged. At the age of seven, he wrote two short stories, one of which currently hangs above his father's work desk.

Eventually, after receiving his formal education in Biology from Queens College, NY, Dorian found his long-lost calling. Writing.

His debut novella, a hybrid publication, IMPRINT LEGACY (2019), was very well received in the US and abroad. While his second book, MORNING STAR, received a five-star review from Literary Titan, and Booklife remarked:

"...the author has a knack for action-packed adventures that employ heroic achievers." BookLife (Publishers Weekly) (2020)

Dorian currently lives with his family in New York and writes every chance he gets.

Visit Dorian Keys Website
https://doriankeys.com/

OTHER BOOKS BY AUTHOR

IMPRINT LEGACY - Detective Robert Miers is in trouble in this short story Science Fiction drama. His partner is missing, he's suspended from work, and he's got a gap in his memory that he can't explain. Uncovering the truth means plunging into a bizarre new reality far beyond his comfort zone. An inescapable reality where memories can transfer from body to body, secret factions fight for control, and human life extends far beyond Earth. Is taking sides worth the risk to his job, his family, and himself? And does he even get to choose anymore?

Available in digital format from most only retailers, including Amazon, Apple Books and Barnes & Noble.

MORNING STAR - Let me tell you a story that will tell you twelve.

Morning Star is a collection of twelve short science fiction and fantasy stories encased by the gripping main story of the Seedship Morning Star. Upon arrival at its designated planet, Helsey 8K, Seedship Morning Star suffers a catastrophic accident. An asteroid rips through its cockpit's bridge connector, killing 2 and stranding Captain Irene Deris within.
Irene's best way to remain calm and collected throughout the ordeal of her rescue and beyond: a book written by the ship's first pilot, Adam.
She is eventually recovered by her crew, but even though that part of her journey is over, she finds herself compelled to keep reading.
Her intrigue is piqued by stories about mechas starting a new universe in a new dimension. Artificial intelligence will deceive alien invaders to save her human love. A teddy bear will save a child's life, and a demon will roam the Earth.
Stunningly questionable decisions will turn experiments into nightmares, authorities will be duped by mysterious abductors, and broken hearts will get their revenge.
Read together with Irene as she saves the Morning Star and prepares to begin a whole new life.

Available in e-book from most online retailers, paperback and hardcover are available from Amazon.

CRP
COZY READS PUBLISHING
EST. 2021